WAR OF THE REALMS

READ ALL THE BOOKS
BY KATE O'HEARN

WAR OF THE
REALMS
A VALKYRIE NOVEL

BY KATE O'HEARN

ALADDIN

New York London Toronto Sydney New Delhi

ALADDIN

An imprint of Simon & Schuster Children's Publishing Division
1230 Avenue of the Americas, New York, New York 10020
This Aladdin hardcover edition January 2018
Text copyright © 2016 by Kate O'Hearn
Published by arrangement with Hodder & Stoughton, Ltd
Originally published in 2016 in Great Britain by Hodder Children's Books
Jacket illustration copyright © 2018 by Anna Steinbauer
Jacket damask pattern by Thinkstock
All rights reserved, including the right of reproduction
in whole or in part in any form.
ALADDIN and related logo are registered trademarks of Simon & Schuster, Inc.
For information about special discounts for bulk purchases, please contact
Simon & Schuster Special Sales at 1-866-506-1949 or business@simonandschuster.com.
The Simon & Schuster Speakers Bureau can bring authors to your live event.
For more information or to book an event, contact the Simon & Schuster Speakers Bureau
at 1-866-248-3049 or visit our website at www.simonspeakers.com.
Jacket designed by Karin Paprocki
Interior designed by Mike Rosamilia
The text of this book was set in Goudy Old Style.
Manufactured in the United States of America 1217 FFG
2 4 6 8 10 9 7 5 3 1
Library of Congress Cataloging-in-Publication Data
Names: O'Hearn, Kate, author.
Title: War of the realms : a Valkyrie novel / by Kate O'Hearn.
Description: First Aladdin hardcover edition. | New York : Aladdin, [2018] |
Series: Valkyrie ; 3 | Summary: With the rainbow bridge closed, Freya and the Valkyries must find another
way to try to stop the war that threatens not just Asgard, but the human world, as well.
Identifiers: LCCN 2017007097 (print) | LCCN 2017033772 (eBook) |
ISBN 9781481447454 (eBook) | ISBN 9781481447430 (hc)
Subjects: | CYAC: Valkyries (Norse mythology)—Fiction. | Mythology, Norse—Fiction. | War—Fiction.
Classification: LCC PZ7.O4137 (eBook) | LCC PZ7.O4137 War 2018 (print) | DDC [Fic]—dc23
LC record available at https://lccn.loc.gov/2017007097

DEDICATION

For my brother John Patrick O'Hearn

March 17, 1955–December 14, 2014

We miss you.

(You met Azrael before me, JP.

Say hi to him from me. . . .)

RAGNARÖK

THROUGHOUT TIME THERE HAS ALWAYS BEEN HOSTILITY within the Nine Realms. Most often it was between the different giant species. Sometimes the frost giants would leave their homes within the walls of Utgard on Jotunheim and attack the Great City in the fire giants' domain on Muspelheim. Occasionally mountain giants would join in the conflict. But, being equally matched, there was never a strong victor and the fight always ended long before they involved the other realms.

At other times there would be tension between the Light and Dark Elves, which would sometimes draw in the dwarfs and turn into short outbreaks of violence. But none of these battles ever resembled anything like the War of Legend—also known as the War to End All Wars—or, in Norse, *Ragnarök*.

So dreadful, so terrifying was Ragnarök, that its name is rarely spoken aloud. Occasionally there would be whispers, uttered late at night by the warriors of Valhalla, telling how this one final war would involve all the realms and eventually consume Yggdrasil, the Cosmic World Tree that was home to all the realms—thus causing the end of everything.

It was fear of Ragnarök that made Odin, leader of Asgard, continue to bring the fallen warriors from Earth's battlefields to Valhalla, to train and prepare for this ultimate conflict. Though they trained and were always prepared, no one, in all the realms, ever thought the legend could truly become real.

Until now . . .

1

"THIS IS IT," FREYA WHISPERED TO HERSELF. "WAR IN THE realms." It was too terrible to consider, but there was no avoiding it.

The young Valkyrie stood outside the closed barn doors at Valhalla Valley, the home of her Earth family. She and Archie had been thrown out by Thor, who was furious with her and held her personally responsible for the start of the war.

Thor was partly right, but she hadn't intended anything like this to happen. All she had set out to do was free her twin brother, Kai, from the Keep of the Dark Searchers before he took his final vow and drank the potion that would destroy his voice forever. She couldn't let him become one of the feared Dark Searchers without offering him the choice of another life. How could she have known that going to Utgard would cause so much trouble?

After a few minutes, the barn door swung open and a large Dark Searcher shoved Kai and their young cousin Mims outside, to join Freya and her best friend, Archie.

"I am no child!" Kai protested loudly as he tried to push his way back inside. "You cannot throw me out while the 'adults' talk. I am a Searcher; my place is in there with you!"

The imposing Dark Searcher said nothing, but held up a warning finger to Kai. After a moment, he closed the door and they heard it lock behind him.

"Thor is really mad." Mims turned to Freya. "He's blaming you for everything."

"Seems like they all are," Archie added. "But if the Searchers in there hadn't followed us from Utgard, Dirian would have killed them, too. They should be thanking us, not treating us like criminals."

Freya nodded and pressed her ear to the door. The discussions inside the barn were heating up as Asgardians, Angels of Death, and humans clashed. Thor was raging, and blaming Loki as much as he blamed Freya.

"Thor is accusing Loki now," Freya reported. "He's saying that Loki and I went to Utgard to cause trouble."

"That's a lie!" Archie said.

A fist slammed against the other side of the door, knocking it into Freya's cheek. "Ouch!" she cried. She rubbed her bruised cheek and punched the door back.

A moment later it opened, and the same Dark Searcher who had evicted Kai and Mims poked his head out. He wasn't wearing his helmet, and his dark blue eyes blazed in threat as he snarled, "You have caused enough trouble, Valkyrie. Leave here, now!"

"Come," Kai said to everyone. "If we are not welcome, we'll go."

They moved away from the barn and headed back to the farmhouse. They climbed the three steps up to the porch and stood there, glaring at the barn.

"We should be in there," Freya said.

Kai nodded. "They only see us as children. But we are warriors, and we are prepared for this war."

"How bad do you think it'll get?" Archie asked. "I mean, you don't think this could actually be the start of Rag—"

"Don't say it! Don't even think it!" Freya said quickly.

Archie was being trained in Valhalla to fight and wield a sword, alongside the soldiers the Valkyries reaped from Earth's battlefields. He was lucky enough to be personally tutored by one of Valhalla's best warriors, Crixus, the ancient gladiator. So it was no real surprise that Archie had the Great War on his mind.

Mims looked at Archie and frowned. "What are you talking about? What is Rag?"

Freya realized that her cousin—the daughter of a wingless

Dark Searcher and a human mother—had never been told any of the Norse myths. She knew nothing of her origin or the stories of her Asgard people.

"It's actually called Ragnarök," Freya corrected. She hated to have to be the one to tell her about the legendary war, but Mims needed to know how bad things could become. As Freya filled her in, all the color drained from her cousin's face. "Ragnarök means the end of everything— all the realms, including Midgard," Kai added.

"But isn't Earth called Midgard?" Mims asked.

Kai nodded. He was taller than Freya, with eyes the color of ice. His long hair was jet black, contrasting with the brilliant white feathers of his wings. He was the only Dark Searcher with white wings, so they had caused him lots of trouble over the years, just as Freya's black wings had done for her, among the white-winged Valkyries.

"I'm sure it won't go that far." Freya tried to sound reassuring.

"But it could," Kai said.

"What a little bundle of joy you are," Archie said. "Look, if everyone in the realms knows about Ragnarök, they'd be insane to start a war that big."

Kai tilted his head to the side. "Are you serious? Weren't you just in Utgard? Didn't you see the frost giants up close? Do you really think they care, or even plan beyond their next meal?"

Freya shuddered as she thought back to their experience in Utgard, the land of the frost giants. She recalled how she and Archie had nearly been squeezed to death in the hand of a giant. Kai was right. Frost giants wouldn't think twice about starting a war that big.

She'd never encountered the fire giants outside of the Ten Realms Challenge, but rumor had it that they were even worse. To all of them, the future was abstract. War, peace—it was all the same. Dark Elves were just as bad. Granted, they were more intelligent, but it was well known that they were as short tempered as the giants. It wouldn't take much to set them off.

"We've got to stop it," Archie said.

"Isn't that what they're discussing in there?" Mims asked.

"Yes," Freya said as she jumped down from the front porch. "And we should be in there. If only they would trust us, I'm sure we could help."

"Gee, where are you going?" Archie called, using his nickname for Freya.

"Back to the barn. I have to hear what they're saying."

"But that roadblock of a Searcher is guarding the door," Archie called after her. "You'll never get in."

"I'm not going to the door. Look—there's a large window into the hayloft. We can fly up there and hear what's going on."

"*Freya, are you determined to have Thor cut off your wings?*" Orus cawed from her shoulder.

"They're talking about the War of the Realms, and that involves all of us. We have a right to know what's going on." She turned to Kai. "I'll carry Archie up if you take Mims."

Freya and Kai flew through the open hayloft window and landed on the upper level of the barn. Creeping forward over the bales of hay, they peered down upon the large gathering.

Thor's voice boomed as he pointed an accusing finger at Azrael, the Angel of Death. "You should have warned us this was coming. Why didn't you say something? You could have told Odin at the Ten Realms Challenge!"

"For one thing, we couldn't be certain," Azrael said calmly. "Yes, we knew something was brewing, but we had no idea who the traitor was or when they would strike. Two, Odin already knew something was in the air. Like us, he wasn't sure who the instigator was, so he remained silent until he had more information. Had he revealed his suspicions too soon, he would have given Dirian the opportunity to plan his attack more carefully. But now, because Freya intervened at Utgard, Dirian has exposed himself before he was ready and has had to move his plans forward, which may cost him dearly."

"It has already cost us dearly, Angel," Kris, Freya's uncle, rasped, his face red with rage. His blue eyes flashed as he pushed through the line of Dark Searchers. Even without their helmets on, they were an imposing sight and an intimidating force. "Dirian has slaughtered our brothers and destroyed our keep with his betrayal. We, the few who remain, can never return there."

"You didn't belong there anyway," Eir, Freya's mother, said. "You are our kin. You should have lived with us in Asgard and not been exiled to Utgard."

Loki waved his hand dramatically. "Not that this family reunion isn't touching, but all this talk is getting us nowhere. Bifröst is closed, and soon the frost and fire giants will march on Asgard."

"They cannot get there with Bifröst closed," Thor said. "Just as we are trapped here until father has Heimdall open the bridge again."

Loki's eyes opened wide in disbelief. He gasped and then started to cough with explosive laughter. "This . . . this is what I've always loved about you, Thor," he gasped. "You're all brawn and no brains!"

Thor's face contorted with rage. "Stop laughing at me!"

The more Thor protested, the harder Loki laughed. "Stop . . . please . . . you're killing me!"

"Thor said stop laughing." Kris caught Loki by the neck and hoisted him off the ground. "Now is not the time for your games," he growled.

Loki clutched at the Searcher's gloves and kicked out his feet.

"Kris, enough!" Freya's younger uncle, Vonni, intervened. "All this bickering is getting us nowhere. You've banished the kids from being a part of this discussion, but you're behaving worse than them!" He caught his older brother's arm and pulled it away from Loki's throat.

Freya studied her two uncles closely. Vonni had been raised on Earth. His wings had been removed by Azrael when he was born and, like Mims, he had never been told his true nature. All he knew was that he, like his mother, was immortal. Vonni was a gentle and loving husband and devoted father, but he also had great strength and all the powers of the Searchers.

Then there was his older brother, Kris. A full-winged Dark Searcher who had been raised in Utgard at the Keep of the Dark Searchers. Trained to be vicious and obedient, he was a powerful fighter. As much as they looked alike, they couldn't have been more different.

"Kris, please," Vonni repeated. "Let him speak. If there is another way to travel beyond Bifröst, we should know about it."

The huge Dark Searcher looked at Thor for direction. When the son of Odin nodded, Kris released Loki.

Loki collapsed to the floor, gasping and rubbing his neck. "You could have killed me, you great big oaf!"

"And you would have deserved it," Thor said. "Now talk. How will the frost and fire giants reach Asgard? Surely Bifröst is the only way—everyone knows that."

"Everyone is wrong," Loki said, rubbing his neck. "There is another way, and you should be thanking me for knowing it."

"There is no other way," Kris rasped.

"Oh no?" Loki teased. "And just how do you think I've been getting in and out of Asgard without Odin's permission when Heimdall is always at his post?"

"You used drugs," Eir said. "Just like you did when you helped Freya cross Bifröst without permission the first time. You used a potion to render Heimdall unconscious."

Loki nodded. "True, because getting Freya killed in the tunnels wouldn't have done me any good."

"Tunnels?" Eir demanded. "Those are an old myth."

Loki turned on her. "Ragnarök is a myth too, but suddenly everyone here is talking about it. And you're right to do so. Now that Bifröst is closed, those hidden tunnels connecting the realms through the roots of Yggdrasil are the only way to reach Asgard from the lower realms. And I hate to say it, but most of them pass right through here in Midgard."

"What are you saying?" Vonni demanded.

"I'm saying that before long, Earth will be crawling with every kind of frost, fire, and mountain giant there is. They'll be coming out of one tunnel and finding their way to another leading up to Asgard. Not to mention the Dark Elves and dwarfs—and anyone else who has sided with Dirian."

Up in the hayloft, Freya inhaled and looked at Archie and Kai. She leaned closer to her brother and whispered, "Did you know about these tunnels?"

Kai shook his head. "I knew about the ones in Utgard

that ran under the keep and the other one that ran under the outer wall. But I've never heard of the roots of Yggdrasil."

Freya flashed back to her visit to the keep in Utgard. To the dark tunnels, cut into the ground with the roots hanging down, smelling of mold and earth. They had barely been wide enough for her to spread her wings. But they were there.

Down below, Thor exploded. "You're lying!"

"Are you willing to risk it?" Loki challenged. "You know I have been deceptive about many things in my life. And perhaps I do enjoy a bit of mischief—now and then. But this is too serious for games."

"This is just another trick," Thor spat.

"I'm not lying," Loki insisted. "There are tunnels that cut through all the realms. I know of at least five entrances scattered across Earth from the lower realms. And if I remember correctly, there are seven leading out of Midgard to the upper realms. If the frost giants want to go up, they need to pass through here first."

"Surely we would have known," Balder said.

Azrael cleared his throat. "Though I am loath to admit it, Loki is correct. There are many tunnels that pass between the realms. I have no doubt that if the giants know about them— and I suspect they do—Earth is in a lot of danger. . . ."

Freya and her friends remained in the hayloft unnoticed for half the night, eavesdropping on the arguing below. They all knew the problem, but there seemed to be no solution. Finally Freya shook her head. "I've heard enough. All they're doing down there is shouting. I need some fresh air."

"Me too," Archie agreed. "Those guys couldn't agree on the color of the sky, let alone how to stop the war."

They flew out the barn window and touched down on the ground outside. The night was cold, but the air was fresh and clear. Stars blazed in the black sky above them and the moon was dipping on the horizon. Freya looked at all the peaceful beauty around her—the trees, the snow-capped mountains, and the lake in the distance. All of it could soon be lost.

"All this is going to be destroyed, and it's my fault," Freya said.

"Gee, stop it," Archie said. "It's Dirian's fault, not yours."

She knew what he was trying to do, but it wasn't working. "It was me, and we both know it. I'm too impulsive—always jumping in without thinking of the consequences. We shouldn't have gone to Utgard."

Freya looked up at the raven on her shoulder. "Orus, you were right. You tried to warn me, but I wouldn't listen. Now look at the mess I've made."

Orus ruffled his feathers. *"Freya, feeling sorry for yourself isn't helping. If we hadn't gone to Utgard, you wouldn't have found your brother."*

Kai nodded. "And I'd be dead now, because I would never

join Dirian. So would all the other Searchers and maybe even Thor and Balder. Is that what you'd prefer?"

"No, of course not. But . . ."

"*No buts,*" Orus continued. "*If what Loki says is true, Dirian has found a way to keep those he kills dead forever. We might have been the trigger that started the war, but it was going to happen anyway.*"

"Only now there are still a few Dark Searchers left to defend Asgard," Kai finished.

Archie nodded. "Gee, this isn't the time to doubt ourselves. Odin needs us now more than ever."

"So does Earth," Mims added. "If it's true that giants are going to come here, what will happen?"

"From the little I've seen and heard of your world, it won't be good," Kai said. "Midgard isn't prepared for this—they don't even know giants exist. It will be down to us to stop them."

"What can we do?" Freya said, still sounding defeated. "There aren't enough of us. A few Valkyries, a dozen or so Dark Searchers, Thor and Balder. I don't know about the Angels of Death and whether they could join us or not. But even if they do, what can we achieve from here?"

"A lot!" Archie insisted. "And before you discount us humans completely, Earth does have its own defenses. We have armies and big weapons. We've even got nuclear warheads. We could do just fine against them, and maybe even stop the giants before they reached Asgard."

"What?" Mims cried. "Fight the war here on Earth?"

"Why not," Archie said, "if the giants are coming here anyway?"

"It won't work," Freya said. "I've been to plenty of Earth's battlefields and seen what your military can do. One frost giant can do more damage than a whole country's army. If they come to Earth, the best thing to do would be to stay out of their way."

"Surrender?" Archie cried. "Are you serious?"

"Very," Freya said.

"She's right," Kai agreed. His blue eyes grew intense. "Do you have any idea how powerful one frost or fire giant is? Even a small one? By their size alone, they could destroy this home with one kick. An army of them will decimate Midgard in days. Even Asgard, with all of Odin's strength, won't be able to stand against the united giants for long."

"You're saying we've already lost," Mims commented.

Kai shook his head. "No. I'm saying that this war won't be won with open engagement. If we were to rely on strength alone, the war is over long before it starts—especially against the giants. We need another plan."

"Well, who do the giants hate?" Mims asked.

"*Us,*" Orus said. "*And everyone who sides with Odin.*"

"I liked it better when giants just hated each other." Freya sighed.

"Exactly!" Kai said. "United, they are a danger to all the realms. They will be unstoppable."

They began walking toward the lake in silence, each lost in his or her own thoughts. They occasionally heard the sound of raised voices coming from the barn, Thor's ringing loudest as they argued and debated a way to save the realms.

They stood by the lake, looking at the dark beauty around them. In the distance, the howl of wolves shattered the silence. Their lonely calls, echoing off the mountains, only added to the deep sense of desperation.

"I've been thinking." Kai stretched and flapped his large white wings. He rubbed his shoulder to massage away an ache. "Not all the giants will join the war or fight against Odin. I had a few giant friends in Utgard. And there are others who make Asgard their home. I wouldn't be surprised if they join Odin's forces to fight against Dirian."

"So there are some giants on Odin's side?" Mims asked.

Kai nodded. "Not all giants hate Odin. Right now Dirian's united the giant kings against him, but I doubt it would take much to set them on each other again. . . ."

The moment Kai finished, there seemed to be a collective understanding among them—a simultaneous idea that offered the faintest glimmer of hope.

"So, if we could find a way to set the giants against each other again . . . ," Freya started carefully.

"*It could stop the war!*" Orus finished. "*That's it! That's how we defeat them. We don't—we let them defeat each other!*"

2

FREYA LED THEM BACK UP INTO THE HAYLOFT. THEN THEY jumped down to the floor of the barn completely unseen. Everyone was too busy arguing—it seemed no progress had been made since they had left the barn.

Loki was still facing off against Kris and several Dark Searchers. Thor and Balder were looking even more thunderous, while Freya's sisters stood back, arguing with their mother and Brundi.

"I don't know about you guys," Archie said, "but I'm not going to interrupt them. We're likely to have our heads chopped off or feel the force of Thor's hammer long before we tell them our idea."

"*Coward*," Orus teased. "*Besides, you're already dead! They can't hurt you.*"

"Maybe not here," Archie agreed. "But you've seen how Thor can hold a grudge. What about when we make it back to Asgard?"

"If we don't find a way to stop the war, there won't *be* an Asgard." Freya caught Archie's arm. "C'mon. We have to find a way to get them to listen to us. We don't have a moment to waste."

In the center of the barn, Balder was holding Thor back to stop him from hitting Loki. Even in this most dangerous of times, it appeared that Loki was causing trouble. He just couldn't help himself.

They saw Azrael standing with his angels, and Freya knew he was the only one who would listen to them. "Azrael." Freya crept up to him, careful to avoid being seen. "We've had an idea, but we need your help to get the others to listen."

"I doubt anyone could do that. What's your plan?"

They filled him in as fast as they could. "We're just not sure how to do it," Freya added. "We don't really know a lot about the giant kings or what it would take to turn them against each other."

Archie added, "Or how to get Thor to listen to us."

Azrael rubbed his chin thoughtfully and started to nod. "You know, it's so simple, it just might work." He caught Freya by the hand. "Come with me. It's your idea. It's only fair you should take the credit."

"No, Azrael, I can't!" Freya begged as she tried to pull

away. "I'm in enough trouble already. There's no telling what Thor will do if he sees us back in here."

"He will listen; that's what he'll do," Azrael said. "This is the perfect opportunity for you to redeem yourselves. You must tell him."

Azrael's grasp was too strong for Freya to break away from him. He led them to the front of the barn, where the loudest fighting was going on.

"Excuse me!" Azrael shouted. His voice rang out louder than Freya had imagined possible. Everyone in the barn stopped and looked at the Angel of Death. Azrael smiled. "Now that I have your attention, Freya and Kai have something to say."

Thor's blazing eyes shot from Azrael to Freya and then Kai. She could actually feel the weight of his anger toward her. "What are they doing back in here? I told them to go!"

Azrael shook his head. "Thor, you should be thanking them for exposing Dirian's betrayal before he had the chance to kill all the Searchers in the keep."

"That remains to be seen," Thor said. "But even so, they are hardly experienced fighters. There is nothing they can say that will help with the war."

"That's the problem," Azrael said. "You're thinking like warriors. But you can't possibly win against the combined strength of the giants."

"Of course we can; I have Mjölnir." Thor lifted up his

hammer proudly. "And the Searchers and Valkyries have their fighting skills, powers, and weapons."

"Granted, your hammer is great," Azrael said. "But it, like you, can't be in more than one place at a time. The giants aren't going to line up for you while you strike them down one by one. They will come at us from every direction."

"So what are you suggesting?" Thor challenged.

"Not me," Azrael said. "Them." He drew Freya and Kai closer. "Tell them what you just told me."

Freya felt everyone's eyes resting heavily on her. She stepped closer to her brother.

"Well?" Thor demanded. "You have our attention. Tell us, what is this monumental idea of yours that will stop the giants?"

The rage in his blue eyes held Freya's tongue. Kai too was left speechless under the intensity of Odin's son's gaze. But then Vonni came over and put his hand on her shoulder. "Go on; just tell us your plan," he encouraged.

"It—it was really Kai's idea," Freya said. "We were talking about the giants and how they always hated each other until Dirian united them."

"We already know that," Thor said, irritated. "What is your idea?"

Freya inhaled deeply. "Well, we know we can never beat them in a fight. They're just too big and strong. But what if we broke their truce? If Dirian could unite the giants, maybe we can turn them against each other again. Then the frost and fire giants would be too busy fighting each other to attack Asgard."

Thor's face was unreadable. His eyes bored into Kai. "You thought of this?"

Kai straightened his back and tried to look like the brave Dark Searcher that he was. But Freya could feel his nerves as he faced Thor. "It wasn't just me," Kai said.

"You know, Brother, this could work." Balder took a step forward. He was known in Asgard as the most gentle and reasonable of Odin's children. The two brothers couldn't have been more different. Because of this, they were very close. If anyone could calm Thor's fiery temper, it was Balder. "I'm sure if a demented Searcher like Dirian could get the giants together, someone could drive a wedge between them just as easily."

"Could it really be that simple?" Vonni asked.

Thor was scratching his long red beard. His bushy eyebrows knitted together in deep thought. He slowly nodded. "It really could." His eyes settled on Freya. "That idea, little Valkyrie, may have just saved your life."

Dawn arrived unnoticed as the fighters in the barn discussed the best way forward. The plan itself seemed simple enough. Working out how to achieve it wasn't.

As morning became afternoon, large picnic tables were set up for food to be served in the barn. The size of the new, winged visitors to the farm meant dining in the house was impossible.

Freya stood with Archie and Azrael, watching the banquet. Her uncle Vonni was dishing out potato salad onto Mims's plate as she sat between her parents. When he finished, he nudged her playfully before passing the dish along. Freya felt a pang of sadness as she watched that simple action. Mims had a father who adored her. He was a powerful Dark Searcher, but his love was obvious.

For most of her life, Freya had wished she knew who her own father was. All her mother would say was that he was a warrior at Valhalla. She yearned to know more, but knew it was forbidden. Valkyries were never told who their fathers were.

"I still can't believe what I'm seeing," Archie complained. "Dark Searchers and Valkyries are sitting with the farmhands like nothing is wrong."

"I know," Freya agreed, pulled from her reverie. "We're wasting precious time. We have a war to stop, but look—everyone is just sitting there eating and laughing like it's a celebration. Don't they realize what we're facing?"

"They know," Azrael said seriously. "That's why they're enjoying themselves. Everyone in this barn realizes this may be the last opportunity for a normal gathering. Some, maybe even most, may not survive what is to come."

Freya looked back at the table, seeing things differently. Azrael was right. Yes, Maya was flirting with a handsome young Dark Searcher, and yes, her mother was smiling as she cradled Vonni's new baby son and spoke with his wife, Sarah. But she sensed beneath their smiles and felt the collective dread.

"I'm sorry," she said softly to Azrael. "I spoke too soon. They know what we're facing."

"There's no need to apologize. We're all frightened for the future," responded the Angel of Death. "Now, if you will excuse us, my angels and I must return to our realm."

"Aren't you going to help us stop the war?" Archie asked.

Azrael nodded. "Of course we are. But we must return to Heofon to tell of what we've learned and to make our own plans. When this war reaches Earth, we must all be prepared to fight for humanity."

Freya felt something heavy settle in her chest at their parting. "I *will* see you again, won't I?" she asked nervously.

Azrael smiled, but it held traces of sadness. "Of course you will. You're my favorite Valkyrie in all the realms. Just call my name and I will come to you, always." He gave Orus a long stroke down his sleek black feathers. "Keep a good eye on this one, Orus."

The raven bowed his head. *"I will."*

After saying his farewells to Archie and the others, Azrael and his angels opened their wings and took off into the clear blue sky.

When he was gone, Freya said nothing for several minutes. She couldn't shake the awful feeling that she might never see him again.

3

BY LATE AFTERNOON, THE FIRST EMBERS OF A PLAN WERE being stoked. Maps were laid out and Loki indicated the tunnel entrances the giants would use to enter Earth and then head through up to the upper realms to reach Asgard.

"There could be more tunnels that I don't know about," Loki admitted. "But these are the ones I've used." He pointed down at the world map. "There's a good one here in the Florida Everglades—that's my favorite. It's big and wide. I'm sure it's going to be the tunnel of choice for the giants. Then there's one in France, one over here in Russia, and then another in China. The fifth tunnel is down here in South Africa."

Thor followed Loki's finger on the map. "What about the exits out of Midgard going up toward Asgard?"

Loki nodded. "The closest one in North America is here, in northern Quebec." He then pointed to multiple places on the map, revealing the giants' routes to the upper realms.

"There are so many," Eir, Freya's mother, said.

"I'm sure there are more that I don't know about," Loki acknowledged.

"And all scattered too far around the world for us to cover," Vonni said. He stared at the map and shook his head. "If they do come, and if they use this entrance through the Everglades, they'll tear a path right up the East Coast of the United States to make their way to Canada. It'll be a disaster."

"They will come," Thor said. "Have no doubt about that. We can wait at the various entrances and fight them there, stopping them from getting any farther into Midgard. Or maybe I could close the entrance with Mjölnir."

Loki glared at Thor and shook his head. "Can't you get it through your thick skull? These are entrances to the Yggdrasil root system. If you destroy these entrances, you'll disrupt the flow of energy that feeds the tree. If the tree dies, we die with it! Your hammer could do more damage than the giants."

"Who are you calling thick skulled?" Thor challenged.

"You, if you can't see the lunacy of your plan!"

"All I see is your finger in this. I'm still not convinced you didn't start this mess with the giants."

"What?" Loki cried. "You're still accusing me of starting the war?"

Thor loomed over him. "That's exactly what I'm saying. Why should we trust you now? You've done nothing to earn it!"

Archie shook his head in disbelief. "I can't believe they're still at each other's throats."

"I'm getting out of here before Thor turns on us again." Freya walked out of the barn.

"Where're you going?" Archie called after her.

Freya sighed. "I don't know, just away from them and their constant bickering."

"It's Loki who always starts it!" Orus said. *"I'm with Thor. I still don't trust him, and I think he might be behind everything."*

"That's just it—he could be," Freya admitted. "But we don't know."

Too restless to stay in one spot, Freya turned to Archie. "Do you want to go flying with me?"

"Now?" Archie said. "Gee, it's still light out. You could be seen!"

"At this point, I don't care. Frost giants could be here any minute; being seen by a few people is the least of our problems. Besides, if I stay here much longer, I'm going to go insane. We won't go far, just up to the mountain where Azrael took us. The view is breathtaking and the air feels clearer up there."

Freya put her arm around Archie and opened her wings.

She sprang up into the air and started to fly. The day was cool and the fresh air felt wonderful on her face. Rising higher over the lake and to the mountains behind it, she felt calmed by the beauty around them.

They touched down at the top of the mountain and gazed over the valley. "Archie, this is real . . . ," Freya started.

"Of course it is."

"No, I mean *really* real. Asgard is at war. Earth is in danger, and I'm terrified that this could be Ragnarök."

Archie hesitated before he responded. "Gee, when I first started to train with Crixus, he told me about Ragnarök. He believes if we all pull together, it doesn't have to be the end of everything."

Freya frowned. "He said that?"

Archie nodded. "That's why he trains me and the other warriors so hard, so that we are prepared to do our part and make sacrifices. He said Ragnarök will bring dark times, but if we hold true to ourselves, from it the light will rise."

"Crixus, the gladiator, told you that?"

"He's not the savage that you think he is. He's really cool."

Freya had only spoken to Crixus once or twice. He had seemed awkward and uncomfortable in her presence, and she was sure she had once caught him looking at her strangely when she and her sisters sang in Valhalla. She never imagined that a gladiator could think so philosophically.

"Do the other warriors feel that way?"

Archie nodded. "Most do. That's why they train so hard."

"All that training will be lost if we don't find a way to turn the giants against each other," Orus cawed.

"And that's the problem," Freya said. "How do we do it?"

She took a seat on the boulder that Azrael had hidden her coat beneath. That seemed such a long time ago, but it was only a matter of months. Archie sat beside her. Saying nothing, he held her hand as they looked out over the mountains.

As the sun slowly crossed the sky and started to descend in the west, they were still no closer to a solution.

"Okay, let's think. . . . What do we know about frost giants?" Archie asked.

Freya shook her head. "Not a lot. Loki is part frost giant. Maybe he knows what can turn them against each other."

"But can we trust him?" Orus asked.

"That's the trouble," Freya said, considering all her encounters with him. "We can't."

"So we're stuck." Archie stood at the edge, peering over the valley. "Earth is about to be invaded and we can't stop it."

As they stood together, Freya heard a sound that was all too familiar—a sound that chilled her blood. It was the heavy thumping sound of large, powerful rotors.

"Do you hear that?" Orus cawed.

Archie frowned and looked around. "That sounds just like . . . Over there, look, just coming over the mountains! Army helicopters."

A large squadron of military helicopters was flying over the mountain range. They crested the highest peak and started to descend down into the valley—their destination clear.

Terror clutched Freya's heart. "They're heading to the farm!"

Freya grabbed Archie and leaped off the side of the mountain. Flapping her wings with all her might, she drove toward the valley. Even before she got close, the sound of gunfire echoed in the mountains.

"It sounds like a war down there!" Archie cried. "Faster, Gee. Fly faster!"

When they cleared the trees and flew over the lake, Freya saw a long line of military trucks tearing down the dirt road toward the farm. As they flew closer, they saw even more were already at the farm. Soldiers were pouring out with their weapons raised. Some were firing into the barn. Helicopters landed in the paddocks as more soldiers arrived.

They could hear Thor shouting and the sound of his hammer smashing the ground. The sides of the barn rattled and soldiers were knocked off their feet.

Freya touched down on the closest shore, and she and

Archie raced into the trees. But before they made it into the clearing of the farm, something attacked Freya from behind and tackled her to the ground.

A hand slammed against her mouth. The grip of her attacker was terrifyingly strong as she squealed and struggled in the viselike arms. No matter how hard she fought, or how much she flapped her wings to cast him off, she could not break free.

"Freya, stop fighting me!" Loki hushed. "Soldiers are everywhere. Stay quiet or they'll hear you."

"Let her go!" Archie cried.

"Not until she promises to stay quiet and not go charging in there."

Freya squealed again and tried to break free of Loki's grip, but he was much stronger than she ever imagined.

"I told you to keep quiet!" he ordered. "I'll release my hand if you do. Will you stay quiet?"

Defeated, Freya nodded reluctantly. When Loki removed his hand, she looked up into his blazing eyes. "Get off me. They're taking my family!"

"That's my family in there too!" Loki challenged, still holding her fast. "Brundi, Vonni, Sarah, and the kids may not be my blood, but they're family just the same. But if you go charging in there, they'll capture you, too."

"Not if you change into a dragon or even a full frost giant and we attack them."

"Then what?" Loki demanded. "More will come. This is not the time to engage the Midgard military. We have a plan and this is all part of it!"

"What plan?" Archie demanded.

"If you promise not to go flying in there, I'll tell you," Loki said. "Do we have an agreement?"

Freya stared into Loki's eyes and couldn't decide if he was telling the truth. Finally she relaxed in his grip. "All right, I'll listen. But if you're lying to me . . ."

"I'm not." Loki let her go and rose to his feet. He offered her his hand.

Freya swatted it away. "I can do it myself."

When she was on her feet, Loki scanned the area, checking that they were still alone. "Follow me. We'll get closer so you can see what's happening. But if you try anything, I'll stop you—and we both know I can."

Loki led them through the trees. Keeping low and hidden, they moved toward the farm. Freya gasped when the large red barn came into view. It was surrounded by rows of armed soldiers.

"Look how many are here!" Archie cried.

Ahead of them, the soldiers pressed forward. They shouted orders into the barn, threatening to open fire and demanding that everyone surrender.

"Thor will never surrender," Freya said softly.

"He'll die before he does," Orus added.

"Just watch," Loki said. "I told you, it's all part of the plan."

No sooner were the words out of his mouth than they heard Thor's booming voice. "Hold your fire—there are innocent humans in here. We are coming out!"

Thor and Balder appeared at the entrance. Both had their hands in the air—though Thor still clutched his hammer. Directly behind him were the Dark Searchers. They were back in their full armor and helmets, though their swords were stowed away in their sheaths. With their hands up and large black wings open, they surrendered.

Freya sought out her brother among them and saw him advancing with the others, though he kept his white wings closed.

Behind them were the Valkyries. Freya's mother and sisters were also in their battle armor, but without their helmets, their wings open and arms raised in surrender.

"Why are they allowing themselves to be seen?" Freya asked. "If they wore their helmets, they'd be invisible and safe."

"Keep watching," Loki whispered.

Soldiers rushed forward and tried to put restraints on the Dark Searchers. Even though they lowered their hands, they refused to allow themselves to be chained.

When a soldier approached Freya's mother, she pulled her hands away. "We're Valkyries. If you touch us, you'll die.

We will do as you ask and go with you, but no one must ever lay a hand on us."

"*Eir, don't do it,*" Orus cawed.

Freya watched helplessly as her family, Thor, Balder, and the Dark Searchers were captured by army soldiers and loaded into the military trucks.

"Now do you understand?" Loki asked. "You know they could easily fight off the soldiers, but they've let themselves be captured. It's the only way."

"Why?" Freya asked.

"We know we can't fight the giants here on Earth alone," Loki whispered. "We need help. But simply asking the military would not work. They have to feel they are in command. After all the sightings of you on Earth, and with the noisy arrival of Thor, Balder, and the Dark Searchers last night, they had to know about us and track us here. So Vonni had a plan. It took some doing to convince the others to go along with it, but they finally agreed to let themselves be captured. Then they'll tell the military command what's coming."

"You don't actually think they'll believe them?" Archie cried.

"They will the moment the first frost or fire giant steps foot on Earth."

"*Then what?*" Orus demanded.

"Then, hopefully, they will work with us to stop the invasion."

"And if they don't?" Archie asked.

"If they don't, Thor and the others will simply break free and go after the giants themselves."

Archie stepped away from them and walked closer to the trees. "I don't like it, and I don't trust you! Why are you here and not there with the others?"

"You don't have to trust me, ghost!" Loki spat. "And I'm not here for you. My job is to stop Freya from doing something stupid like getting herself captured along with the others. . . ."

"Why?" Freya demanded.

Loki sighed and combed his fingers through his long dark hair. "Because we have our own mission."

"What mission? What are you talking about?" Orus cawed.

Loki grinned. "We're going to cause the trouble between the giant kings and stop this war!"

"What?" Freya cried.

Loki slammed his hand across her mouth and shoved Freya up against a tree. "Shut up! Are you trying to get caught with the others?"

"I'm warning you, let her go!" Archie charged at him.

"Or what?" Loki challenged. His eyes burned red with fury as he turned on Archie. "What will you do, ghost?"

The tension between Archie and Loki was quickly getting out of hand. Freya reached up and pulled Loki's hand away from her mouth. "Stop it, both of you!" she said. "All right, I'm listening."

Loki glared at Archie a moment longer. He stepped away from Freya and reached for a package hidden behind a tree. "Not here. Let's go somewhere we can talk without fear of you doing something stupid!"

Freya looked back toward the barn to see her mother and sisters climbing up into the back of a large truck. Mims was among them, looking frightened. The worst thing, though, was seeing Vonni, Sarah, and the baby being separated from the rest. They were taken to a car and put in the backseat. Even before the trucks moved, the car pulled away from the farm, taking her uncle, aunt, and infant cousin to an uncertain future.

Every nerve in her body screamed for her to do something. Anything. That was her family being taken away. Even though it was part of a greater plan, it was still tearing at her heart to watch.

"All right," she finally said. "It's almost dark out. I know where we can go." She faced Loki. "But if you're lying to me, I swear I'll kill you."

4

BY THE TIME NIGHT FELL, FREYA, ARCHIE, AND LOKI WERE
back at the top of the mountain.

"So this is where you hang out," Loki said, putting his
large bundle down.

"I don't hang out," Freya countered. "But we do come
here to think." She turned on the troublemaker. "All right,
you wanted to talk—so talk."

Loki paused, and then something strange happened. His
air of self-confidence slipped away. His shoulders slumped
and his expression became unreadable. He wouldn't look up
to meet her eyes. "I know what you and everyone else thinks
of me," he started. "I've known all my life and usually I don't
care. But I do now."

Freya knew him too well to be completely fooled. But

still, there was something in his expression that seemed genuine. "What changed?"

"This—the war."

"You mean because everyone thinks you're behind it?" Archie said.

Loki's eyes darkened for a fraction of a second, but then he nodded. "I'm not. But I can't convince the others."

"Everyone is suspicious of you because of your behavior," Freya said. "You constantly cause trouble, and Ragnarök would be your ultimate trick."

"Ragnarök is the end of everything! What would I stand to gain? Thor, Odin, and everyone else, *including me*, would die! There's no point in causing trouble if, ultimately, I'm not around to enjoy the fruits of my labor."

In a strange kind of way, it made a lot of sense. There would be nothing for him if war destroyed everything. "But why cause trouble at all?" Freya asked.

Loki sighed, and it made Freya uncomfortable. She was used to his arrogance, his bravado. Not this new, almost defeated, Loki. "Because it's fun," he finally said. "And because it keeps people sharp. Look at what I did for you."

"Are you serious?" Archie cried. He started to count off on his fingers. "You nearly got her de-winged, blinded, and banished! She was almost killed by Dark Searchers, and then nearly died being squashed by frost giants—"

"No, no, no! Those were side effects," Loki said. "Because

of me you are braver and more independent. Odin knows you now; so do Thor and the other senior Asgardians. They know your name, who you are, and what you are capable of, and they respect you for it. You can claim the head Angel of Death as a personal friend! Tell me, what other Valkyrie has ever achieved that—and at such a young age?"

Freya hated to admit it, but part of what he said was true. Because of Loki, she had accomplished things she never dreamed possible, including having Archie, her brother, and Azrael in her life.

"Did you tell this to the others?" Freya asked.

"They don't trust me. Nothing I say will ever change their minds. They think I'm behind all this trouble and won't consider anything else."

"If they think that, why did Thor send you on this secret mission?"

Loki turned his back and walked up to the cliff edge.

"Loki?" Freya asked.

"*He didn't!*" Orus cawed. "*There is no mission—you ran away from the barn so you wouldn't be captured by the soldiers!*"

"What a liar!" Archie cried. "You're here to save your own skin!"

"All right, it's true. I lied!" Loki admitted. "There isn't a mission for us. But there should be. I have an idea that I know will work, but they wouldn't listen to me. They thought I was just trying to escape capture. But not this time—this time

I'm fighting for all of us. I'm fighting to stop Ragnarök."

"So my mother and Thor don't know you're with me?" Freya asked.

Loki shook his head. "No. They think I fled in fear. But they must be relieved that you haven't been captured with them."

"Gee, if we leave now, maybe we can follow the convoy. We can get them out of wherever they are taken!"

"You stupid ghost," Loki cried. "They can break free anytime they want. No human prison could ever hold them—especially Thor! It's all part of the plan to engage the human military. But that strategy will only slow down the giants. It won't stop them. My plan will!"

"What plan?" Freya asked. "You keep talking about a plan. What is it?"

"It is a plan that will only succeed with your help."

"*You're stalling,*" Orus cawed.

"Just tell us," Freya demanded.

Loki looked at her. "How good is your memory?"

That surprised her. "It's all right. Why?"

"Think back to your early history lessons. Do you remember the stories about the Aesir-Vanir War?"

Freya frowned, trying to remember. "We of Asgard were the Aesir, and the people of the lower realm, Vanaheim, were the Vanir. I don't remember why they were fighting, but the war went on so long, they finally called a truce. We sent two hostages to their realm and they sent two to Asgard. There's been peace ever since."

"So? What is your point?" Archie asked. "We don't have all night, you know."

Loki shot him a withering look, but continued. "The Aesir-Vanir War started because Odin and his people were jealous of the magic of the Vanir. They wanted that power to help rule the realms, but the Vanir didn't see it that way and rebelled. The war ended only because each side grew tired of fighting. The Aesir used brute force, swords, and steel, whereas the Vanir used magic as their weapon. If I'm honest, the realms would be completely different—and maybe better off—if the Vanir had won."

"They didn't and we're all peaceful now," Orus said.

"But we aren't, are we?" Loki said. "Obviously there has been some resentment of Odin for some time. Otherwise Dirian couldn't have compelled the other Dark Searchers to join him—and he wouldn't have been able to convince the giant kings, who are notorious for hating each other, to work together against Asgard."

"What does this have to do with the Vanir?" Freya asked.

"Everything!" Loki said. "Don't you see? The moment the giants start moving through the realms to reach Asgard, the Vanir will be drawn in. We can't be sure whose side they'll take. They've been a silent mystery for millennia, never leaving their realm, even to join in the Ten Realms Challenge. As far as I know, no one from Asgard has ventured to Vanaheim in many generations. We don't know how strong their magic has become, or what their feelings are toward Odin or Asgard. But I believe it's there that we will find the solution to the war."

"You want us to go to Vanaheim?" Freya cried. "Are you crazy? We can't—it's forbidden for anyone to go there!"

"When has that ever stopped you?" Loki said. "You went to Utgard knowing full well that the Valkyries weren't allowed there. You even entered the Keep of the Dark Searchers. Suddenly you care about rules?"

"Utgard is one thing, and I was looking for my brother. Vanaheim is another! It's wild and savage. Magic rules there, not logic—"

"Exactly!" Loki said. "And it's going to take a lot of Vanir magic to get the giants to stop." Loki bent closer and his intense eyes bored into her. "Freya, we are fighting for all the realms. If we fail, those who survive will wish they'd died. Giants will overrun the Earth, maybe even destroy it. They will capture Asgard and enslave those they don't kill. You've experienced them up close. Would you want to see that happen?"

Freya looked down into the dark forest beneath them. Her Valkyrie vision let her see everything—the beauty and wonder of the world around her. The thought of frost or fire giants here was too terrible to consider.

"What's in it for you, Loki?" Archie asked. "You don't do anything without a reason."

Loki's hand flashed out to strike Archie across the face, but since Archie had no substance on Earth, Loki's hand passed right through him.

"You missed!"

"Archie, stop, please," Freya said. "This is too serious for you two to keep bickering."

"That's the point—it's deadly serious!" Loki turned on Archie. "Nothing's in it for me! Nothing but the protection of my family and those I care about." He focused his whole attention back on Freya. "I have burned a lot of bridges in my life. I know it. No one trusts me, especially you. But I am not lying—not about this. The Vanir can help end this war before it goes too far."

"Why do you need our help?"

Once again Loki's shoulders slumped. "Because I can't do it alone. As one of Odin's Battle-Maidens, you might be able to convince the Vanir Elders to take our side in the war. I imagine they'll trust you more than me. I'm sure the giants are expecting them to remain neutral, if they've even considered them at all. But their involvement could mean the difference between peace or Ragnarök."

"You've really thought this through, haven't you?"

"Yes!" Loki cried. "I'm not trouble all the time, you know! Occasionally I try to do something good. This is one of those times. We can't win this war without the Vanir on our side. It's as simple as that."

Freya felt conflicted. She didn't trust Loki—they'd been through a lot together, and he'd always been deceitful, always had his own agenda. But at the same time, what he said made sense. She looked up at the raven on her shoulder. "Orus, you've lived in Asgard just as long as me. You've seen everything and know the history. What do you think we should do?"

"Why are you asking me?" Orus cried.

"Because whatever I do, you have to do too. This is too big a decision for me alone. You know I trust your advice."

"You're going to listen to a bird?" Loki cried.

"Orus is more than a bird, and you know it," Freya said.

"But why now?" Orus cawed. *"After all the times I told you not to do something and you did it anyway, why would you care what I have to say now?"*

"Because this is more than us—it involves all the realms."

"Freya," Orus finally cawed. *"What does your heart tell you to do? That has never steered you wrong before."*

"He's right," Archie said. "Your instincts are good. You know I'll go anywhere with you and support whatever you decide. But this is up to you."

Freya looked at Archie and then up to Orus. This was the biggest decision of her life. Stay and fight with her family and maybe make a difference. Or go off with Loki on a crazy quest to an unknown realm that could get them killed—but if they succeeded, could save all the realms.

Finally, she turned to Loki.

"All right, let's go!"

5

LOKI STARED AT FREYA FOR SEVERAL HEARTBEATS, HIS
expression unreadable. Freya wasn't sure if she saw gratitude
in his eyes, or doubt. Whatever it was, it lasted for only a
second, then vanished.

A moment later he said, "Good. Now, before we leave,
you need to change. You can't go to Vanaheim dressed as a
Midgard country bumpkin." He handed the bundle he was
carrying to her. "Don't take too long. Every moment counts."

Freya looked down at the clothes she was wearing from
Mims's wardrobe: a floral skirt and lacy top with slits cut in
the back for her wings to fit through. He was right—it wasn't
exactly standard Valkyrie attire.

Inside the bundle she found the clothes she had worn
during her visit to Utgard. It was a Dark Searcher uniform,

complete with black helmet. She sighed at the thought of having to wear it again. She lifted it and gasped. Hidden underneath was her golden, flaming sword—the one she'd won at the Ten Realms Challenge—along with her dagger and Valkyrie armor. "How did you get my armor? I left it in Utgard."

"I went back, remember? I collected it from where we hid it. Good thing I did, too. You may need it where we're going."

Freya frowned. "How did you know I would agree to go with you?"

"You're not stupid. I knew you'd see that this is the only way to stop the war."

Freya wasn't sure if she should be flattered by him saying she wasn't stupid. She took the bundle and went behind the boulder to get changed. She emerged wearing the Dark Searcher uniform, with her armor breastplate over it. She drew the gauntlets up her arms and then pulled the heavy black cloak around her shoulders to cover her wings. Finally, she wrapped the sword belt around her waist and stowed the helmet away for later. "All right, where do we go to find the root down to Vanaheim?"

Loki looked up into the star-filled night. "It's going to be a long flight, but there's only one exit I know of that goes down to that realm."

"Where is it?" Archie asked.

"A small island off Greenland called Kaffeklubben Island. It's the closest landmass to what the humans call the North Pole."

"We're flying to the North Pole!" Archie cried. "That's thousands of miles away from here. Gee will never make it in one night."

Loki looked Freya up and down and then glanced back to Archie. "She could if she tried, but she won't have to. I'm going to carry her . . . and you too, I guess." He stepped away from them and started to shimmer and grow. A moment later, the large black dragon was standing before them. It lowered its head to the ground and invited them up onto its back.

Freya stole one final look down into the valley— knowing this might be the last time she saw it. Finally, she nodded and climbed up onto the dragon's back.

As Dragon Loki climbed high into the sky, Freya used one hand to hold on to a tall spinal plate, while the other held tightly to Archie. Orus was tucked under her cloak. Having never ridden a dragon before, Freya had not realized how uncomfortable it would be. Loki not only had slippery, pointed spinal plates, but he also had razor-sharp scales running down his sleek dragon body. The scales caught her cloak and cut painfully into her legs. Yet despite the discomfort, with each powerful wing beat they were moving faster than she'd imagined possible.

Heading north and then east, they watched the midnight sun sitting sullenly on the polar horizon. This time of year it set only briefly, never rising high in the sky, casting the area in a kind of strange twilight.

"It's beautiful," Archie said, gazing around. "Look, it's the middle of the night and you can still see. It reminds me of Utgard."

They were flying over snow-covered ground. Freya reckoned they were soaring over northern Canada. This far north, there were no signs of human habitation, and the terrain remained wild and untouched. Well above the tree line, very little grew, with only the hardiest of animals able to survive in the harsh environment.

Hours later, they were passing over the ocean and then approaching Greenland. Continuing north, they saw a few scattered islands along the shores. Loki started to descend as they passed over water again. In the distance, the small outline of a narrow island appeared. Ice floes were floating in the water, making it difficult to distinguish between land and water.

The dragon glided smoothly over the rocky surface of the island until he approached the northern tip. Tucking in his leathery wings, Loki touched down. While the dragon shimmered and returned to human shape, Freya and Archie looked around.

"Wow," Archie said. "It's hard to believe we're still on

Earth. I never dreamed a place could look this barren. I bet it's cold, too. It's a good thing I'm a ghost and can't feel it."

"I can," Freya said. "It's not as cold as Utgard, but it's sure not warm either."

Loki stepped up to them. "Well, it's better than being in the center of New York City. At least here no one will follow us to Vanaheim. Come. Time is not our friend."

"Where?" Freya asked, turning in a circle. "There's nothing here. No fjords, caves, or mountains. It's all flat and empty. Where's the entrance to the root system?"

"It's not on the island," Loki said, charging forward. "It's under it. I'm afraid we're about to get very wet."

"*Figures,*" Orus complained, flying up to Freya's shoulder. "*Have I ever told you how much I hate water?*"

Freya patted the raven's back. "Every chance you get."

"*But still, here we are—about to go for a swim in the freezing ocean.*"

Loki stopped and turned on the bird. "If you're not happy, you can always stay here."

"*No way,*" Orus said. "*I'm not letting Freya go anywhere alone with you.*"

"Then stop complaining and shut that black beak of yours!"

Orus was about to protest when Freya grabbed his beak. "Let it go, Orus. I'm not looking forward to getting wet either, but I don't think we have much choice."

"No, we don't," Loki snapped.

At the shoreline there was more frozen slush than free-running water. It became solid ice just a few yards out. "In a couple of weeks, it'll all be frozen over," Loki said. "At least now we can still reach the entrance. Any later in the year and we'd need to burn our way in. Come. It's this way."

Showing no reaction to the cold, Loki entered the water and waded out to chest level. He turned. "Well, are you coming or not?"

Freya caught hold of Orus and tucked him into her breastplate. Then she reached for Archie's hand. "Come on, let's get wet."

Despite living in Asgard, which was much colder than Earth, Freya inhaled sharply from the shockingly cold water.

"You should see your face." Archie laughed.

Freya shot him a withering look. "Just wait till this is over. We'll go back to Utgard and I can laugh at *your* face."

"No one is going anywhere if we don't stop this war," Loki said. "Hurry up—the water's not that cold."

"Says who?" Freya called. Her teeth were chattering and she was sure her lips were turning blue.

"It's going to be a treacherous swim," Loki said. "But I'll be there to guide you. Now, hold on tightly to Archie and Orus. If you let go, you won't have enough breath left to go back for them." He gave Archie a dark look. "And don't expect me to come back for you, because I won't."

"Don't worry about me," Archie said. "But if this is a trick—"

"How deep are we going?" Freya cut in.

Loki glared at Archie a moment more. "Deep enough that I'll have to transform into a whale to get you there. When I change, I want you to put your hand in my mouth and keep it there. I'm going to bite down on you, hard. But it's so I don't lose you."

"You're going to bite her?" Archie cried.

Loki narrowed his eyes. "Consider yourself lucky that I can't bite you!" He turned to Freya. "Now, do you understand? Don't pull your hand free of my mouth."

"I won't."

Loki closed his eyes and started to shimmer. A moment later, a beautiful white beluga whale floated in the water beside her. It let out a high, squeaky whistle and opened its mouth.

Freya caught hold of Archie's hand and looked down at Orus, hidden in her breastplate. "I hope you can hold your breath long enough," she said to the raven.

"*Me too,*" Orus agreed. "*But if I drown, don't worry. I'll come back to you.*"

"Promise?"

"*I promise. Just don't let Loki eat or bury me.*"

"I won't."

The beluga whale whistled impatiently and spat a mouthful of water at Freya.

"I'm coming!" She looked at Archie. "You ready?" When he nodded, Freya placed her left hand in the whale's mouth. Loki closed it on her hand, and his sharp teeth cut into her skin.

"Ouch!" Freya cried. "Loki, not so tight!"

The beluga whale whistled again but didn't lighten his grip. Instead, he took a deep breath through his blowhole and dived down into the icy waves.

Freya barely had time to take her own breath before she was pulled down beneath the surface. Her hand was stinging from the salt water and the ferocious bite of the whale. But as they sank deeper into the dark water, she found she was grateful for the tight grip.

Deeper and deeper they descended. Freya could feel Orus squirming and his fear rising as he ran out of breath and slowly suffocated. Every nerve in her body shouted for her to go back to the surface, to get him back to air. But Loki wouldn't let her go.

Forgive me, Orus . . . , Freya called with all her heart. Soon the raven stopped squirming and passed out.

There was little time for Freya to worry about Orus as she felt the pain coming from her own lungs. But still Loki drew her deeper into the ocean depths.

Thought soon slipped into dizziness as she started to struggle against the grip that kept her in the water. Her lungs screamed for air. Suddenly her mind was cast back to the Ten

Realms Challenge, when Dirian strangled her to death. This was just the same.

The sound of blood started rushing in her ears. The pain in her chest intensified as her body fought for breath. A strange disorientation hit, and then, finally, nothingness.

6

"GEE, WAKE UP. . . ."

"Come on, Freya, we don't have time for this!"

Freya felt warm lips pressing against her mouth and a full, painful breath of air being forced into her lungs.

"Breathe!" Loki commanded.

The lips and then warm breath again . . . This repeated several times as Freya struggled back to consciousness. Suddenly feeling very sick, she rolled over and coughed up a lungful of bitter, salty water.

"Finally!" Loki said, sitting back on his heels.

"Gee!" Archie cried. "Talk to me! Are you all right?"

Freya's head was pounding and her lungs felt like they were still filled with brine. "I—I'm fine. . . ." She coughed. "What happened?"

"You disappointed me," Loki said. "I thought you would be able to hold your breath longer than that."

"Wha—what?"

"You drowned," Archie said. "Loki had to resuscitate you. But I don't think you died."

"Almost," Loki agreed. "But not quite."

"Drowned . . ." Freya suddenly sat up and winced, as she was crushing her wings. "Orus!"

Loki handed the limp body of the raven to her. He was wet and deathly still as his head lulled to the side. "We should bury him down here and get going. We still have a long journey ahead of us."

"No!" Freya cried. Her senses told her that a small spark of life remained in Orus. She opened his beak and, as Loki had done to her, she breathed air into his tiny lungs. "He's still alive. He's going to be okay!"

Loki stood. "If you're sure . . . But if he dies, don't expect me to carry his smelly carcass around."

"I won't," Freya said as she clutched Orus to her and gave him another breath. "You promised," she whispered to the raven, breathing into him again. "Come back to me, Orus. I need you."

With each breath, Freya felt more of the raven returning. Soon he was breathing on his own, but he remained unconscious. Satisfied that he was going to pull through, Freya climbed painfully to her feet. They were in a spacious cavern with a high ceiling rising far above their heads. "Where are we?"

"In a big cave under the island," Archie said. "Come here—this is so cool!"

Freya followed Archie over to a massive, rough wall. Looking along the length, she couldn't see the end of it. The texture was different from what she'd expected. When she touched it, it was warm and seemed to hum and vibrate. "This isn't rock. What is it?"

"Yggdrasil," Loki said. "That's one of its smaller roots."

Freya gasped. "This is the Cosmic World Tree?"

"No," Loki said. "I told you, it's one of its roots."

Freya touched the root with great reverence. Then she pressed Orus to the wall. "Feel it, Orus. That's Yggdrasil. Feel how warm it is. It's humming to you, telling you to wake up."

"It's warm because it's alive, and those vibrations are all the lives in all the realms it supports," Loki said. "But it won't last long if we don't stop Ragnarök. Now, come, put the bird away. We've got to move before we find we have very unwelcome company in here."

"What do you mean?" Archie asked. "Will the giants come this way?"

"Not giants, but Nidhogg," Freya explained as she tucked Orus gently inside her breastplate. "Do you remember the dragon Azrael fought during the Ten Realms Challenge? That was Nidhogg. It's said that he guards the roots of Yggdrasil. That he patrols all these tunnels and will kill anyone he encounters. But I honestly thought it was just stories."

"No, it's all true," Loki confirmed. "I've met him down here more than once, and each time was unpleasant. I'm hoping that, with the giants using the other roots, he'll be too occupied with them to come after us."

"But couldn't he help us?" Archie asked.

"Not really," Loki said. "Nidhogg won't take sides. His duty is to protect Yggdrasil from everyone—he'll kill anyone he finds. But if the tunnels are filled with giants, he may be overwhelmed and defeated."

"Then we'd better hurry," Freya agreed.

As they traveled deeper into the tunnels, a kind of glowing lichen grew on the root and cast a greenish light. It was not enough to read by, but certainly enough to guide them down toward the lower realm.

Time became immeasurable; whether it was night or day, they didn't stop. The tunnel was too treacherous and winding for Freya to use her wings, so they had to keep walking, which slowed them even more.

"How much farther is it?" Archie asked.

Loki stopped and looked around. "By my estimate, we've only come a third of the way at most."

"Wow, it's a long way."

"Of course it's a long way, you idiot!" Loki snapped.

"We're traveling between realms. This isn't a short walk around the park, you know. We are going to a new world."

"Hey, there's no need to be a jerk," Archie said. "I was just asking."

"Well, don't!" Loki snapped.

Archie looked at Freya and shook his head. She was thinking the same thing. Maybe this wasn't such a good idea after all.

They continued in silence as they carefully picked their way through the seemingly endless tunnel. At one point the way ahead narrowed and they had to squeeze around a particularly tight corner. Freya felt part of the root cutting into her wings and back as she pressed forward.

"It's a good thing we're not claustrophobic," Archie commented. "Mind you, if it stays like this much longer, I'm gonna be." He pulled himself through an opening that was almost too small, and a sharp part of the root cut the back of his hand.

"Ouch!" he cried.

"Archie, you're bleeding," Freya cried.

"It really stings!"

Loki walked back to them and inspected the wound. "And you wonder why I call you an idiot!" He shook his head and walked away.

"What?" Archie said. "What is it? Tell me."

Loki paused. "You really are that stupid, aren't you? You're hurt because you've regained your physical form. We've left the influence of Midgard, where you were just a ghost, and we're now within the power of Vanaheim. Meaning you have a body again. A body that can be hurt and killed."

Of course! It made complete sense. Freya felt like the idiot for not realizing it sooner. She could even feel Archie's presence with her again. She focused in on her Valkyrie senses and picked up on other things that she never felt on Earth. There were people ahead, but definitely not human. And she sensed a density of life that she'd never experienced before, even in the thickest of Earth's jungles.

Knowing they were drawing closer to their destination, they put on more speed through the narrow passage until Freya was sure she could see a faint light shining in the distance.

"I think I see something."

Archie frowned and leaned forward. "All I see is the green glow. I don't know if I'll ever see normally again!"

"Stop complaining," Loki snapped. He looked past Archie to Freya. "Put your helmet on and keep walking. I'm going ahead to see where we're going to come out of the tunnel."

Before she could say anything, Loki shimmered and turned into a colorful hummingbird. His tiny wings were flapping so fast, she could no longer see them. A moment later Loki darted away.

"I really don't like him," Archie said.

"I don't think he cares much for you either," Freya said.

"Or me, for that matter. But he needs us and—I hate to say it—we need him if we hope to stop this war."

"And that's what really bugs me," Archie agreed.

Freya and Archie kept walking toward the pinprick of light. Finally, she felt movement against her chest.

"Orus!" Freya reached inside her breastplate and freed the large raven.

"Did you get the name of the giant that hit me?" Orus moaned. *"My head is pounding!"*

Freya hugged the bird tightly. "You really scared me," she said. "I thought you'd drowned."

"Me, drown? Never," Orus said. *"I was just taking a long nap."*

"Well, the dive almost killed Gee," Archie said. "But Loki gave her mouth-to-mouth and she came back much faster."

The raven's eyes went wide. *"Loki kissed you?"*

"Oh, gross!" Freya cried. "No, he didn't. He gave me mouth-to-mouth resuscitation so I could come back faster. But that's not kissing."

"It's miles away from kissing," Archie agreed. "It was first aid."

As Orus recovered, he rolled over onto his legs, but he remained cradled in Freya's hands. *"Maybe, but he didn't offer to give me first aid, did he?"*

"No, I did that," Freya said. "Would you have preferred Loki?"

"*Are you kidding? No, thank you.*" The raven looked around. "*So, where are we?*"

"We're nearing the entrance to Vanaheim. Loki's gone ahead to see where we are. That little light, way ahead, is the exit."

"*Way up there?*" Orus cawed. "*Good. I'm tired and I'm going to take another nap. Wake me when we get there.*"

Freya leaned forward and kissed the back of his feathered head. "I will. Just rest and recover."

She tucked Orus safely behind her breastplate and carefully picked her way through the tight passage. Eventually it opened and the light shining from the entrance grew brighter. They paused long enough for Freya to put on her helmet.

Around them the walls of the Yggdrasil root grew wider and more cavernous. The air started to smell different too. Gone was the stale "green" aroma of the lichen and a tunnel that had never known wind or fresh air, replaced by the beautiful, sweet fragrance of flowers, rich earth, and growth.

Archie paused and inhaled deeply. "That's much better," he said. "I thought I was going to puke from the smell in there."

"You're lucky," Freya said. "You haven't been solid for most of the journey. I've had to endure it the whole way. I'm sure we're going to stink of it for a while."

Thick layers of vines grew down from above and obscured the exit. Freya realized that unless you knew what the tunnel actually was, you'd never know it was the hidden route to another realm.

"I wonder where Loki is," Freya mused.

Archie shrugged. "I don't think he'll go far. He seems a bit freaked by everything that's happening."

Freya nodded. "He's not the only one."

Pushing back the vines, Freya and Archie stepped into the blazing daylight and discovered they were high on a lush, green mountain. The ground dropped away just ahead of them into a sharp cliff. Across a great divide, they saw a stunning waterfall that started from the top of the neighboring mountain. As they walked up to the edge of the cliff, their eyes followed the waterfall down into a large, crystal-clear lake, hundreds of yards below.

Behind them, and all around, they were surrounded by thick, dense jungle. Trees taller than they'd ever seen before rose high in the air, with leaves almost as big as Archie. The air was humid, sweet, and filled with birdsong. The sunlight beating down on them was warm and came from a sun much larger than that of Asgard or Earth.

"Wow," Archie breathed, turning a full circle. "Vanaheim is awesome!"

"It sure is," Freya agreed. She could feel the area around them teeming with life—too much for her to comprehend. It was like nothing she'd felt before, and she was overwhelmed.

"There's too much life here," she said. "I can't take it all in; it's making me dizzy."

"Don't try," Archie said. "Turn off your senses."

"Really? That's your solution—to turn off my senses? Can you stop your nose from smelling all these flowers, or turn off your hearing from the birdsong?"

"Well, no, that's silly," Archie said. "I can't turn them off. They're part of me."

"And my senses aren't part of me?"

"I just meant that maybe you can turn them off."

"Unfortunately, I can't. I can focus them if I need to, but they're always with me and always picking up things."

Suddenly the jungle behind them exploded with sound and movement. Voices shouted in an unfamiliar language, and Freya and Archie were scooped up into the air.

Freya tried to open her wings but couldn't. Her feathers caught painfully on something invisible that wouldn't give. She reached back to free her wings and touched the braided edges of what felt like a net.

"Hey!" Freya cried. "Let us go!"

Freya wriggled and fought in the confines of the net. As Archie struggled alongside her, his elbow smacked her in the helmet.

"Archie, move," Freya cried. "Your elbow's killing me!"

"Me?" Archie cried. "What about you? Your knee is

digging into the middle of my back! And I won't tell you where the hilt of your sword is pressing!"

They squirmed and struggled in the tight net, but couldn't break free. Still unable to see their attackers or the net imprisoning them, they were carried higher in the air. Soon they were gliding over the treetops.

Archie grunted as he tried to move. "What was that you were saying about not being able to shut off your senses, and how you're feeling everything?"

"Not funny, Archie!"

With Archie's arm pressing her helmet up against the ropes of the invisible net, Freya peered around, searching for signs of their captors. But like some of the Asgardians, she couldn't feel anyone around her. It was as though they were simply floating in the sky.

"Hey, what's happening?" Orus awoke. *"Let me outta here!"*

Freya tried her best to pull the cloak away from the raven as he crawled out of her breastplate. She whispered to him, "Orus, quiet. We've been captured."

"By whom?"

"I'm not sure."

Orus crawled up to her shoulder. Finding the edge of the invisible net, he pecked at it a few times and then poked his head out. *"Hey, let us out of here!"*

"We've already tried that," Freya said. "They won't answer."

Freya thought she heard fluttering wings very close to her. But when she turned her head to follow the sound, she couldn't see anything. They floated over the waterfall and followed along the path of a winding river that fed it. In the distance, she spied a small clearing. Smoke rings curled in the air from small cooking fires.

As they drifted closer, Freya had her first glimpse of the people gathered in the clearing. From afar they looked just as normal as Asgardians. But when they got closer, she realized they looked like nothing she'd ever seen before.

"Cool!" Archie cried. "Hey, Gee, can you see them? They're butterfly people!"

"They're the Vanir," Freya said. "And I think they know we're coming."

The net carried them down toward the group of tall figures with colorful butterfly wings on their backs. They carried no weapons, but they didn't need to. The Vanir were a race that used magic, not steel.

"Look at that girl," Archie breathed. He squirmed in the net to get a better look. "She's gorgeous. Her wings look like a swallowtail!"

A girl of about Freya's age stood with the other butterfly people. Her hair was long and as black as Freya's feathers. Her large wings were open—also solid black, but down at the bottom, near where the extra bits of wing swooped out gracefully, there was a large dot of the deepest sapphire blue.

The girl moved into position with the other Vanir people, making up a large receiving circle. Freya was reminded of the ring of angels circling Dirian in Chicago. Only this time they were the prisoners, and not the Dark Searcher.

Just before they touched down, they stopped. As they hovered no more than a few feet aboveground, the invisible net came away and they landed unceremoniously on the leaf-covered earth.

Freya rolled away from Archie and climbed to her feet. Suddenly, her invisible captors and the large net they carried became visible. They were a mix of butterfly people and those with four see-though insectile wings that reminded Freya of the dragonflies that lived in Asgard. She reached for her sword, but the moment her hand touched the hilt, she found she couldn't remove it from its sheath.

"That's enough, Searcher," a deep voice called. "You will not draw your weapon here."

A middle-aged butterfly man moved forward. He had black, white, and orange hair and wings.

"He looks like a monarch butterfly," Archie commented softly.

"But tell me, what is this?" he said, stepping closer. "A Dark Searcher that isn't a Searcher at all, but a Valkyrie." He waved his hand, and Freya's helmet slipped off her head.

There was a short intake of breath from the circle around them as Freya was exposed.

"I am Freya, daughter of Eir, the head Valkyrie of Asgard. We come in the service of Odin. It is urgent that I speak with the Elders of Vanaheim."

"I am Kreel, leader of this community. If you are in the service of Odin, why have you come here in disguise as one of his Searchers?"

"Because we didn't know what to expect."

"So you thought to come as a dreaded Dark Searcher, bearing a weapon?"

"We intended no harm," Freya said. "But it has been an age since an Asgardian has come here."

"True," Kreel said. "And why has Odin not come himself?"

"Bifröst is closed and he's unable to leave Asgard."

"This we already know," Kreel said. "Tell me, with Bifröst closed, how is it that a Valkyrie and her servant have arrived in our realm?"

"Hey, I'm not her servant," Archie said.

"You are a dead human traveling with a Valkyrie. You bear her mark on your hand. That makes you her servant."

"Yes, Gee gave me her mark, but we're friends. I'm not her servant or slave."

"Archie, that's enough," Freya warned. "It's true. Archie is my friend and not a servant. Orus here is my raven advisor. It is imperative that we speak with the Elders."

"Why?" Kreel demanded. "Could it be that foolish squabble the giants have started?"

Freya gasped. "You know about the war?"

"It's not a war, just the giants moving on Asgard again. What happens there won't affect us here."

"You're wrong. All the giants are working together. They'll take Asgard and then come here. If we don't stop it now, it will draw in all the realms, and Yggdrasil could be destroyed."

Kreel shook his colorful head. "Ragnarök? I hardly think so. No, I think you are here to start your own trouble with the Vanir, Freya of Asgard. You, the boy, and Loki have come to Vanaheim without permission."

Freya was shocked to hear Kreel mention Loki. Once again her doubts about Loki rose to the surface. Had he set them up?

"Yes, Valkyrie, we know about Loki as well. His presence and yours is a pollution of our world that we won't tolerate. You have broken our laws and will be punished." Kreel looked at his guards.

"Take them away and lock them in a cage, where they belong!"

7

"PLEASE LET FREYA BE OKAY," MAYA WHISPERED TO herself over and over again. Since arriving in the military installation deep beneath a Utah mountain, she had heard nothing of her missing sister. Had Freya been captured and taken somewhere else? Was she all right?

So far the Asgardians had been treated well, although they'd been subjected to countless medical tests and examinations. Blood and other tissue samples had been taken, and they were constantly being questioned.

The doctors had taken special care with Maya. She was put through a machine called a CT scanner, which gave them a full look inside her body and at the injuries she'd sustained during the attack from the hunters at the farm. After that her shattered wings were treated more effectively than the farm's veterinarian had been able to do. The moment they were properly set, Maya felt the healing process begin.

Maya's raven, Grul, was also in the final stages of healing. At first the soldiers had tried to take him away from her, but Maya had turned on her charm and talked them into letting her keep him close. As the minutes passed, Grul was getting better.

After her final treatment, Maya was returned to the holding cell she shared with her Valkyrie family. Peering through the thick iron bars, she looked into the opposite cell. The Dark Searchers stood at the bars, looking ready to do battle with anyone who challenged them.

Her brother, Kai, stood among them—a bit smaller, but just as imposing. He was still a mystery to her. But it was clear that Freya was already devoted to him. If there was one thing Maya knew, it was to trust her youngest sister's instincts. She just needed time to get to know her "new" brother for herself.

The Dark Searchers remained in their full armor and helmets. It was only Vonni's strong negotiating skills that convinced them to surrender their weapons peacefully. Looking at them—powerful and intimidating—she didn't think they needed them. They were a ferocious sight—even when they were simply standing still.

Thor and Balder had been locked in the cell beside the Searchers. But earlier in the day they had been escorted out of the cell block. If the situation weren't so serious, watching the soldiers trying to get Thor to surrender his hammer would have been funny. When they threatened him, Thor slammed the hammer down on the ground so hard, it caused the whole mountain to shake and cracked open the floor of the holding facility.

Thor was allowed to keep his hammer after that. The soldiers led Thor and Balder away, and the brothers hadn't returned since.

"You don't think they'll hurt my little brother, do you?" Mims asked, wringing her hands beside Maya. "They wouldn't let me see him or Mom. What if they're dissecting him?"

Maya took her cousin's hand. "Don't think like that. They wouldn't dare hurt him. They may study him, but these are not stupid people. They know what we'd do if they damaged even one feather on his tiny wings."

"But—"

Maya shook her head. "No buts—little Michael is going to be fine. You know, despite his noise and bad temper, Thor loves children. If they dared to hurt the baby, nothing could stop him from using his hammer to tear down this mountain."

Mims nodded and descended into silence, but Maya could still sense her cousin's fear. They were all in a situation they'd never experienced before. Would the military side with them? Or were they facing a battle with the humans as well as the giants?

They'd been held in their mountain prison for two days, and the military wouldn't believe them despite their warning of the impending giant invasion. Instead, they pursued their continuous questioning and examination.

As the hours of the day ticked away, they heard the heavy door at the end of the corridor open and Thor's booming voice echo down the passageway. "Foolish humans, what will it take to convince you? This realm is in grave danger."

"Thor, calm down," Balder said.

Soldiers streamed into the prison block and lined the walls of the corridor as Thor and Balder were escorted to their cell.

"You're more stupid than trolls," Thor called out as they streamed past the Valkyries' cell. Everyone knew the bars would not hold against the strength of the Dark Searchers if they tried to break out. There was little chance they would hold against the Valkyries either. The human soldiers knew it too, yet they continued with this charade.

The Searchers stood to attention as Odin's sons passed by.

"Stand down," Thor ordered. At his word, the Dark Searchers relaxed—but refused to sit.

"What news?" Brundi called to Thor.

"These fools refuse to believe us," Thor answered. "I almost wish the giants would arrive. Remaining here is wasting precious time. There's no telling what's happening in Asgard!"

"Perhaps now is the time to leave," Kris called with his broken voice. "Vonni's plan has failed. If they will not believe us, we must go."

"Give Vonni a little more time," Brundi called to her oldest son. "He will convince them. I know he will. He may not have trained in the Keep of the Dark Searchers like you, but he has served in the human military many times. He knows how they work and how to speak their language."

"One day more," Thor said darkly. "We will give him one more day to convince these fools. After that we will make our own way back to Asgard and leave Midgard to the mercy of the giants!"

8

FREYA COULDN'T TAKE HER EYES OFF THE VANIR AS THEY
marched her and Archie away from the small village and into
the dense jungle. They were the most unique beings she'd
ever encountered: a parade of color with delicate, insectoid
wings. She was mesmerized by their enchanting appearance,
but she knew there was more to them than met the eye.
Freya could feel that they were capable of great power and
ferociousness.

"You don't understand. We must speak with your Elders.
It is a war, and it will destroy Vanaheim as well as Asgard and
the other realms!"

"Silence!" ordered one of the dragonfly guards.

Freya looked around at the guards. Most were middle-
aged or older, but one looked to be around Archie's age. He

had intense gray eyes and four clear, narrow wings, folded tightly down on his back. He was barefoot and wore roughly woven shorts and a tight top that blended in with the lush green jungle environment. He wore a flat cap of leaves over his long brown hair. His eyes found and held Freya's for a moment before he turned and looked away.

"What do we do now?" Archie whispered.

"I'm not sure," Freya answered. "Maybe we can break away."

"Drowning must have addled your mind worse than mine," Orus cawed from Freya's shoulder. *"This is Vanaheim, where magic reigns. You won't get anywhere."*

The dragonfly boy stepped closer and shoved Freya in the wings. "Do you not realize that we can hear you?"

She shot an angry look back at him. "Well, you wouldn't listen to us about the war—so I figured you weren't paying attention now."

"You're talking nonsense." The boy snorted. "There isn't going to be a war."

Archie turned on him. "Listen, Peter Pan, how stupid can you be! Of course it's a war. And before long, I bet this Neverland of yours will be crawling with frost and fire giants."

"You're lying," the boy said. "All who come from Asgard lie."

"I'm not from Asgard," Archie said. "I'm from Earth."

"Where?"

"Midgard," Freya corrected. "And whether you believe us or not, it won't matter when the giants get here."

"Enough chatter," the leader of the guards said. "Quinnarious, get away from them before they poison you with their words." The leader pointed at Freya. "And you, Valkyrie, stop talking before I am forced to do something unpleasant to stop you."

The boy nodded to his commander and stepped back into the ranks while Freya shut her mouth and turned forward. They continued in silence.

They were led through an area of dense trees and bushes. Vines grew along the ground and tangled around their feet while exotic, monkey-like animals and birds pressed in all around them, unbothered by their presence. Everything they had seen of Vanaheim was wild and untamed. Including its citizens.

The leader of the guard stopped. He waved his hand in the air, and two large cages appeared. They looked to be made of bamboo and were held together with thin string.

Loki was locked in one of the cages. He walked up to the bars and nodded at Freya but said nothing.

"Inside," the leader of the guards commanded as the door to the empty cage swung open on its own.

When Freya hesitated, the leader raised his hand. She and Archie were shoved inside by an invisible force. Then the door slammed shut and string secured it tightly—all without anyone laying a single finger on them or the cage.

"You will remain here until we figure out what to do with you," the leader said.

"Wait," Freya cried. "You must believe us—Vanaheim is in danger! Once the giants conquer Asgard, they'll come here. You must realize that."

"What happens here is no concern of yours," the guard said. Just before he turned away, he raised his hand again. Freya's sword and belt came away from her body and flew between the bars of the cage and into the leader's hand.

"You won't need that again," he said. The guard turned away and opened his dragonfly wings as he and his men launched into the air.

"Wow. They're like big faeries. You can't even see their wings move," Archie said, turning his head to follow their departure.

"But they're infinitely more dangerous," Loki called.

Freya moved to the side of the cage closest to Loki. "When did they get you?"

"Moments after I left you. They caught me when I was still a bird. I'm surprised they let me return to this shape."

Freya inspected the bamboo bars and the string holding them together. It didn't look that strong. She grasped a bamboo joint and started to pull. No matter how much strength she used, the bars didn't even bend.

"You think I haven't tried that?" Loki sighed. "These cages could be made of paper, but they're still too strong for us to break. There's powerful magic binding us in here."

"How did Vanaheim not win against Asgard during that battle all those years ago?" Archie wondered. "If they had all this magic, they could have easily defeated Odin!"

"They are most powerful in this realm. When they leave Vanaheim, their powers weaken. Even so, I don't remember them being this strong."

"How do you know all this?" Archie asked.

"Foolish ghost, you still don't know who I am? I was there!"

That surprised even Freya. She knew Loki was old, but she had never imagined he was *that* old. "You saw the war?"

Loki casually inspected his fingernails. "Of course. Thor was very young and didn't have his hammer yet, and I myself was just a boy, but I saw enough to know that the Vanir have changed a great deal since then. I doubt even Odin knows how powerful they've become. If we somehow manage to stop the war with the giants, Asgard may have another unexpected problem—Vanaheim."

Freya shook her head. "Let's take it one war at a time!" She started to inspect every inch of her cage. It didn't make sense. It was made of sticks and string—how could magic be strong enough to keep them inside?

"What about you?" Freya asked. "Can't you turn into a bird or something and fly out between the bars?"

Loki slapped his hand to his head. "Why didn't I think of that?" He shook his head and snapped, "Of course I've tried that! I've also turned into a giant to break the bars. But watch . . ."

Loki shimmered and turned into a fly. Long before he could reach the bars, the cage magically shrank to meet the fly's size. Another change and Loki turned into an elephant. Once again, the cage altered to meet the size with larger, thicker bars that the elephant couldn't break free of.

He returned to normal. "Any other brilliant ideas—O wise one?"

"There's no need to be sarcastic," Freya said. "I was only trying to help."

Loki flopped down to the ground and crossed his legs. "Escape is impossible. We have to find another way, and soon. Each moment counts."

Freya didn't need Loki to tell her how urgent the situation was. But in all her life, she had never encountered circumstances like these. There was magic in Asgard, present within the Light Elves and faerie communities, but nothing like this. Not even her Valkyrie strength could break the bars.

As the day passed and the shadows of the large jungle leaves grew long, Freya was startled by the return of the guards. They didn't fly in; they just appeared out of thin air.

"Has anyone ever told you how annoying that is?" Loki snapped. He climbed to his feet and approached the bars of his cage. "Now are you ready to surrender to me?"

Archie nudged Freya. "Is he serious? That attitude isn't

helping. If he's not careful, he's going to get us all shot!"

"They don't need guns here," Freya whispered. "But I think I know what he's doing, and it's rather clever."

"What?" Archie asked.

Freya was about to answer when she became aware of Quinnarious watching her. The young guard was standing near their cage and staring right at her. The expression on his face was unreadable. Freya tried to feel what he was thinking. For an instant she could sense him. Then he seemed to realize what she was doing and forced the connection to break. He continued to stare at her and shook his head ever so slightly, as if trying to convey a message to her.

Freya nodded imperceptibly and stepped away from the bars, wondering what this was all about. She had a feeling there was more to Quinnarious than met the eye. She turned from him and focused on Loki's exchange with the commander of the guards.

"I told you, we're not spies. Can't you get it through that thick, bug head of yours? War is coming. If you don't get involved now, you'll go down with the rest of us."

"Silence," the guard commanded, waving his hand so that the door magically opened. "Come forward."

Loki crossed his arms over his chest. "Ah, no. Thanks all the same, but I think I'll stay. You bugs can fly away and find a big spider's web to play in."

"Come!" the commander ordered.

Invisible arms caught hold of Loki and dragged him out of the cage. The moment he was free, Loki turned into the large black dragon and inhaled deeply to release a stream of fire on his captors. But even before he could let it go, the guard raised his hand and the cage behind him grew and enclosed the dragon. When Loki released his flame, it was contained within the cage and bounced back at him. The dragon roared in pain and rage and returned to Loki's human form. His clothing smoldered and his hair was singed shorter. He patted out a lingering flame on his sleeve.

"Shall we try this again?" the guard said calmly. "Or should I make it really uncomfortable for you?"

Smoke and the stink of burned dragon followed Loki as he exited the cage again. "I don't like you very much."

The guard opened his dragonfly wings and prepared to fly. "I don't care." He reached for Loki's arm and lifted him lightly off the ground. In moments, the guards took to the air and carried Loki away.

"How can these morons not know what's coming?" Archie said, kicking the side of the bamboo cage. "They've gotta know what'll happen if the giants beat Odin."

"Maybe they believe their magic will protect them," Freya suggested. "It's really powerful. Perhaps it will."

"Will magic save them if Yggdrasil is destroyed?" Orus asked.

"No." Freya looked up, watching the guards carry Loki away. "I wonder what they'll do to him."

{ 81 }

"Torture, probably," Archie said. "Get him to talk."

"But we've already told them why we're here. We're not holding anything back."

"*We're* not, but what about Loki?" Archie said. "Do you really trust him?"

Freya considered a moment and shook her head. "No, not completely. He seems sincere, but I just don't know."

"Me neither."

As the warm sun started to set, Freya and Archie inspected every inch of their cage. They tried lifting it to get under the bars. They tried untying the binding and anything else they could think of. But nothing worked.

Night arrived and, with it, other jungle sounds. There was no light, and with the full jungle canopy above them, they couldn't see if Vanaheim had a moon or stars. Large, unseen creatures moved noisily through the trees around them, but even with her Valkyrie vision, Freya couldn't see what caused the sounds.

She started to pace the confines of the cage as her thoughts went to her family. What was happening on Midgard? Were they safe? Had the giants arrived yet? Had the war started? There were so many questions, with no way of knowing the answers.

Sometime during the long night, the wild sounds of the jungle stilled. The silence was worse than the loudest noise.

"I don't think we're alone," Archie whispered as his eyes scanned the area. "Gee, what can you feel?"

Freya cast out her senses, but once again, with Vanaheim teeming with life, it was hard to focus on any one thing. "I feel everything; that's the trouble. But I agree with you. We're not alone."

She stepped up to the side of the cage. "Whoever you are, show yourself! We know you're out there!"

Freya waited, but there was no response.

"Coward!" Archie shouted.

"Silence!" a hushed voice called. Quinnarious suddenly appeared beside the cage. His eyes were wide and wild, and he was carrying a small satchel made of woven leaves.

"If you're here to cause trouble, you can just turn around and fly away, bug boy," Archie said.

Quinnarious frowned. "I am here because I need to understand."

"Understand what?"

"Everything," the dragonfly boy said. "Vanaheim is in danger. I know it. But the Elders won't tell us what's happening. They've taken your friend to the Well of Knowledge, but they've been gone ages and haven't returned."

"Loki's not our friend," Archie said. "We're just traveling with him."

"What is the Well of Knowledge?" Freya asked.

"It is where the truth is drawn out. No one can resist its

powers. After Loki, they are planning to take you both there."

"That doesn't sound good," Archie said. "What'll happen to us?"

"They will make you drink from the well and then ask questions. If you tell the truth, you are safe. But if you lie, you will die in agony."

Archie looked at Freya. "Loki wouldn't know the truth if it bit him! He's toast!"

"Why are you telling us this?" Freya said. "What does it matter to you what happens to us?"

"When we first captured Loki, I heard Kreel talking with the others. They remembered him from stories of the ancient war. They said Loki caused a lot of trouble back then and will do so again. But then you came and everything changed. There is a lot of fear and hushed talk in the villages."

"Good!" Archie said. "There should be. War in the realms is real. You won't escape it, and locking us away won't change it."

"Some of us already know there is great trouble coming. But the Elders are trying to suppress our knowledge of it. They will seek to silence Loki and you before you can warn everyone. Even if he tells the truth, I know they will kill him. You too. But it has gone too far. Killing you won't change what is coming."

Orus cawed, *"They are going to kill us!"*

Quinnarious nodded. "The Vanir hate the Aesir. They won't tolerate you here."

"But why?" Freya asked. "The war between our realms was a long time ago."

"It's because of what you represent," Quinnarious said. "You coming here could mean a change to our way of life. The Elders don't want that. They want things to remain the same."

"But it won't stay the same if the giants invade Vanaheim," Archie said. "Quinn, you've got to let us out of here now!"

"My name is Quinnarious," the boy corrected. "Not Quinn, or that other name you called me, Peter—"

"Okay, I'm sorry I called you Peter Pan," Archie snapped. "But honestly, have you looked in the mirror lately? You look just like him."

"What are you saying?" Quinnarious challenged.

"Both of you, stop it," Freya said. "Archie called you Quinn because it's easier than your full name. But it wasn't meant as an insult." Freya paused. "At least I don't think it was." She turned to Archie. "Who is Peter Pan?"

"He's from a book. He dresses just like Quinn and can fly too."

"Hello?" Orus cawed. "Does that really matter right now? Didn't you hear him? The Vanir are going to kill us!"

Freya turned back to Quinn. "Please, you must set us free. We know how to stop the war. That's the only reason we came here. Not to change your way of life or to challenge the Elders. Just to stop the war."

"How?"

"The combination of Vanir magic and Aesir strength should be enough to stop the giants."

Quinn shook his head. "Vanaheim will never join forces with Asgard. We called a truce long ago, but that doesn't mean we trust Odin or would fight beside him."

"Then it's over," Archie said. "The giants will destroy us all."

Quinn considered for a moment. "Not necessarily. Even now some of us are planning to challenge the Elders. If you promise to help me, I will release you. Then I'll show you the way out of Vanaheim."

"How can we possibly help you?" Freya asked. "It seems you have a lot more power than we do."

"Promise to help me, and I'll tell you everything."

"Why should we trust you?" Orus demanded.

"Because if you don't, Kreel and the others will come for you, question you, and then kill you—not because you spoke about the war, but because you come from Asgard. For them, that is crime enough."

Freya looked at Archie and Orus. "We don't have much choice, then." She turned back to Quinn. "You have my sworn word as a Valkyrie. If you let us out, we'll help you. Then you'll help us get out of Vanaheim."

"Agreed."

Quinn waved his hand in the air and the cage door swung open. "I really hope I can trust you. This is too serious to risk a mistake."

When Freya walked free, she nodded. "You can. Loki, I'm not so sure about. But if Archie, Orus, or I give you our word, we always keep it."

"So do I," Quinn agreed. "Come, we must move. They'll be here for you at dawn." He opened his clear, insectile wings. "It's this way—you'll have to fly."

Freya put her arm around Archie and opened her own black-feathered wings. She leaped into the air and, with Orus flying at her side, followed behind Quinn. They kept close to tree level, and Freya realized he was trying not to be seen.

All through the long night they flew. A canopy of bright stars shone above them while three sullen moons rested on the distant horizon. After a time, there was the blush of pre-dawn glow rising behind them.

"How much farther?" Freya called.

"Not far," Quinn said. He pointed ahead of them. "Just beyond that mountain range."

They had flown only a short distance farther when Freya and Archie felt powerful, invisible hands catch hold of them and start to drag them from the sky.

Freya flapped her wings hard and fought against the unyielding force, but nothing could halt their descent. Their screams echoed together as they were pulled through the canopy of trees and crashed down to the ground far below.

9

FREYA HIT THE GROUND HARD. BUT WEARING HER
breastplate kept her from serious injury—though it didn't
stop the pain in her shoulder when she landed on her side.

"Are you all right?" she said to Archie as she rolled over
and saw him lying beside her.

"Ooof—I landed on something hard. . . ." He sat up and
pulled a fist-sized rock from beneath him. "This is one time I
wish I were still in ghost form."

Quinn touched down lightly beside them and reached
for Freya's arm to help her up. "I'm sorry we had to do that to
you, but we needed to ensure we weren't being followed and
that you weren't working with others."

Freya climbed painfully to her feet. "You did that to us?
You nearly broke my wings!"

Quinn looked alarmed. "I didn't mean to hurt you, but we must be careful."

Freya tried to massage the ache away from her shoulder. "This isn't the best way to get us to trust you."

"But it was the only way to ensure you weren't being followed," an elderly voice called.

Behind them, two women emerged from the trees. One looked as old as time itself, with a tattered brown cloak that dragged along the jungle floor, collecting leaves, sticks, and dead insects. Her face was almost impossible to see under all the wrinkles in her skin. The other woman was much younger and carried an air of elegance. "I am sorry, Freya and Archie, but it was necessary."

"Do you know us?"

The older woman nodded. "I have known both of you from before the time of your birth." Her ancient eyes settled on Orus at Freya's shoulder. "And you, young Orus, I watched you hatch."

"Who are you?" Freya asked.

"I am Urd," the old woman said, "and this is my sister Verdandi."

Freya's eyes flew wide. "Urd and Verdandi? You can't be serious!"

The younger woman nodded. "We're quite serious."

"But—but you don't belong in Vanaheim," Freya cried. "You are supposed to be at the base of Yggdrasil at the

Urdar Fountain. You feed the Great Cosmic Tree."

"Who are they?" Archie whispered.

The older woman took a step closer to Archie and stroked his cheek. "We are the Norns." When confusion rose on his face, she continued. "You might know us as the Fates. We have many names."

"Fates?" Archie said. "I think I've heard of you . . . from the myths."

"We are no more myth than Freya." She nodded to Freya. "Normally, we *do* reside at the base of Yggdrasil, keeping the tree fed and healthy. But something has happened to disturb our work."

Archie frowned. "Wait, aren't there always three Fates— Past, Present, and Future?"

Urd nodded. "Indeed there are. Our youngest sister has been taken from us, and we need your help to rescue her."

"Skuld is missing?" Freya cried.

The two sisters nodded. "She was taken by a Dark Searcher. He tried to abduct all three of us, but succeeded only in capturing our youngest sister."

"Was it Dirian?" Freya said.

Verdandi nodded. "He must have used some kind of enchantment to approach unnoticed. He attacked us before we could prepare a defense."

"What does he want with Skuld?" Archie asked.

Urd sighed, and it carried the weight of ages. "I do not

think you understand just who or what we are. We are the Norns. I, the eldest, know everything that has ever been. My dear sister Verdandi knows all that currently is. Skuld knows all that is yet to come. . . ."

Freya understood that this was important, but she couldn't grasp how. "And . . . ?" she said softly.

"And," Verdandi said, "now that Dirian has our sister, by controlling her, he controls the future."

"But if Skuld can see the future, why couldn't she see this coming?" Archie asked.

"We believe powerful Dark Elf magic is involved," Urd explained.

"I still don't understand," Freya said. "If Dirian took your sister, why are you here in Vanaheim? Surely you should be going after her?"

Quinn came forward. "Vanaheim has enough magic to keep these two safe. If they were to be captured and united with their sister, Dirian would possess the past, the present, and the future. He could take ultimate control of all time across all the realms."

Archie's mouth hung open. "That's intense. . . ."

It seemed inconceivable that one insane Dark Searcher could cause so much havoc and incite a war of epic proportions. Suddenly a terrible thought came to Freya. "Tell me, does Skuld have the power to alter or end someone's future?"

"She wouldn't do that," Urd said. "She can see it and advise on it, but she mustn't get involved."

"But could she, if she were forced?" Freya pressed.

The two Norn sisters looked at each other. They nodded.

Freya gasped. "This is too terrible. . . . That's how he's doing it!"

"I don't understand," Quinn said.

"Yeah, Gee—doing what?" Archie repeated. "What are you talking about?"

"That's how Dirian is keeping fallen immortals dead!"

Orus cawed as the realization struck him. "*It all makes sense now. It's just like Loki said when he came back to the farm—Dirian killed those who wouldn't join him, and when they died, he found a way to keep them dead. Skuld is doing it! She is ending their destiny.*"

Urd cried out, "Of course! Our sister has control of everyone's fate. She could end their destiny. But she wouldn't do it."

"Not unless she was being forced," Quinn said. He turned to Freya. "This is much worse than even I feared—we must warn the Elders. With Dirian controlling Skuld, he could demand that all the realms surrender to him or he will force her to bring on Ragnarök!"

10

LOCKED IN THE MILITARY FACILITY, MAYA FELT THE
tension from her family and the other Asgardians growing.
Despite their best efforts, the humans still refused to believe
the danger facing their world.

Being so deep underground, there were no windows, but
somehow everyone knew it was late in the night. Come the
morning, Thor planned to break out and lead everyone to
the tunnel heading up to Asgard. After that, Earth was to be
left to fend for itself.

Just before dawn, the doors at the end of the cell block
burst open. Vonni charged in, followed by a large group of
soldiers.

Maya hadn't seen him since their capture, and she was
stunned when he arrived wearing an army uniform. She

had been on the battlefields long enough to recognize his rank. Vonni Angelo, a Dark Searcher born of a Valkyrie and secretly raised on Earth, was a colonel in the United States Army.

"Open them," Vonni ordered. "All of them!"

He moved down to Thor's cell. "Thor, Balder, they're here. The giants have started invading Earth. The first wave just arrived in Florida. Now they're appearing all over the world. It's just like Loki said; they're using the roots of Yggdrasil. The military are ready to listen to us now. Please, will you stay and help Earth?"

Thor looked at his brother and then nodded. "Get us out of here."

Maya stayed close to Mims as they were led away from the cell block. For the first time since their arrival, the soldiers around them kept their weapons down. She and the Asgardians were no longer perceived as the threat. She could feel that the soldiers were terrified and looking to them for hope.

They passed through the research center of the vast facility and up the stairs into the full military level, entering a large, open hangar. Hundreds of chairs had been set up, and leaders from all the military forces filed in and took a seat.

"This way," Vonni said.

All eyes rested on the Asgardians as Vonni led them up to the front. He took his place at the podium next to four higher-ranking officers. Occasionally they would turn to stare back at the Valkyries and Dark Searchers.

"Good morning, everyone," Vonni started. "My name is Colonel Giovanni Angelo. Before we get started, I must tell you that I, like those standing behind me, am immortal." Murmurs of shock rippled through the audience.

Vonni nodded. "I have served in the United States military since its beginnings in the Revolutionary War. In addition, I served in the American Civil War under General William Tecumseh Sherman, the Spanish-American War under Major General William Shafter, then on to World War One and Two."

Not a sound was heard in the hangar as the guests stared in open shock. Finally the crowd erupted in calls and questions. One of the higher-ranking officers beside Vonni raised his hands to calm the gathering and came forward and started to speak.

"Good morning, everyone. For those of you who don't know me, I'm General Wilcox. I appreciate how all of this must sound, but what Colonel Angelo says is true. We've checked our archives and found detailed records of him and his military service, covering hundreds of years. He and his people"—the general waved his arm back to include the Asgardians—"are here to help us with this giant situation."

The general stepped back and handed the microphone to Vonni. Vonni began, "Seeing what is happening around the world is difficult to believe or accept. But it is time the people of Earth knew the truth. . . ."

Maya stood back with Mims and her family and listened to Vonni explain about Asgard, Odin, the existence of Yggdrasil—and Earth's place within the Nine Realms.

"The people of Earth have lived in isolation for so long that the stories of the realms have become little more than myths and fodder for comic books and movies. But these aren't myths. The giants invading our world aren't comic book monsters. They are very real and very dangerous. It's difficult to believe that we could be part of such an amazing collective as the realms. But we are. The Valkyries have been coming to Earth—or Midgard, as they call it—unseen, since the dawn of time. Our ancient Vikings knew of the realms and told the stories of Odin, Asgard, and Valhalla." Vonni paused and stepped back to Thor. "Many of you have grown up hearing the tales of Thor and his mighty hammer, along with his brother, Balder, and their fights against the frost and fire giants. I am here to tell you now—those aren't just stories. It is my honor to introduce you to the very real Thor and Balder, sons of Odin—here on Earth, from Asgard."

There was stunned silence in the room as all eyes fell on Thor and Balder.

"And here," Vonni continued as he walked along the line of Searchers, "these are the servants of Odin. His Dark Searchers and the Valkyries—my family."

The room exploded into noise. Comments and questions were once again fired in quick succession. "How do we know the giants haven't sent them? Why are you here? Is this an alien invasion? Where is Odin? If it's all true, where are your wings, Colonel?"

The general came forward and again held up his hands. "Silence! Silence! We have a lot to get through today. I'm sure there will be time for questions later. But right now we are in crisis. I assure you, Colonel Angelo is what he claims to be. He's here to explain what we're up against."

Vonni looked at the soldier who'd asked the last question. "General, I will answer a question now, if I may." He focused on the crowd and removed his military jacket, undid his tie, and started to unbutton his white shirt. "Just like you, I was born on Earth. It's the only home I've ever known, and it is the world I love." He pulled off his shirt. "But do not doubt what I say. I was born a Dark Searcher. To keep me safe and hidden, my wings were removed when I was a baby." Vonni turned his back to the crowd to reveal the two large scars where his wings should have been. He faced the crowd and then reached for an empty chair. Vonni lifted it up and easily bent the thick metal legs like a pretzel to prove his non-human strength. "But I hide no more. Earth and all the realms are in danger and if we are to defeat the giants, we must all work together."

Maya cast out her senses over the crowd of military

personnel and felt their fear and doubt. She couldn't blame them—it was a lot to take in. But as the minutes turned to hours and the briefing finally drew to a close, she felt the emotions in the hangar change. The soldiers were moving on from shock, fear, and doubt to determination to fight for their world.

She watched them with increasing sadness. These soldiers had no concept of what they were about to go up against. All their bravado and their bravery would vanish the moment they engaged the giants.

By late afternoon, the hangar had become the Central War Room of the US military services during "Operation Giant-Stop." It was in here that Vonni and the generals coordinated battle strategy against the invaders.

Maya stayed with her family, making their own plans for confronting the giants. Their weapons had been returned, and as large maps were laid out on tables, they were shown all the locations where the giants had been spotted emerging from the tunnels.

"There are so many," Eir said, strapping her golden sword to her waist. "There must be more tunnels than Loki knew about."

"I'm sure he couldn't know all of them," Brundi said.

"It doesn't matter." Thor was stroking his beard. He pointed to the map and the Florida entrance. "This is where we'll go first. This tunnel is the largest, and has the shortest route to the next tunnel going up to Asgard. It's the most dangerous for all of us."

Long before the assignments were doled out, Vonni came rushing over with a private close behind him. His face was ashen.

"There's big trouble," he said. "Reports are in that a large group of giants are heading this way. They're moving fast—it's only a matter of minutes before they get here. We're evacuating the mountain."

"It's us," Balder said grimly. "The giants can feel us here. Capturing me and Thor would be a great prize in this war. In this mountain, there will be no escape. We must go."

"Transports are waiting to take you away, sir," the private offered.

"No," Kris growled. "We will use our own wings, not Midgard machines, to move Thor and Balder."

"Mom!" Mims cried. She dashed away from Maya's side and ran up to her mother, who had just entered the hangar. Sarah was clutching her baby.

"Von," Sarah called, joining them. "We've just heard. Giants are coming. We're being evacuated."

Vonni nodded and turned to the private. "I want you to get my family out of here." He stopped and looked at Maya. "You too. Those wings of yours aren't healed yet. You can't fly. Go with Sarah and the baby, Mims, and your gran."

Maya shook her head. "I can't fly yet, but I can fight."

"Yes, you can. And I need you and Kai to fight to protect your Earth family."

"Me?" Kai said. "I am no child minder. I will stay with my brothers, the Dark Searchers."

Kris turned to Kai. "You will do as Vonni commands. Once the infant Searcher is secure, you will join us in the fight. Until then you are ordered to escort the others away from here."

Disappointment showed on Kai's face, but as a fully trained Dark Searcher, he obeyed his orders. "As you command."

The good-byes were brief as Maya and her family were led away from the other Asgardians. Walking beside her brother, she could feel his disappointment.

"Don't worry, Kai. There will be plenty of giants to fight soon enough. Let's just get the others to safety and we can come back."

Kai stopped and looked at her. "I don't care about fighting. Freya is missing—I was hoping to slip away to look for her. I haven't felt her in too long and I'm starting to worry."

"You're worried about her too?" Maya asked. "I've been frantic. But you haven't said anything."

"Of course I'm worried," Kai said harshly. "She is my sister, my twin. We have a bond that I can neither explain nor deny. I must find her." He paused, and his eyes bored into Maya's. "And I will, with or without permission."

"I'm coming with you," Maya said sharply. She looked at

her brother with a new understanding. They hadn't known each other very long and hadn't had a chance to speak. All she knew about him was what she knew of the Dark Searchers. They were cold and distant. She was shocked to find out he cared. Then she caught on to what he said. "Wait, what do you mean you haven't felt her? When we're in Midgard, I can't ever feel her—do you mean that you can?"

Kai nodded. "I've always felt something, but I didn't understand what it was. It became clearer at the Ten Realms Challenge, when we first touched, and this bond has grown ever since. I can feel her when we're in the same realm. But now that's gone. I fear she and Archie may have left Midgard."

Maya's eyes went wide. "How? Where?"

Kai leaned closer. "Don't forget, Loki is missing too. Last time they were together, they came to Utgard to find me. I am convinced they are doing something together again."

Maya looked back at the Valkyries as they were being led away. "We should tell the others."

Kai shook his head. "No. They will try to stop us—but I won't be stopped by anyone."

Maya was struck by his strong will and determination. He was just like Freya. "All right. We'll get Sarah and the baby to safety, and then you and I can set out. Do you know where she is?"

Kai shook his head. "All I know is that she's not in Midgard."

11

DEEP IN THE VANAHEIM JUNGLE, VERDANDI WAS convincing Quinn not to take Freya and Archie to the Elders. "No, child. By the time you do, it will be too late. You must rescue our sister first. Only when Skuld is free do we stand a chance of ending the war before it goes too far."

Freya shook her head. "I'm sorry, Verdandi, but we must speak with the Elders first. We know how to stop this war and we need their help!"

Verdandi addressed her. "Getting the giant kings to turn on each other is a viable solution. But it will only succeed if Skuld is free and there is no chance of Dirian replacing the giant kings with those who will do his bidding."

"How do you know our plan?" Archie demanded.

"We are the Norns," Urd said. "We know all. I have seen everything you have been through. . . ."

Verdandi nodded. "And I know all that is current. I know you came here to engage the Vanir in this struggle, but it will take more than your word and certainly more time than you have to get them on your side. Their distrust of the Aesir runs too deep."

"So what do we do?" Archie said.

"We put aside our old resentments and work together to free Skuld. It's the only way." Quinn turned to Verdandi. "Where are they holding your sister?"

"She is being held in a keep in the desert in Muspelheim," the younger woman said.

Freya gasped and Orus cawed.

"What?" Archie said. "Where's Muspelheim?"

"It's the realm of the fire giants."

"The fire giants?" Archie choked. "The same guys we saw at the Ten Realms Challenge? The ones always on fire?"

"That's them," Freya said.

"*Muspelheim is the most dangerous of all the realms*," Orus cawed. "*We'll be killed!*"

"It is," Urd agreed. "Your journey will be fraught with danger, and you will be risking your lives. If Skuld is doing Dirian's bidding, should you be killed, I fear you will not rise again."

Freya nodded. "I'm sure Dirian would love to kill me for good if he got the chance."

"Me too," Archie said. "Remember, I nearly cut his hand off."

"He will kill all of us if he learns of our intention to free Skuld," Quinn said.

"We should free Loki," Freya suggested. "He could help us."

"No way!" Archie cried. "Gee, how do we know he's not working for Dirian? That bringing us here wasn't just a distraction to get us out of the way?"

Urd shook her head. "Your suspicion of Loki is justified. He has done many bad things in the past. But I can assure you, this time his intentions are genuine. He is on the side of peace and was not leading you to harm in bringing you here."

Verdandi nodded. "Unfortunately, the Vanir do not trust him any more than you do. He is now suffering at their hands."

"If he's innocent, we must save him," Freya said.

Verdandi shook her head. "No, child. You must go to free Skuld. Whether Loki survives his ordeal or not will make little difference if Dirian gains control of all the realms. Urd and I will present ourselves to the Vanir Elders and explain what has happened. We will plead for Loki's life. But your quest is set. You must leave here now."

*　*　*

Freya had no reason not to trust the Norns. They were renowned for never taking sides—they were observers of all, but never became personally involved. Since Dirian had taken their youngest sister, they had been drawn into the fight. Freya just hoped it wasn't too late.

They sat in the small clearing as Quinn pulled out several maps, drawn up on a roughly woven fabric. The first and largest map was a detailed picture of Yggdrasil, the Cosmic World Tree. There were circles drawn on the tree to show each of the Nine Realms and their placement within the branches of the Great Tree. At the top was Asgard and Valhalla. Midgard appeared beneath it. Below and to the left of Midgard was Vanaheim, and then along the bottom from left to right was Jotunheim, realm of the frost giants; Helheim, realm of the ancient dead; Nidavellir, the realm of the dwarfs; and then Svartalfheim, realm of the Dark Elves. Finally, on the far right, was Muspelheim—realm of the fire giants.

Quinn pointed to Muspelheim. "This is where we must go. We can travel through all the lower realms to get there."

Freya looked at the map and shook her head. "It will be too dangerous for us to journey through all those realms, especially while we're at war. Look, the best way is for us to go back through the tunnel we took to get here, and return to Midgard. Then we can find the secret tunnel that will take us directly to Muspelheim. It will cut out all those other realms."

"What are these tunnels?" Quinn said.

"The roots of Yggdrasil," Freya said. "That's how we got here."

Quinn looked at the two Norns. "Is this true? Do the roots of Yggdrasil connect all the realms?"

Urd nodded. "They have existed since the beginning of time. But very few know of them. Most believe them to be a myth."

"It's no myth," Archie said. "We used one to get here. Loki thinks the giants will use them to get to Earth and then take other tunnels leading up to Asgard. It's kind of like a weird game of snakes and ladders. You arrive through one tunnel and head up through another."

"Loki is correct. The giants have already started using them," Verdandi said. "They are in Midgard now, making their way up."

"What?" Archie cried. "No, they can't be. It's too soon!"

"I do not lie, child," Verdandi said. "I tell only what I see. It is happening right now. Frost and fire giants are entering Midgard as we speak. They are bringing their allies—the Dark Elves, dwarfs, and trolls—with them." Verdandi closed her eyes and lifted her head, as though she were focusing on something very distant. When she opened them, her face revealed great sadness. "Midgard forces are trying to fight them, but they stand no chance."

"What about Thor?" Freya cried. "He's in Midgard right now. So are the Dark Searchers who are standing against Dirian. What about my mother and sisters? Can you see them?"

Verdandi shook her head. "Fear for our sister is distracting me. I cannot see them."

A stone settled in Freya's stomach. Had the giants killed her family and those fighting for Asgard?

"We have to go back!" she cried, getting to her feet.

"Wait," Quinn said. He searched in his pouch and pulled out a blank, woven parchment and quill and handed them to the Norns. "If you know of these tunnels, please, show us where they are. Freya says she can lead us back to Midgard. When we get there, how do we find the passage to Muspelheim?"

Verdandi hesitated for a moment. "These are sacred tunnels, meant to be kept secret."

Urd nodded. "Show them. The secret is out."

Verdandi started to draw on the parchment. Freya immediately recognized the continents of Earth. The Norn put a small dot on the map. "This is the only root that will take you to Muspelheim. And when you have our sister, you must go back to Midgard and take this tunnel to get you straight up to Asgard. This is an especially secret root that only we, the Norns, use. No others know of it. But it is the fastest way to Asgard and Odin's protection of our sister."

Freya looked at the map and frowned. "What about a root from Muspelheim directly to Asgard? Surely that would be faster."

Urd nodded. "Indeed it would. But that tunnel will be filled with Dirian's servants. You must keep Skuld safe and away from them."

Verdandi nodded. "Once Skuld is free, Dirian will lose his power to keep his enemies dead. Then, when you set the giants against each other, the war will end."

"So we know our plan," Quinn said. He rose to his feet and tucked the precious map in his bag. "Let's get going. We don't have a moment to waste."

12

BY THE TIME THEY LEFT, THE SUN WAS HIGH AND HOT IN the brilliant blue sky. Freya hated leaving the two Norns in the jungle, looking so vulnerable and alone, but Urd insisted they go. She said rescuing Skuld must be their only priority.

Freya, Archie, and Quinn took off, heading in the direction of the tunnel where the security team had first captured them. As before, they remained close to the canopy of leaves to help hide their presence.

Despite the teeming life around them, Freya's senses were in overdrive as she reached out to feel for any Vanir fighters in the area. When they were just over halfway back to the mountain, she felt the presence of others.

"Quinn, they're coming!" she cried. "Get down!"

Freya heard Quinn call something back, but with little time to waste, she tucked in her wings and dived headfirst down into the dense carpet of trees. She clenched her eyes as thick branches and vines bit into her skin and the wings on her back. Archie cried out as the same branches scratched his face and arms.

When they pulled free of the trees and reached the ground, they heard Quinn calling. A moment later he landed beside them without a scratch. "Are you deaf? I told you to wait. . . ."

Moments later, three young winged warriors landed. Two had the same dragonfly wings as Quinn, while the other was the butterfly girl she had noticed earlier, with the black wings and big blue dots. Freya searched for a weapon. But even before she reached for a thick branch, invisible hands wrapped around her and held her tight.

"Freya, stop!" Quinn said. "They're with me!"

"*Freya, help me!*" Orus cawed. The raven was high in the trees overhead and trapped in a tangle of vines.

The young girl with the butterfly wings floated up and freed the raven from the tangle. "You're all right," she cooed softly, stroking his feathers. "We're not going to harm you."

She released him, and Orus flew to Freya's shoulder.

"These are my friends," Quinn said, releasing his grip on Freya. "That's Parsi, Skyrian, and Switch. Everyone, this is Freya and Archie."

"*And Orus,*" the raven said.

"Yes, of course—and Orus," Quinn corrected.

The girl who had freed Orus stepped closer to Archie. "If it's easier, you can just call me Skye."

"I'm Archie," Archie stuttered awkwardly. "Everyone just calls me, er, Archie. I'm from Earth—I mean Midgard."

Skye blushed lightly and her butterfly wings fluttered. Her black eyes sparkled. "I've never met a human before. You have no wings?"

"Nope. Humans don't." Then he added, "But yours are really cool."

Switch nodded to Freya. "We know something is happening that the Elders aren't telling us."

"It's worse than we imagined," Quinn reported. He, Freya, and Archie explained what they knew. "We must free Skuld," he continued. "Nothing else matters if she remains a prisoner of Dirian."

"I never liked what I heard about the Dark Searchers," Parsi said. "They're all feathered Aesir scum!"

"Don't blame the Aesir for this!" Freya shot. "We're in more danger than you are."

"Why shouldn't I blame you? A Dark Searcher started this war," the tall dragonfly boy spat.

Freya's hands balled into fists as she advanced on the tall boy. "My brother is a Dark Searcher, and in case you hadn't noticed, I have feathers!" Freya opened her wings threateningly. "So take that back, Vanir, before I make you!"

"What are you going to do, Valkyrie, reap me? Turn me into a slave, like this dead human?"

"Hey, I'm no slave!" Archie cried. He stood beside Freya and faced down the troublemaker. "It's called friendship and loyalty. Something I'm sure you know nothing about!"

"Enough!" Quinn cried.

Freya wouldn't back down. She poked her finger into Parsi's chest. "Listen, bug boy, it's not our fault that Dirian's insane. He's working against all of us."

Parsi looked at his friends. "That's so typical of the Aesir, ready to use violence first."

"You wanna see violence?" Archie said as he raised his fist. "Keep going after Gee like that and I'll show you what humans can do!"

Skye stepped between them. "Everyone calm down! Fighting among ourselves isn't helping." She looked back at Quinn. "We know what the problem is, so how do we solve it?"

"First, we stop accusing each other. Then we free Skuld. After that, Freya has a plan that the Norns said would work. We're going to turn the giant kings against each other."

"We?" Archie said. "After your guys just blamed us for everything? You still expect us to work together?"

"We must," Quinn said. "This war will involve all the realms. The Vanir can't avoid it, no matter what the Elders say. Only together will we stand a chance of stopping Ragnarök."

Freya nodded. "Quinn's right. Unless we put our old resentments aside, we don't stand a chance." She turned to Parsi. "I'm willing to try if you are."

Parsi nodded reluctantly. "I'm in." He paused, and a slight smile came to his lips. "As long as you don't call me 'bug boy' again."

"Fine, just as long as you stop insulting my feathers," Freya said.

"Agreed," Quinn said. "Here's our plan." He pointed to his two dragonfly-winged friends. "You two will go to the Norns and make sure they get safely to the village. You must make the Elders release Loki and convince them what will happen if we don't side with Asgard."

"What about me?" Skye asked.

"You're coming with us to Muspelheim."

"Are you sure about that?" Archie asked. "It's going to be very dangerous."

"Yes, and . . . ?" Skye prodded. "Don't you think I'm a warrior or brave enough?"

Archie blushed. "Of course you're brave enough, but, um . . . I mean, that's not what I mean. Look at you. You—you're so—so delicate. Your wings look like they can be damaged very easily."

Skye smiled, and Freya could see it had a devastating effect on Archie. "Don't worry about me, Archie. I am quite capable of taking care of myself."

Quinn nodded. "She is. In fact, Skye's got more magic than the rest of us."

"I—I'm sorry. I didn't mean to hurt your feelings . . . ," Archie stuttered.

Freya watched her friend and smiled. In all their time together, she'd never seen Archie this flustered.

"*I can't believe what I'm seeing,*" Orus whispered in her ear. "*Look at him! Archie is tongue-tied around her.*"

"I'm sure she'll do fine," Freya said. "Archie, we're going to face dangers we never imagined before. I for one am happy to have Skye with us. We're going to need all the help and magic we can get if we hope to save the realms."

"It is agreed, then," Quinn said. "Let's get moving."

"Wait. I have something for Freya." Skye reached back between her two large butterfly wings and pulled out Freya's sword and belt. "I think you might need this."

"My sword!" Freya cried. "How did you get it?"

"Kreel is my father," Skye explained. "He had it in our home. He says weapons like this are crude, ugly, unnecessary things. But since we're not staying in Vanaheim, I thought you might want it back."

"Thank you." Freya accepted the sword. "But won't your father be angry when he finds out what you've done?"

Skye nodded. "But saving the realms is more important. He'll understand when we get back."

"*If we get back,*" Orus cawed.

Grateful to have her golden sword back, Freya fastened the belt around her waist and felt instantly better. The Vanir might use magic to defend themselves, but she was still a Valkyrie, raised on the battlefield and trained to use weapons.

"Now, does everyone know what they're doing?" Quinn asked.

Parsi nodded. "We'll get the Norns to the Elders and convince them to side with Asgard. Good luck freeing Skuld."

Quinn raised his hand and used magic to lift them all back up through the dense trees and into the open sky.

"For Vanaheim," he cried, as the two groups parted on their missions.

"For all the realms!" Freya echoed as she opened her wings and led her team toward the cave.

13

MAYA AND HER FAMILY WERE EVACUATED TO A SAFE house on the beach along the California coast. Just north of Los Angeles, it was far from where the giants were entering the country.

Standing on the balcony that ran the length of the house, several yards above the sand, Maya gazed out over the Pacific Ocean. The water before them was calm and the beach was empty. But it was an illusion. The world was anything but calm.

Kai stood at her side lost in thought—though his emotions were running wild with concern for Freya.

Hours earlier they had received a call from Vonni to say he and the others had made it safely out of the mountain facility moments before the giants arrived. They were now on the East Coast, near Boston, preparing to engage the enemy. Vonni said there was a steady stream of frost and fire giants coming up from the south.

"Have you felt anything at all from Freya?" Maya asked, breaking the painful silence.

Kai shook his head. "Nothing." He turned to her, and his ice-blue eyes were filled with worry. "But I'm sure she's all right."

Maya nodded, knowing he was trying to convince himself more than her. "Of course she is. Freya is resourceful. It's the rest of us I'm worried about."

The television in the lounge behind them droned on— filled with news reports from all over the world, talking about the invasion. Giants, Dark Elves, and a terrifying assortment of other creatures were appearing on every continent.

"There's Thor!" Mims cried.

Maya and Kai ran back into the house. The large television screen on the wall showed Thor taking on four frost giants at once. Hammer in hand, he was dodging their attempts to kill him while he attacked them with lethal hammer blows.

"I've never seen him use Mjölnir like that before," Maya said. "He's only ever fought with swords at Valhalla. He's unstoppable."

"He's never had to," Brundi said. She was sitting on the sofa between Mims and Sarah, who was holding the baby. "Thor is an army unto himself."

"Thank heavens he's on our side," said one of the soldiers

assigned to them. "Look at him. He's minuscule compared to them, but he's bringing them down."

"Look, there they are!" Kai cried, pointing at the television. "It's the Searchers—and there's Mother!" The camera changed angles and was showing the Dark Searchers and Valkyries fully engaged with the giants. Their blades moved so fast, they couldn't be followed by the cameras. Though the giants were massive in comparison, by working together, the winged Asgardians were able to bring down two fire giants and were taking on a third.

The report cut away to other battles around the world, and the news wasn't as encouraging. London was under attack as giants arrived from a tunnel in the Scottish Highlands and left a path of destruction through Edinburgh and all the way down to the south coast. The giants then entered the English Channel to cross to France. From there they stormed through to Germany, where Maya and Kai knew a hidden tunnel led up to Asgard.

Tanks and jet fighters from the world's united military forces took on the giants but couldn't stop their advance. Despite humanity's best efforts, their weapons had little effect on the large invaders—though they were having success against the trolls, Dark Elves, and dwarfs.

With each passing moment, Maya felt despair coming from the three soldiers in the room. "We can't win against them, can we?" the corporal asked her.

Maya shook her head. "Not even Asgard will stand long against the united giants."

"I should be there," Kai said as his white wings fluttered, and he punched the back of the sofa. "I'm doing nothing here but watching my brothers fight!"

One of the soldiers nodded. "So should we."

"You are where you must be," Brundi said. "I am sure Vonni will send for you when you are needed."

Maya stayed to watch a little longer. But with each new report showing the path of devastation left by the invaders, she felt despair crush her. Finally she walked back out to the balcony to be alone.

"I know what you're thinking," Grul said. The raven was finally recovered and back on her shoulder. *"You want to join your mother and sisters in the battle and be there too."*

Maya nodded. "Midgard is overwhelmed, and I feel help-less here." She walked up to the railing and grasped it tightly as she slowly opened her wings. They were stiff and sore but healing quickly now that they'd been properly set. She winced as she flapped them lightly.

"It won't be long," Grul said.

Maya massaged her right wing and nodded. "They're feeling much stronger. I'm ready to try to fly tomorrow—just a short flight at first."

"Then what?" the raven asked. *"Please don't say you're going to join the fight. You're not ready for that."*

Kai arrived back on the balcony. "That's exactly what we're going to do. The moment Maya can fly again, we're leaving."

"But what about Brundi and Mims? What about the baby? They need your protection."

"They have the human soldiers. Grul, we can't stay here doing nothing while the world falls," Maya said.

"Then it's decided," Kai said. "Tomorrow, if you can fly, we'll go."

They remained glued to the television, watching the reports of the invasion until late into the night. Of the combined forces of Asgardians and humans, the only ones with any success against the giants were the Asgardians, finally winning them acceptance as allies.

When Maya retired to bed and lay down in the room she shared with Mims, she was unable to sleep. She was more conflicted than she had ever been in her life. Part of her wanted to join her family in battle, but another part was called to find Freya. Neither option held any hope of success. Finally, she decided what she would do. She would join her family against the giants, but she had no illusions. They were fighting a losing battle.

Maya turned onto her stomach and flexed her wings open and closed. She could feel them getting stronger with each passing moment. By morning, she was confident they would be healed enough to carry her to the East Coast.

When she had finished her exercises, she rolled onto her side and tried to sleep. She needed all the rest she could get. But just as she started to doze off, she felt a blaring alarm going off in her head.

Maya jumped up and went to the window. The moment she and Grul looked out to the dark ocean, her jaw dropped. Two frost giants were emerging from the water.

"Mims, get up!" She ran for the door and out of the bedroom. "Everyone up!" she shouted. "It's the frost giants—they're here!"

Kai was first to appear in the hall. "From where?"

"The ocean! There must be a tunnel entrance we didn't know about just offshore—"

Any further comment was cut off as the timber beams of the house creaked and the ground beneath them shook. Suddenly a frost giant's voice boomed like thunder. "Kill the Valkyries!"

"They're tracking us!" Brundi entered the hall, pulling on her robe.

There was no time to react or move as the ceiling suddenly exploded. Timber flew in all directions and debris rained down. The last thing Maya saw before darkness overwhelmed her was the horrifying sight of a massive frost giant fist smashing down through the house.

14

"SO THIS IS THE ROOT OF YGGDRASIL?" ASKED SKYE, staring at the rough walls covered with glowing green lichen. Freya had led the group into the cave leading to Earth.

Freya nodded. "If you touch it, you can feel it vibrating with life."

The two young Vanir stopped and touched the living wall. "I can hear her singing!" Skye cried.

"Who?" Archie asked, pressing his ear to the root. "I don't hear anything."

"It's Yggdrasil. If you know how to listen, you can hear her. She's beautiful."

Archie shook his head. "I still don't hear anything."

"Me neither," Freya agreed as she touched the dark brown root. "But I can feel it humming with life."

Quinn closed his eyes and listened to the song of the Great Cosmic Tree. "Let us never forget, this is what we are fighting for."

When they reached the halfway point, Archie became a ghost again. "I hate this!" he complained. "One moment I'm solid, and the next I'm not. I just wish the realms would make up their mind. Am I alive or dead?"

"You're both," Freya said.

Archie gave her a black look. "That doesn't help."

"You're alive to me," Skye offered.

Color rose on Archie's face.

"Who'd have thought a ghost could blush?" Orus teased.

Freya smiled at her friend but said nothing as she took the lead, guiding the Vanir through the tunnel. Soon the passage began to incline up toward an opening. Spread out before them was the underground lake that would take them to the surface of Midgard.

"All right," Freya said, standing on the shore. "I should warn you. To get to Midgard, we have to swim. The water is freezing cold, and you're going to need to hold your breath for a long time. Can you do that?"

Quinn nodded. "We swim a lot back home."

"But this water is freezing—will you be able to cope with it?" Freya asked. "I heard it never gets cold in Vanaheim."

Skye shook her head. "It doesn't, but that doesn't really

matter here—we won't get wet. Take our hands and we'll show you how."

Freya tucked Orus into her breastplate and took Quinn's outstretched hand. Then she caught hold of Skye.

"And you, Archie." Skye offered her free hand to him. "Join us."

The moment their hands were all linked, Freya felt a strange sensation, as if an electric current were flowing through them. Her hair started to stand on end. Beside her, Quinn's hair also started to rise.

"Show us the way," Skye said to Archie.

They entered the water together, and it was as if they were traveling in a big bubble of air. The freezing water never touched them as Archie gave instructions to Skye on the route that Loki had taken.

Safe within the protection of the bubble, they looked around in wonder at the Arctic Ocean. Soon they burst through the surface of the water. To Freya and Archie, it seemed they had only just left. But here the ocean water was almost solid ice, and Kaffeklubben Island was covered in snow.

When they touched the shore, Skye let go of Freya's hand and the bubble vanished.

"That was awesome!" Archie said. He slapped Freya playfully on the arm. "Why can't you do cool stuff like that?"

"Sorry to disappoint you," Freya said, "but I'm just a

poor Aesir, remember? We use crude weapons and brute force, not magic."

Quinn looked at Freya and grinned mischievously. "Just so long as you remember that."

They walked around the small arctic island. The sun was sitting sluggishly on the horizon, giving no clue as to whether it was day or night. There were no signs of life anywhere. "Well, at least the giants haven't been here yet," Quinn said.

His comment brought home the danger. Urd and Verdandi had said that the giants were already on Earth. What damage had they done? "We're too far north," Freya explained. "The tunnel to Asgard is much farther south. That's where we'll see the real damage."

Orus cawed, *"I hate to imagine what they've done."*

"Well, we won't know until we get there." Freya looked at the two Vanir. "How are you two for endurance flying? It's a long way south."

Quinn grinned. "We'll keep up with you, Aesir. Don't worry about us."

Freya grinned back at him. "Really, Vanir? My feathers against your insectoid wings—the first person who needs to land loses!"

"Deal!" Quinn cried as he flapped his four dragonfly wings and launched into the arctic sky.

"Go get 'em, Gee," Archie cried.

Freya caught hold of Archie, flapped her larger, feathered wings, and took off behind Quinn and Skye.

The journey south was much longer than the journey up had been. Then they'd ridden a large black dragon. This time they were using their own wing power and could fly only as fast as Skye's butterfly wings could manage.

Freya could sense Quinn and Skye growing fatigued. For all their bragging, they obviously weren't used to long-distance flying.

The sun had set hours ago, and with thick storm clouds above them, they were traveling in total darkness.

"There is no shame in stopping for a rest," Freya called as she maneuvered closer to the two Vanir. "I'm used to this. You're not."

"We're fine," Quinn panted.

"Don't be a jerk!" Archie called. "Skye's really struggling. Her wings aren't built like yours or Gee's—it's harder for her to keep up with us."

Quinn looked back at his companion and saw Skye battling to match their speed. But with her light wings, she fluttered in the windswept sky, unable to fly in a straight line. She nodded to the others but was too tired to speak.

"All right," Quinn said. "Let's take a short break."

Freya slowed down and glided over the snow-capped mountains of northern Canada. They touched down at the top of one of the mountains.

Quinn waved his hand in the air, and suddenly a large, warm campfire appeared in the thick snow. He pulled out a small cloth and wiped a film of sweat off his brow. "I don't think I've ever flown that far before."

"Me neither," Skye gasped as she fluttered down to the ground and gulped air. Her butterfly wings drooped and her shoulders sagged. "I hate to admit it, but I'm exhausted. It's true, feathers are better for long distances."

Freya wanted to say "I told you so," but she didn't have the heart. After all, she was the best flyer in Asgard. Mentioning it would only sound like bragging. "But I can't use magic," she said instead.

"True," Quinn said. Then he grinned at Freya. "Which means we can do this and you can't!" He waved his hand again, and a banquet of food appeared on a leafy blanket beside the roaring fire. From breads to exotic fruit Freya had never seen before, it all looked delicious. "I'm starving. Let's eat."

As Freya took a seat on the leaf cover, Archie harrumphed. "It's just not fair. It all looks delicious, but I can't eat!"

Orus emerged from Freya's breastplate and cawed, *"But I can—I'll enjoy it for you!"*

While they ate, Quinn and Skye stared around them. "We've never been to Midgard before," Skye said. "Does it all look like this?"

Freya shook her head. "No. This realm is really special.

It seems to have a bit of all the realms in it. There are even a few jungles that look just like Vanaheim."

"Really?" Skye asked. When Freya nodded, she continued. "When this is over, I want to come back here and see more."

"I'll be glad to show you around," Archie offered.

Quinn watched the exchange between Skye and Archie. He frowned. "Archie, aren't you and Freya . . . you know, together?"

"Me and Gee?" Archie choked. "Are you serious? No way. We're just friends."

Freya couldn't resist kicking his foot. "Thanks, Archie, but you didn't have to make it sound like the idea was a fate worse than death!"

Archie blushed. "I didn't mean it like that! I just wanted Skye to know that we were just friends."

"She knows now; that's for sure," Freya teased. She looked at Quinn, who was looking down and smiling to himself, as if pleased to hear this new piece of information. Freya flushed and cleared her throat, changing the subject. "So, after all these years without contact between our realms, what do the Vanir think of the Aesir?"

Quinn shrugged. "Not a lot, really. But we're always preparing for war."

"With Asgard?" Archie asked.

Skye nodded. "We're raised to be ready for any kind of

attack. From the moment we can fly, we're required to train for battle and use our magic skills to fight."

"So you're all in the army?" Archie cried.

"He means you're all warriors," Freya corrected.

Quinn nodded. "Whether we want to be or not."

"What *do* you want?" Freya pressed the Vanir. "You seem like a leader to me."

A slight blush of pink rose in Quinn's cheeks. "I always dreamed of exploring the other realms and cataloging the wildlife. There's so much to see. But we're forbidden to do anything like that. We can't leave Vanaheim."

"What'll happen if you're caught here with us?" Archie asked.

"We'll be executed," Skye said softly. "And because my father is the leader of our village, he'll be executed too."

"What?" Archie cried. "You never said that would happen. You shouldn't have come here!"

"We had to," Skye said. "If this war escalates to Ragnarök, nothing will survive. We must try to stop the giants, even if it means punishment for breaking our laws."

Freya looked at her new Vanir friends. She hadn't realized the risk they were taking coming with them. Vanir punishments were much harsher than Odin's.

Silence fell as they gazed into the fire.

"Speaking of giants," Archie finally said, "Gee, can you feel them? Are they really here?"

Freya had dreaded that question from the moment they arrived. But Archie knew how acute her senses were. When he asked again, she nodded reluctantly. "Yes, they're here. So are the Dark Elves, dwarfs, and others."

Quinn raised his eyebrows. "Can you really feel them? I can't. Where are they?"

"Everywhere—all around us." Freya pointed south. "But most are down that way. There are a few behind us, but not on this continent. They'll be using the other tunnels."

A renewed silence fell over the group. The War of the Realms had started, and the giants were moving on to Asgard—via Earth.

"I wonder what the military is doing about it?" Archie asked. "The people here don't even believe in the other realms. How can we possibly fight them?"

"You can't," Freya said. "The safest thing for everyone would be for the military to stay out of their way and let the giants go for the other tunnels."

"You know they won't do that, right?" Archie said.

Freya nodded but said nothing. She stood up. "I can't eat any more. If you're all up to it, we should get moving."

"And about time, too!"

Freya turned and saw Loki striding up to them.

"Loki!" Before Freya realized what she was doing, she ran forward and threw her arms around him.

"Puh—lease!" Loki said as he pulled free of her embrace. "A little decorum, if you don't mind."

Freya looked him up and down. He was dressed in the leather armor she hadn't seen him wear since her First Day Ceremony. He carried his staff in his right hand. It was taller than him and had a large jewel at the top.

"How did you get away from the Vanir? Verdandi said they were torturing you."

"It was just a minor, but rather unpleasant, misunderstanding. When the Norns came and explained the situation, they released me. To make up for their actions, they re-created my armor and staff. Urd told me about the plan to rescue Skuld, and I had to catch up with you. Of course you'll need my help."

Freya smiled at his bravado. "Yes, I guess we do."

"Do the Elders know that Skye and Quinn have left Vanaheim to come with us?" Archie asked.

"They do now," Loki answered. He looked at the two Vanir. "I wouldn't want to be in your shoes when you get home."

"I don't care what the Elders say or do," Quinn said bravely. "If we fail, Vanaheim will fall just like Asgard. Then breaking the law will mean nothing."

"What about the Elders? Will they side with Asgard?" Freya asked.

"I believe so," Loki said. "The Vanir will be drawn in whether they want to be or not. I can't see them joining the giants." Loki reached down for a piece of bread. "Now, if you've finished your little picnic, we should get going."

"Loki," Freya started, "Skye and Quinn aren't used to this much flying. Do you think . . . ?"

Loki held up his hand. "Don't say it. You want to hitch a ride."

"Not for me," Freya said. "I'm fine. It's for the others."

Loki made a point of sighing dramatically. "All right, all right. You don't have to cry about it."

Freya frowned. "I wasn't."

"Sure you were—just like you were worried about me and frightened the Vanir might hurt me. Admit it—you actually like me, and it's so gosh darn sweet!"

Within seconds of his arrival, Loki had managed to irritate her again. "If you're just here to cause trouble, you can turn around and go back to Vanaheim!"

"Loosen up, Freya. You're too uptight." Loki laughed. He rubbed his hands together eagerly. "Now, where are we going?"

"Muspelheim," Archie said.

"I know that, ghost! I meant via which root of Yggdrasil. I don't know of any direct tunnel to Muspelheim from here. Urd said she told you where it is."

Quinn pulled out the Midgard map and lay it down on

the ground. He pointed to the spot Urd had indicated.

Loki studied it for a moment and nodded. "Machu Picchu—that makes a lot of sense. The Incas knew all about the realms. Some of them must have found the tunnel and tried to reach Muspelheim. Maybe they even saw a fire giant or two. They would have viewed them as sun gods."

Archie frowned at the map. "Is that Brazil?"

Loki looked at him and snorted. "No wonder you're an idiot! Is that what they're teaching in school these days?"

"Hey," Archie cried.

Freya quickly stepped in. "No, Archie. It's in the Andes of Peru. By the time I was old enough to go on the reapings, Machu Picchu was already abandoned. But Mother says it was once a wondrous place."

Quinn picked up the map and stowed it away. "And that's where we're going."

15

FLYING ON THE BACK OF THE BLACK DRAGON, THEY reached the first of the northern settlements just before sunrise.

As they passed over the homes, Freya immediately felt powerful emotions rising from the people below. The closer they got to cities, the more intense the feelings became.

"I can feel the people from here," Freya said. "Everyone is terrified."

"Of course they are," Archie said. "Earth is being invaded by monsters—it's like a disaster movie!"

By midmorning they approached a large city and witnessed the source of everyone's fear. "Look!" Quinn shouted. "Are those frost giants?"

"That's them," Freya said.

Ahead of them was a long line of frost giants standing taller than the highest buildings and moving steadily north. Military jet fighters flew at them from all directions, launching their rockets. But the weapons did little more than irritate the giants. When the jets flew closer to use their guns, the giants simply swatted them away like flies.

"They look so much bigger here than they did in Asgard. Earth doesn't stand a chance," Archie moaned.

Suddenly Loki veered sharply in the sky, nearly tossing Freya and the others off his back. Seconds later a rocket shot past the dragon's side.

"Hey, they're shooting at us!" Archie cried.

"They can't tell us apart from the invaders!" Freya leaned forward on the dragon's back. "Loki, take us higher—away from the fighting!"

Instead of following Freya's advice, Loki glided lower in the sky and used his large, powerful wings to maneuver expertly between the giants and the military fighters.

They glided up to a tall building and landed on the roof. Even before everyone had climbed off his back, he was returning to his normal form. They ran up to the edge of the roof and witnessed the sickening sight of a world in trouble. Frost giants were storming through the city, kicking buildings out of their way and challenging anything that came at them. Perched on most of the frost giants' shoulders were masked Dark Elves. Their hands were moving too fast to follow. But with each movement, a jet fighter was knocked magically out of the sky.

Beyond the long line of frost giants was an even more terrifying sight. Fire giants—looming taller than the frost giants, their skin and hair flaming red and glowing, while their clothing was engulfed in living flame. All they had to do was touch a building and it became a raging inferno.

"Where are we?" Archie asked, gazing all around.

"Montreal, Quebec," Loki answered. "Or rather, what's left of it."

"I've never seen a fire giant before," Skye said in a whisper. "They're even more frightening than the frost giants."

"They're meaner, too," Loki said.

As the long line of giants swept past them on their journey north to the Asgard tunnel, several stopped and turned in their direction.

"Uh-oh," Archie said. "I think they can feel us. Get ready to fly, everyone."

"Not yet," Loki said. "But stand back. I want to see just how much power the Vanir gave me to work with."

"They couldn't give you power," Quinn said.

Loki looked back at him. "Wanna bet?"

He turned forward again and raised his staff. The jewel at the end glowed brilliant green. When the closest giant was no more than two steps away, Loki called, "Alpeera."

The jewel exploded in a blazing flash of green lightning

that struck the giant and knocked him backward into the others. The ground shook as three giants lost their balance and fell, landing on a multistory parking garage and collapsing it to the ground. The giant who took the blast lay still as his chest smoldered.

"Wow!" Archie cried. "It worked."

As the other giants saw their companions go down, they roared in fury. The stomping of their feet charging toward the building rattled the ground like an earthquake.

"Uh, Loki . . . ," Freya cried as she drew her flaming sword. "Would you please use that thing again and stop those giants before they get here and squish us!"

Loki raised his staff. "Alpeera!"

Once again, the green jewel sent a blast of lightning at the frost giants. It knocked them to the ground with explosive impact.

Everyone on the roof cheered as the giants went down. But their joy was short-lived as fire giants charged in their direction.

"Loki!" a fire giant roared. "I know it's you! You're dead!"

For a third time, Loki used the staff, but even though the blazing green lightning struck the approaching fire giant in the chest, it had little effect on him.

"Well, isn't this disappointing," Loki said, casually inspecting his staff. "It doesn't seem to work on fire giants. I think we might be in trouble. . . ."

Freya looked back to Quinn and Skye. "I've got my sword, but it won't do much against them. What can you do?"

"More than that," Quinn cried. "Skye, you're with me. Freya, do what you can to slow them down—we need time to prepare a spell!"

Freya looked up at Orus on her shoulder. "Get into the air and stay back. They're too big for you."

"They're too big for all of us!" Orus cawed, and he launched off Freya's shoulder and took flight.

"Archie, stay here," Freya ordered as she flapped her wings and took off. She circled around him once and called, "Remember, you're a ghost. They can't hurt you. Even if this building goes down around you, you'll be okay! Stay here and I'll be back for you."

"Be careful!" Archie cried.

Freya nodded and focused on the first fire giant. Quinn and Skye were beside her. "Do what you can to keep him focused on you," Quinn ordered. "We're going for his legs."

Freya nodded and let out a loud Valkyrie howl, calling the giant's attention to her. The closest fire giant saw her in the air and shouted, "I hate Valkyries!"

He swatted at her, and Freya felt the blast of searing-hot air. But she was fast enough to dart out of the way of the giant's fiery hand.

"Come on, you can do better than that!" Freya teased. "Here I am—come and get me, Fire-Face!" She raised her sword and dived forward toward the giant's burning ear. The heat from his flaming head singed her skin, but in a quick maneuver, she was able to pierce her sword right through his earlobe. "Now you can wear an earring!"

The giant screamed and slapped his hand up to his ear, missing her by a breath. Distracted by the pain in his ear, he failed to see Quinn and Skye at his knees. As Freya moved in for a second attack, she stole a look down and saw that the two Vanir had joined hands and were casting a spell.

Moments later the fire giant roared as he tried to move and found that his two legs were magically fused together.

"Freya, knock him over!" Quinn shouted.

Freya dived at the giant again. But she didn't need to touch him. The fire giant behind him swatted at her but missed. His hand struck the trapped fire giant with a blow so hard, it knocked the restrained giant off his feet and into a large, round building. The impact was enough to tip the building over, taking the flaming fire giant down with it.

There was little time to celebrate. No sooner had one fire giant gone down than there were two more to take its place. Working as a team, Freya, Quinn, and Skye managed to bring down four more giants. But they weren't down for long, as Dark Elves arrived quickly and used their magic to release the spell restraining their legs.

"It's the Dark Elves," Quinn cursed. "There are too many here. Their combined powers are greater than ours."

"Just do what you can!" Freya called as she flew at another giant.

Fighting the giants was like trying to push back the ocean with a spoon. They couldn't possibly win, even with the Vanir's powers and her skill with a sword.

Above them, jet fighters saw Freya and the Vanir fighting against the giants and joined in the attack. But even working together, they were badly outmatched.

Behind Freya, frost giants roared Loki's name. When she circled back, she was stunned to see the Loki she knew was gone. He had changed and grown into one of the largest, most ferocious-looking frost giants she'd ever seen.

Everyone knew Loki was part frost giant. But Freya had never seen him in his true form. He was as terrifying as he was big. In fact, he towered over the other giants around him. Loki still had his recognizable long dark hair, but his face had taken on frost giant features: a large bulbous nose, protruding forehead, and full lips. His eyebrows were so bushy, she could barely see his eyes. His body was heavily muscled in his large green leather armor. But there was no mistaking the fact that this was still Loki.

The magic of the staff had grown with him. Loki wielded it like an expert and knocked over any giant who dared to come near. When he fired a blast of power at the frost giants, the effect was devastating and killed every frost giant it struck.

The frost and fire giants lost interest in Freya and the Vanir and started to go after Loki.

"Loki, look out!" Freya shouted.

Loki turned toward his attackers and charged. In the middle of the dense city, the powerful giants came together in an explosive, rolling battle that completely destroyed everything around them. Buildings fell like dominoes, and roads and bridges were torn up under the strain of the fight.

From somewhere in the middle of the melee, Loki shouted her name. His voice was deep, guttural, and rolling like thunder—but his message was clear. "Freya, get everyone outta here; you know what you must do!"

Freya had grown up on the battlefields of Earth and thought she'd seen a lot. But she'd never witnessed anything like this. The violence of the fight was worse than anything she could imagine. Nothing could withstand the impact of the wrestling giants, and before long, the beautiful city of Montreal lay in ruins.

"Go!" Loki roared again.

Freya turned away, flying toward Quinn. "Where's Skye?"

"She's gone to get Archie," he called. "Loki's right; we can't stop the giants. We have to go!"

Moments later Skye fluttered back to them with Archie clutched in her arms. Freya flew closer. "I'll take him. It's easier for me to carry him."

Archie shook his head. "No, Gee, not right now. You

need to keep your sword arm free in case more giants come after us. I'm too much of a burden."

"But Quinn and Skye have their magic—it's stronger than me and my sword."

"Not now," Skye admitted. "The Elders were right. In Midgard, the Vanir lose their powers. Ours are fading fast. You must protect us until we reach Muspelheim, where they should be restored."

"They're right," Orus called. *"Let's go—we can't help Loki or Midgard now."*

Freya hesitated a moment longer and watched Loki fighting the other giants. Though he was taller and, by the looks of it, a lot stronger than the others, he was badly outnumbered.

It wasn't long before he was overwhelmed by giants. The last thing Freya saw was Loki going down and all the others moving in to tear him apart. She was sickened to realize there was nothing she could do.

Loki and Earth were lost to the giants.

16

MAYA AWOKE TO THE SOUND OF SCREAMING. OPENING her eyes, she discovered that she was buried in thick rubble. She started to cough as the settling dust filled her lungs. She took stock of the situation. She was sore, but nothing new was broken. Lying on her side, she found she was buried, but not trapped, in the rubble.

She could feel that the giants had gone. In the ruins of the house, Kai was buried to her left and just starting to stir. Grul was on her right. The raven was alive, but barely. The soldiers in the house were dead. Farther down the long corridor, Brundi was unconscious but very much alive. Mims was conscious and starting to panic as she tore through the remains of the house.

"Mom!" Mims cried again. "Where are you?"

"*Maya?*" Grul moaned.

"I'm here," she said urgently. "Just hold on. I'll get us free!"

Maya started to push back debris. A heavy ceiling beam was lying across her body, but the rubble beneath it kept its weight from crushing her. She'd been lucky. If it had hit her fully, she knew it would have broken her wings again, maybe even worse. With a bit more digging, she freed herself and then started to dig for Grul.

By the time she found him, Grul was in rough shape. His back was broken and a wing was bent at a terrible angle.

Maya's hands trembled as she freed him. "Is it very bad? Are you in much pain?"

"*I—I can't feel anything.*" The raven panicked. "*Maya, I can't move!*"

"Calm down, Grul. You're alive—that's all that matters to me."

Kai climbed from the debris beside her. His face and black hair were gray from building dust. "How is he?"

Maya fought to keep control. "His back is broken. He's paralyzed. But he's alive!"

"Mom!" Mims screeched as her panic intensified. "Maya! Kai! Where are you? I need your help!"

"Go." Grul moaned. "*Leave me and help Sarah.*"

Maya refused to release Grul and carried him through to the back bedroom that housed Sarah and the baby. The strong sound of Michael's cries was a relief to her. At least he was alive. But as she stumbled through the remains of the doorway, she felt Sarah's life force fading.

"Maya, over here. Hurry!" Mims cried. "Please, we have to save her."

The house had been cast into darkness by the attack, but with her Valkyrie vision, Maya was able to pick her way through the bedroom. Mims had cleared most of the rubble away from her mother.

Sarah was lying on the floor beside the bed with Michael sheltered in her arms. It was obvious to see that Sarah had protected him from the collapse with her body.

"Mom, please . . . ," Mims cried.

Maya handed Grul to Kai and then lifted the baby away from Sarah. She placed Michael in Kai's other hand. "Get them both out of here and stay on the beach. If the giants come back, don't wait for us—just fly away. We'll be right out."

Mims was holding her mother's hand. "Maya, please, help her."

Kneeling beside her young cousin, Maya looked at Sarah. The damage to her human aunt was fatal. Nothing could save her now. Mims's growing Valkyrie senses already told her the truth, but she couldn't accept it.

"I'm so very sorry I can't save her. I just don't have that kind of power," Maya said.

Mims shook her head. "I can't lose her. Please . . ."

Maya sighed sadly. "You know there's only one thing I can do, and that's to end her pain."

"She's going to die?" Mims sniffed.

Maya nodded. Her aunt had been struck by the giant's fist. That she managed to save her baby was proof of her love. It tore at Maya to have to tell Mims the truth. "Her time has come. It's too soon, but I can't change that."

"Will you reap her?" Mims choked through her tears. "Please, don't let her suffer."

Maya felt her own eyes welling up. Sarah was a good woman who didn't deserve this violent end. "She named you, so you've already given her your name. We'll reap her together, you and me, so you can always be together." She took Mims's hand and spoke the words she'd said so many times before. But this time, their meaning had never meant more.

"Sarah Angelo, your time has come. Let us end your suffering."

Together they reached up and gently caressed Sarah's forehead. Maya made certain her little finger grazed along the dying woman's skin. Her throat constricted as she said, "Come, join us now. . . ."

"Mom . . ." Mims wept as her mother took her final, unsteady breath.

Soon her spirit rose and looked around in wonder. She glanced down at her body and then frowned at the gold-and-black Valkyrie symbol blazoned on the back of her hand. "Am I dead?"

Maya nodded. "I'm sorry, Sarah. It was the giants."

"What happens now?" she asked in confusion. "I don't want to leave you."

"You won't," Maya said gently. "That symbol on your hand means you belong with the Valkyrie Myriam-Elizabet. Mims reaped you, so you will stay with her."

"But the baby?" Sarah panicked.

"Michael is unharmed. You kept him safe. He's with Kai outside."

"Mom . . ." Mims threw her arms around her ghost mother and held her tight. "I'm so sorry I couldn't save you . . . ," she sobbed.

Sarah held her daughter the same way she had in life. "It's all right, sweetheart. The worst is over and they can't hurt me anymore." She looked at Maya and nodded. "Thank you. Now I can stay with my family."

"Sarah . . . ?"

Brundi climbed unsteadily into the bedroom. There was a large cut on her forehead and she was moving stiffly, but she wasn't seriously injured. When she saw Mims and Sarah, her head dropped. "I'm so sorry, child."

"Don't be," Sarah said gently. "When I was alive, I was a liability to you. Now I might have more strength to join in the fight against the giants."

Leaving the wreck of the house behind them, they walked down to the beach and joined Kai with the baby and Grul. Maya took her raven back and cradled him gently. "You'll fly again, my sweet Grul. I promise you will."

The sun was just coming up to reveal the full damage done to the house. Beyond it lay a trail of complete destruction as the two giants made their way inland. Seeing the devastation wrought by the giants, Maya was surprised that any of them had survived.

Her senses told her that they were alone. The million-dollar beach homes surrounding them had been abandoned as their inhabitants had fled the moment the giants arrived. A soft, sweet ocean breeze was coming off the calm water. At any other time, it would have been beautiful. But now it only reflected the desolation of the area and the eerie silence around them.

Maya looked back out over the ocean with an uneasy feeling. "More giants are coming—we must leave here now."

Brundi nodded. "And I want to call Vonni to tell him what's happened."

Sarah shook her head. "Please don't. It will only distract him. I'm fine. The baby and Mims are fine. He's needed where he is."

"But he should be told what happened to you."

"He'll find out soon enough," Sarah said. "Earth needs him now. We can't ask him to come back when there's nothing he can do for me."

Kai stepped forward. "She's right. Our first priority is getting away from here." He looked at Maya. "Are you strong enough to fly?"

Maya opened her wings and gave them a full workout. She nodded. "They'll work. Just as soon as I get all these bandages off them, we'll go."

With Mims to help her, Maya's wings were soon freed from the bandages. She took a quick test flight along the beach and came right back. Landing with the others, she nodded. "All set. Let's go."

17

BACK IN THE RUINS OF MONTREAL, FREYA RELUCTANTLY turned away from the terrible sight of Loki going down. For all the trouble he had caused her, all his sarcastic barbs, he had become a big part of her life, and she realized she would miss him.

"Come on, Gee," Archie called from Skye's arms. "You can't help him now. None of us can. But he's given us the chance to get away. We can't waste it."

Archie was right, but it was still hard to leave Loki behind. Freya maneuvered in the sky and hung poised, ready to fly away. Now that she'd experienced fighting the giants, she was able to come up with a strategy. "Remember, the giants can't move very quickly, and they aren't agile. Keep low and fly no higher than their knees. We're too small and fast for them to hit us. Follow me!"

Freya led her small group of fighters away from the city and continued to fly south. Along the way they saw a straight, wide path of destruction. East Coast cities that had stood for hundreds of years were burning ruins as the giants followed a course leading from the Florida Everglades up to northern Canada.

In the sky above them, military fighters took on the giants, but their struggle was in vain. Rockets couldn't wound or even slow their progress, and on the ground, large military tanks lay quashed by giant feet. Humanity could do nothing to stop the invaders.

Occasionally they saw evidence of a small victory as they encountered a dead giant. It seemed that when a fire giant died, its flames were extinguished. In death they looked just like frost giants. Freya and the others knew that the immortal giants would rise again, but they didn't know how long this process would take. Hopefully, the war would end before then.

As they flew over the ruins of Boston, they spied several giant corpses whose wounds gave Freya hope. She called the others to land and flew up to the head of one of the dead giants.

"Look." She pointed at the wounds. "There is only one thing in all the realms that could do that kind of damage to a frost giant."

Archie came up beside her and peered at the wound. "Could it be?"

"What?" Quinn asked. "What killed him?"

"Thor," Freya and Archie said as one.

Archie continued. "Only his hammer could make this kind of dent in a giant's head. Thor's fighting them here on Earth. The military must've let him go."

"Or he escaped when the giants arrived," Freya said. "Either way, he's free and fighting. Maybe my family is free as well." She looked around, hoping they might still be in the area.

"I wonder where they are," Archie mused.

"I can feel Kai. He's alive, and not very far from here." She closed her eyes. "But something is wrong."

"Of course something's wrong," Archie said. "There are giants on Earth!"

Freya shook her head. "No, it's more than that. . . ."

"I am sorry, Freya, but whatever you're feeling means nothing right now," Quinn said. "We must get moving if we are to stop this war."

"I know," she reluctantly agreed. "I just wish I could let my family know what's happening."

"They could be anywhere," Orus said. *"Quinn's right; we don't have time to look."*

A furious roaring of giants sounded behind them, followed by explosions and gunfire. The battle was starting again as the next wave of giants descended upon the area.

"Hey, you kids, get out of there!"

Battle-weary soldiers ran at them but slowed when they saw the wings on Freya and the Vanir. They raised their weapons and their leader came forward.

"Who're you fighting for?" he demanded.

"We fight for you," Freya said carefully. She could feel their despair. They were fighting a losing battle. She tried to sound reassuring as she extended her wings. "We are with Thor and the Asgardians. You might know of my mother and sisters, who also have feathered wings. We all serve Odin and are on the side of peace."

The soldiers lowered their weapons. "I'm sorry, miss. I'm Sergeant John Romin," the soldier said. "These days I can't tell the good guys from the bad." He looked back at his men. "They're on our side." As an afterthought, he warned them, "But don't any of you touch them. This young lady is lethal."

"So you know my mother and sisters?" Freya asked hopefully. "Have you seen them?"

"Not personally," Sergeant Romin said. "But we've all heard of what happens to those who touch Valkyries. We've been ordered not to fire on anybody with wings until we know who they're fighting for."

"How long have the giants been here?" Archie asked.

Freya shook her head. "Archie, you're a ghost—he can't see or hear you." While Archie cursed, she repeated the question to the sergeant.

"A couple of weeks," he said. "They're appearing all over the world. Here in the United States, they're crawling out of a big hole in Florida, and we've just heard reports of more coming out of the Pacific Ocean."

"And they're heading to a tunnel in northern Canada," Freya finished.

"That's right," the sergeant agreed. "But nothing we try seems to stop them. So far the only thing that has been able to kill them is your people."

"But it's not enough." Freya called Quinn and Skye forward. "Sergeant, I need you and your men to find Thor or my mother, the head Valkyrie, and get a message to them—"

"Look, miss, I'm grateful for what your people are doing, but we've got a war to fight. We ain't a courier service."

"If you don't pass along this message, the war is over and the giants have already won. This information is crucial to the survival of Earth."

The soldier hesitated for a moment and then nodded. He pulled out his mobile phone, dialed a number, and then handed the phone to Freya, careful not to touch her. "It's the command center—give them your message."

"Hello?" a voice called over the phone.

"Hello, I'm the black-winged Valkyrie your people saw in Chicago some time ago," Freya explained. "It is imperative that this message reaches my mother, the lead

Valkyrie, and Thor, leader of the Asgard forces and his Dark Searchers."

"Hold a moment, please. . . ."

A couple of minutes later, another voice started to speak. "I am General Pickers, central commander of the International Coalition of Defense Forces for the United States. Who am I speaking with?"

"I'm Greta, the black-winged Valkyrie that caused a lot of trouble in Chicago," Freya said.

"I remember reading the reports about you," the general said. "And I've seen more than a few photos of you in action. You caused quite a stir back then."

"But that's nothing compared to what the frost and fire giants are doing to Earth right now."

"True," the general agreed. "What can I do for you?"

"It is critical that you get a message to Thor and his people. This information could change the outcome of the war in the realms."

Not being face-to face with the man meant Freya couldn't read him fully. But her senses were acute enough to hear his breathing change. "You know what I'm talking about, don't you?" she asked.

"Ragnarök," the general breathed.

"Yes," Freya agreed. "Now, please, listen to me. Thor and my mother must hear this. It's desperately important information."

The tone of his voice changed again. "Greta, I'm recording this conversation right now. Tell me what you want them to hear. . . ."

"Mother, Thor, it's me, Greta," Freya started. "I'm sorry I disappeared from the farm, but I've been with Loki. He was on our side all along—though I just watched him fall in battle in Montreal." Freya's voice caught for a moment as she recalled the sight of Loki being overwhelmed by the giants. "Loki took us to Vanaheim to ask the Vanir to help us defeat the giants. While we were there, we found out Dirian and his men attacked the Norns at the base of Yggdrasil. Urd and Verdandi escaped, but he's taken Skuld to Muspelheim and is using her to end the destinies of those who oppose him.

"There is only one thing we can do to stop this war. We're going to Muspelheim to try to free Skuld. Once she is safe, we hope the fallen immortals will rise. Or, at least, we hope that those who fall after she is free will be able to rise. Then we will go to the giant kings. I'm with two Vanir warriors. They'll use their magic to get the giants to turn on each other again."

Freya paused, knowing the reaction that this news would bring to her family. "Mother, we know the danger we're facing, and it's likely we'll die and perhaps stay dead in the attempt. But it's the only way to save the realms. Urd and Verdandi agree with us. Skuld is the key to ending the war. If we fail and are killed, you must follow us to Muspelheim and free her. As long as Skuld is a prisoner of

Dirian, none of us are safe and all the realms will fall.

"We're leaving now, and must travel down to the Andes. There's a hidden, direct tunnel to Muspelheim. It's in the ancient city of Machu Picchu. When we find the entrance, I'll mark it with my crest, so you'll be able to follow us.

"Thor, please forgive us for doing this without you. But you are so desperately needed here on Earth. We've seen the damage the giants are doing. Midgard needs you, just like Skuld needs us."

Freya took a deep breath and looked at her companions. "Have I forgotten anything?"

Quinn shook his head. "No. That's everything."

Freya focused on the phone again. "That's all. Thank you, General. Please ensure that the message reaches Thor and my family as soon as possible."

Just as she was about to hand back the phone to the sergeant, she heard the general call, "Greta, wait."

"Yes?"

"I will ensure your family hears this message. You have my word," he said. "And I want to thank you on behalf of the people of Earth for your efforts. But please, let us help. There's nothing our Earth forces can do to stop the giants; we know that. Nuclear weapons have been discussed, but we've been told by Colonel Giovanni Angelo and Thor himself about Yggdrasil and that the tunnels are the roots of the Great Tree and that to kill the roots is to kill the tree and end all of us.

"It's still so hard for us to accept, but considering what we've seen, I must believe in the existence of the Cosmic World Tree and the damage nuclear weapons pose to it. So we will do what little we can to support the Asgard fighters." He paused for a moment and then said, "And you."

"I don't understand," Freya said.

"I'm asking you to let us help you," he continued. "You are in the Boston area, and it's a very long way to Peru. Let us take you there in military transport. If you are going to fight for us, I don't want you exhausted from flying thousands of miles before you engage the enemy. I can make all the arrangements now. We can have you in the air in half an hour. Will you let us do this for you?"

Freya's initial instinct was not to trust humans. But this time was different. They were united in war. She told Archie what the general had said. "Do you think we should trust him?"

"Are you serious?" Archie cried. "Of course you should trust him! This could save us a lot of time!"

"*Do it, Freya,*" Orus cawed. "*I know it goes against everything you believe, but this time, we must trust them.*"

Freya said into the phone, "Thank you, General. We would all be grateful for the ride."

Six hours later they stood at the back of a large military transport airplane, escorted by multiple fighter jets. Freya had been on an airplane only once before and it had terrified her then. This was worse.

The aircraft was larger than the one her uncle Vonni had flown, but it was bumpier and much noisier. They were surrounded by soldiers who looked at them with a mix of fear and awe.

Little could be said on the flight as it was too loud to be heard above the noise of the plane. But as she stood holding on to cargo netting for balance, she watched her new friends' faces. Quinn was taking it all in his stride and wasn't bothered by the sights and sounds around him. Skye was more anxious but just as determined.

"How much farther?" Freya called to one of the soldiers escorting them to Peru. They had been flying all night and the sun was already up.

"Just over an hour," answered a female soldier with her dark hair tied back in a neat ponytail. Even though she looked to be only in her early twenties, Freya sensed she had seen more than her fair share of battle. "We're taking a bit longer to stay on a route that's giant-free, so we don't encounter any trouble."

The hour dragged and the tension grew. It was one thing to plan to go to Muspelheim; it was another to actually get there. What horrors lay ahead in the land of the fire giants? Yes, she had her silver breastplate and armor for protection, but Quinn and Skye were exposed. She'd heard that Muspelheim was hot. But just *how* hot was hot?

Finally they felt the tilt of the airplane, signaling their descent.

"Greta, we're approaching the jump point," the female soldier called to her.

"Thank you, Corporal . . . ?" Freya noted the corporal's name wasn't on her uniform.

"Corporal Biederon." She smiled, but her expression held the same anxiousness Freya felt. "But you can just call me Tina."

"Thanks, Tina."

They heard the large airship groan as the rear cargo doors opened and a long, wide ramp slid out into the open air. Morning sunlight blazed into the darkened hull, and all the soldiers around them rose to their feet and prepared to jump out of the airplane.

Freya had argued that she and her team should travel alone. But the general had insisted on a protective escort to see them safely to Machu Picchu. He reasoned that their mission was far too important to risk locals attacking the winged visitors.

Sergeant Romin had requested that he and his soldiers be the ones to escort Freya. Permission had been granted, and as they prepared to jump from the transport ship, the sergeant leaned closer to her. "Greta, let me and my people jump first and then you and your team can follow us. I'm sure, with your wings, you could land before us. But please don't. Stay with us and land when we do. We know this area is seeing a lot of activity from frightened people escaping the giants and coming here to pray. There may be trouble when they see you."

Freya nodded and watched the soldiers check their parachutes a final time. When they got the green light, one by one they ran down the ramp of the open cargo doors and jumped into the blazing blue sky. The sight of the parachutes opening reminded Freya of the wild mushrooms that popped up in the Asgard forests. When the last soldier had jumped, Freya nodded to her team. "Ready?"

Skye caught hold of Archie again, and Orus launched off Freya's shoulder and was the first out of the cargo exit.

"Let's go!" Freya said. She ran after Orus and, keeping her wings closed tightly, dived off the ramp and into the sky. Turning around in midair, she watched Quinn and Skye follow behind her.

When she turned to see where they were going, Freya was struck by the sight. Machu Picchu was a magnificent stone city at the top of one of the mountains. As with most ruins, the roofs were missing, but the walls and structure of the ancient homes, temples, and meeting places were still intact.

Tiers had been cut into the side of the mountain, which

held all of Machu Picchu stable and kept landslides at bay. Freya wished she'd been old enough to see it when it was still a thriving city.

Halfway down to the ground, Freya opened her wings and started to glide. High in the Andes, they were surrounded by tall mountains covered in tropical and subtropical vegetation, with two distinct peaks directly beside the ancient ruins. The sights were stunning as they dropped down into the lush green area.

Freya maneuvered closer to the parachuting soldiers and stayed with them as they headed toward their destination on the open, grass-covered Central Plaza of the old city. As she glided past the soldiers, they waved at her and gave the thumbs-up signal.

"Who'd have ever believed this?" Orus cawed as he stayed close to Freya. *"For years we've remained invisible to human soldiers. Now we're actually flying with them and they're here to protect us."*

"I guess war does change the rules," Freya admitted. When they approached the plaza, she understood what the soldiers were concerned about. There were hundreds of people gathered in the area. Their feelings of fear confirmed to Freya that they weren't tourists visiting old ruins. These were desperate people looking for any kind of protection from the invaders.

"Greta," the sergeant shouted. "Keep your team in the

air until we secure the area and make it safe for you to land."

Freya acknowledged the message and flapped her wings to climb higher in the sky. With Quinn and Skye close beside her, they heard the crowds shouting and saw their fists waving in the air at the sight of the winged visitors. These people didn't see her as a black-winged angel, as so many in the past had. To them, Freya and her friends were part of the invasion.

"This isn't good," Orus cawed. *"They'll tear us apart if they get the chance."*

"We won't give them the chance," Freya said.

When the soldiers touched down, the crowds rushed forward, and the soldiers were forced to fire their weapons in the air to drive them back. But with tensions running so high, it wouldn't take much to turn the situation into a violent riot.

"Quinn, Skye, follow me," Freya called. She descended and landed on the tallest stone structure above the flat plaza. "Keep your wings open and get ready to fly if they try to climb up after us."

Freya stood at the edge of the stone structure and looked out at the people rushing at the soldiers. She took a deep breath and released the loudest Valkyrie howl she could manage.

Civilians and soldiers alike covered their ears and tried to escape the harsh sound. But they couldn't—the howl of a

Valkyrie could be heard for miles, and it echoed through all the Andes Mountains.

"Hear me!" Freya called, using the special Valkyrie power that allowed her to be understood by anyone, no matter what language they spoke.

The gathered masses shook their heads and tried to clear their ears.

"We are here to defend Earth, not conquer it," she started. "You need only look at the soldiers with us to see the truth. We are on a special mission. If we succeed, the giants will leave Earth. I am from Asgard, and my companions are from Vanaheim. Our realms are in as much danger as yours. We, like you, are fighting the giants, and our worlds, like yours, will fall if we fail."

Freya's senses told her that the people were listening. Many still had doubts, but at least their hostility was fading. "We know a way to defeat the giants and we know that there is a special place we can go to stop them. The tunnel to that place lies here, buried deep below the ground of Machu Picchu."

Confusion rose in the crowds. An older man came forward and shouted in Spanish, "How can we trust you? It's demons like you that are destroying our world."

"We are not demons," Freya called. "And we are united with you in our struggle against the giants! Please, will you help us find the tunnel that will lead us to the realm of the fire giants? It is there that we will stop them."

"Freya," Orus cawed. *"You can't promise that when it's likely we'll fail."*

"If we fail, it kinda won't matter what Gee promises," Archie said. "Earth will be toast anyway."

"Look at them," Freya said. "They're terrified and helpless to stop the giants. Let me give them a little hope, if only for a while." She turned back to the crowds. "To help us is to help yourselves. It's the one thing you can do against the giants."

That struck a chord with the people. They nodded, and their posture changed.

"Greta," the sergeant called. "Where do we go? Where is the tunnel?"

"Quinn, use the map. Where's the tunnel?"

Quinn pulled out Urd's map. It showed the details of Machu Picchu, including the two peaks behind them. Using them as the starting point, he looked at the map and then toward the stone structures. "It's down there, just past the Central Plaza, in a place called the Temple of the Sun."

Freya opened her wings and jumped off the structure. She landed among the soldiers. "We need to find the Temple of the Sun."

"Temple of the Sun?" a middle-aged woman asked nervously in perfect English with a strong Spanish accent. She was small and round and dressed in a colorful poncho and full skirt that was characteristic of the area. "It is down here, not far at all. I can show you."

The woman turned to the crowds and called out in Spanish. Freya understood she was telling everyone they needed to find the Temple of the Sun.

Soon the masses of crowds parted and formed a path. The soldiers completely surrounded Freya and the two Vanir to ensure that no one came within touching distance. After a short walk, the woman stopped and pointed to a cluster of walled-off ruined structures. "It is that one," she said.

"Gee, look, it's the only place here with a round tower."

Archie was right. While the other structures were square, angular buildings, the Temple of the Sun was a perfect semicircular structure built into the surrounding rock to match the natural environment.

"How do we get into the tunnel?" the sergeant asked Freya.

Freya shrugged. "I don't know. But if the Incas knew that this was the tunnel to Muspelheim and knew what would happen to anyone who ventured there, it's likely they would have blocked it off completely."

"There is a large sacrificial stone inside," the woman said. "It is in here that the priests performed the sacrifices to the gods for a prosperous harvest and to gain insight into the future. No one was allowed inside but them."

Freya turned to the woman. "How do you know so much?"

"I am a tour guide here. Or at least I was until the giants

came. Now we all come here seeking protection from the Ancient Ones." She looked at Freya and the Vanir and bowed her head. "Ancient gods like you."

"We aren't gods," Freya said. "We just come from another realm."

"Isn't that the same thing?" she asked.

"Not to me," Freya said. "Would you please take us in and show us the stone?"

The woman bowed again and led them into the maze of structures that surrounded the entrance to the temple. "It is this way."

They entered the temple and went into a small chamber with two large windows on opposite ends.

"Wow!" Archie cried as they went toward the area of sacrifice. "That's not a stone. It's the top of the mountain! How're we going to lift it?"

The altar stone was lying on the floor and took up most of the chamber. It was at least three yards long and two yards wide. To the casual viewer, it looked as though it was a natural stone that was part of the mountaintop and that the temple had been built around it. But as Freya bent down and inspected the stone more closely, she could see it had actually been placed there. Casting out her senses, she could feel a cavern beneath it. Grasping the corner of the massive stone, she started to lift.

The stone shifted a bit, but as she continued to strain, Freya realized that she couldn't lift it.

Panting, she stood up and looked at Quinn. "It's under here. I can feel it. But I'm not strong enough to lift it on my own."

"We can all help," the sergeant said. "Hook ropes on it and pull through that window."

Freya shook her head. "It will take more than all of us together to shift it."

"Gee, you're not giving up, are you?" Archie asked.

"No, but it's going to take more than strength to move it."

"Like what?" the sergeant asked.

Quinn and Skye were doing their own inspection. "Magic will shift it," Quinn informed them. "Whoever placed this here didn't want others moving it to access the tunnel."

"Maybe it was to stop the giants from coming up," the sergeant offered. "There haven't been any sightings of them here in Peru."

Freya shook her head. "Believe me, if they wanted to come through here, that rock wouldn't stop them. No, they either don't know about it or, more likely, they can't fit through the tunnel and had to take another route."

"But we'll fit through it," Quinn said. He looked at the sergeant. "Would you take your people out of here and move the crowds back? We don't want anyone hurt."

The sergeant nodded and ordered most of his soldiers out of the temple. A few minutes later, one called through the window, "All clear out here, sir!"

"All right," he said. "It's up to you now."

Freya stepped up to Quinn and Skye. "Please tell me you have enough power left to do this."

"I hope so," Quinn said. He took Skye's hand and then looked at Freya. "Give me your hand as well. Let's see if that Aesir blood of yours holds any power."

Freya took Quinn's hand and stood facing the ancient stone. As the two Vanir started to cast a spell, she felt a strange tickling sensation go through her.

Her mind burst with wild, vivid colors, and she could feel a power older than time itself. It was a natural power that came from all around them—from the earth below their feet, the blue sky above them, from the trees in the mountains surrounding them, from the animals and all the people anxiously waiting outside the temple. Finally she felt the presence of the Great Cosmic Tree itself.

As the moments ticked by, the Vanir's spell grew louder and more intense. Because it was spoken in an ancient tongue, Freya couldn't understand the words, but she could see the result. The stone that had lain undisturbed for millennia started to tremble. Dust rose from the dry ground, and a rumbling arose from deep inside the earth. Soon the massive stone started to lift.

Freya stole a look at Quinn and saw his eyes were closed in deep concentration. Skye's were the same. The stone was moving slowly, as though it were on a hinge. The back edge was staying put, but the front was lifting like a trapdoor. Higher and higher it climbed until the bottom of the stone finally lifted out of the pit, revealing the narrow tunnel beneath it.

A whoosh of stale, hot air blasted Freya's and the Vanir's hair back. It smelled of sulfur and earth.

When the stone was secured, standing on its long edge, Quinn and Skye opened their eyes. Their faces were covered in a thin film of sweat from the effort.

"Awesome . . . !" Archie breathed.

The soldiers beside them were speechless. They stared at the massive stone and then back to the two Vanir who had moved it with only the power of thought. The sergeant came forward and touched the edge of the stone to ensure it was secure. It wouldn't move.

He looked back at Freya and the Vanir. "Remind me never to annoy you kids."

"It wasn't me," Freya said. "It was them."

"It was all of us," Skye said. "We can manipulate the energy of life. Without it, we have no magic." She turned to Freya. "I never knew Valkyries had so much power in them."

"Me? Really?" Freya said. "All I have are strong senses."

Quinn shook his head. "No. You have much more than that. But it's wild and untrained. With a little practice you could be as powerful as the Vanir."

"Cool!" Archie cried. "Gee, you gotta learn to do that!"

"*We've got to survive this war first,*" Orus cawed.

"And to do that, we have to go down there." Freya pointed into the dark tunnel.

The sergeant nodded. "I'll gather my soldiers together. We'll leave as soon as you're ready."

"Wait," Freya said. "You're not coming with us."

"Yes, we are," the sergeant said. "We're your escort. We've signed on to support your mission, and we're going to follow that through."

Freya shook her head. "You can't. Earth is the only realm that can support human life. I assure you, you'll die if you try to follow us."

The soldier looked doubtful. "We have our orders. We'll take you as far as we can, and then if we see signs of trouble, we'll stop."

Freya could tell there would be no arguing with him. He was a dedicated soldier, trained to follow orders. "I won't stop you from following us, but this is foolish."

"Let me be the judge of that," the sergeant said.

While the sergeant pulled his team together, Freya walked out of the stone temple and drew her flame sword. Having been crafted by the power of the dwarfs, nothing could hurt or dull the enchanted gold blade. She used the tip to carve her ornate Valkyrie mark on the wall. If her mother or the others tried to follow, they would know where to start.

When it was time to enter the tunnel, Freya led the way,

with Archie, Quinn, and Skye close behind. The eight soldiers followed at the rear. As they descended deeper, the soldiers turned on their flashlights.

Tina gasped as she touched the wall. "Sir, feel this—it's warm."

The sergeant touched the wall with his bare hand. "It feels organic, not like rock."

Freya looked back at them. "It is. We told you, we are following one of the roots of Yggdrasil. That wall is a living root."

"That tree you keep talking about is actually real?" the sergeant asked.

Freya nodded. "Of course it's real. Yggdrasil connects all the realms. Without it, we'll all die. So it must be protected."

Awe rose from all the soldiers as they each took turns touching the root of Yggdrasil.

Archie burst into laughter. "Look at their faces—that's priceless! Maybe we should tell them that Santa Claus is real too. I bet they'd believe us!"

Freya grinned and whispered to him, "Be nice. Remember, your expression was exactly the same the first time you saw me."

Orus was on Freya's shoulder, watching the soldiers with concern. *"I don't know if it's a good thing that humans learn that the realms and Yggdrasil are real. It could make things difficult for us."*

"How?" Freya asked. "They can't live outside Midgard, so visiting or even making war on the other realms is impossible."

"I've seen human determination," Orus said. *"They'll find a way eventually."*

"And we'll be ready for them if they do," Freya finished.

After two days and nights in the dark, narrow tunnel, the temperature increased and the soldiers started to suffer the first signs of realm-change difficulties. Progress slowed, and Freya was feeling the pressure to keep moving without them. But at the same time, she knew she couldn't leave them behind.

As they stopped for a break, Sergeant Romin couldn't catch his breath. He was in his fifties and feeling the pressure more than the younger soldiers. Freya sensed his heart was beating too fast, struggling to pump his thickening blood around his body. It would soon become dangerous for him.

"Now do you believe us?" she asked the panting sergeant. "By tomorrow we'll be out of the influence of Midgard completely and heading toward Muspelheim. You must believe me when I say it will kill you. Look at your people. You're all sick. If you go much farther, I promise you you'll die."

The sergeant lifted his head and frowned, not at Freya but at Archie, standing beside her. He squinted and then jumped. "There's someone beside you!"

Freya nodded. "This is my friend Archie. He's been with us all along."

"I don't understand," the sergeant said. "How? I haven't seen him."

"That's because, technically speaking, I'm dead," Archie explained. "On Earth, I'm a ghost, which is why you couldn't see me. But as I pass into the other realms, I regain my physical presence. Now that we're in an area of transition between realms, I'm becoming solid just as you're getting weaker."

"You're—you're really a ghost?" the sergeant asked.

Freya nodded. "I reaped Archie when he was critically wounded in Chicago. This is what I've been trying to tell you. Midgard is unique. Only in death can humans visit the other realms—otherwise, the journey to the realms kills them."

"So you've gotta go back," Archie insisted. "Look at you. It'll only get worse if you stay."

"But our orders . . ." The sergeant panted.

"Your orders weren't to die," Freya insisted. "Your commanders wouldn't expect you to go to the bottom of the ocean without proper protection. This is the same thing. Living humans can't survive this environment."

The sergeant struggled to his feet. Like all the other soldiers, he was ghostly pale and could barely breathe. His lips and fingertips were turning blue. "So," he gasped, "if you touched me, you would reap me, and I could continue this mission."

Freya nodded. "Theoretically, yes, but I wouldn't touch you because it would kill you. So you must all go back."

Before Freya could stop him, the sergeant grasped her bare hand. She shouted in protest, but it was too late. In an instant, and completely against her will, Freya's Valkyrie powers reaped him.

"No!" she cried as she watched his body fall to the ground, dead.

18

"WE NEED TO GET TO SAFETY!" MAYA CALLED TO KAI AS they headed east in the sky. Between them they were carrying Brundi, Mims, Sarah, and the baby. They followed the trail the giants had made and saw that they were moving north, heading toward the tunnel to Asgard in northern Canada.

Maya changed direction and led them south toward Colorado Springs, in the direction of the Cheyenne Mountain Air Force Station. It was one of the most secure places in the country and central command for all the defending military forces. They had originally declined its sanctuary and chosen the California safe house instead. But now Maya and Kai agreed it was the safest place for Brundi, Mims, and the baby.

They flew down toward a large circular tunnel entrance

where a carved sign read, CHEYENNE MOUNTAIN COMPLEX. They soared over the security gates and past the armed soldiers posted there. There was furious activity below as the various military forces arrived and left in response to the giants.

They touched down a few yards from the entrance and were immediately surrounded by armed guards in camouflage uniforms. A captain ordered the others to stand down and rushed forward toward Kai, but when his eyes landed on Maya, he headed straight to her as if she had some magnetic pull over him.

"I'm Captain Miller. Are you the Valkyrie I've heard of . . ."

"You can call me Mia," Maya said, being careful not to give him her real name.

The captain frowned. "I was told your wings were broken and that you were grounded."

"They've healed," she said. "We were at the safe house in California, but the giants destroyed it. I'm sorry, but the soldiers with us were killed, and my raven has been gravely wounded."

"I heard about that," he reported. "More giants have appeared on the coast, and California has fallen to them. Like all the others, these giants are moving north."

Kai stepped forward, thrusting his chest out and confronting the soldier. "Captain, we have brought our family to you. You will protect them with your life, or you will answer to me."

Maya realized Kai had no experience with talking to humans and still had a lot to learn. "Please excuse my brother's manners. What he means is that we hope you can offer sanctuary to this baby and these two wingless Valkyries. And I would be in your debt if you would have your medical people help my Grul. He is very precious to me."

"Of course," Captain Miller said. "You're all welcome here. We've been authorized to offer sanctuary to all Asgardians"— he smiled radiantly at Maya—"including their ravens."

Kai shook his head. "Mia and I aren't staying."

Brundi choked, "Of—of course you're staying! You're both too young to be going off and fighting giants."

Kai shook his head. "We're not going to fight the giants. I can feel Greta. She's back in Midgard and needs our help."

"Where is she?" Maya asked.

Kai shrugged. "I don't know Midgard well enough to tell you. Only that I will be able to track her through our link."

"Greta and her team are in Peru," the captain offered.

"What?" Maya cried. "What's she doing down there? And what team?"

Captain Miller called for a jeep to transport them into the tunnel. "We received a message from Greta explaining everything. Let's get inside and you can hear it."

They drove deep inside the busy mountain facility. Everyone they encountered, be they from the air force, army, or foreign services, all reacted in the same way to the winged visitors. They nodded in respect and, in a few cases, even saluted.

Maya acknowledged them with a nod. She could feel from them the hope the Asgardians offered. She just prayed they could live up to the expectations of humanity.

They took an elevator down two thousand feet below the surface. When they emerged, they were escorted to the command center. The room was cavernous, with an incredibly tall ceiling, and filled with large wall screens showing different locations where the giants were marching through the world. Seeing the devastation playing out on the large screens stole Maya's breath away. Cities were being decimated by the storming frost and fire giants.

Other screens revealed military jets and helicopters trying to engage the giants, but their rockets were useless against them.

"We can't stop them," the captain admitted sadly. "Nothing we've tried works. Thor and Balder have been the most effective against them, and then the Dark Searchers and Valkyries, when they fight together. All we can do is offer support."

Everyone stood in silence, watching the screens until a senior officer arrived. They were introduced to General Pickers, the central commander of the International Coalition of Defense Forces for the United States. He was the one who had spoken personally to Freya and recorded the message. He held up his phone for everyone to hear.

Maya heard her sister's voice and the desperation it held. Freya had been to Vanaheim and had engaged two of the Vanir in their mission. The greatest shock was hearing that Dirian had taken Skuld. Suddenly the war made sense. With Skuld under his control, no one stood a chance against him.

"Muspelheim!" Brundi cried when the message finished. "That's insanity! She'll be killed!"

"They all will," Maya agreed. "I swear that sister of mine is going to be the death of me. General, have you heard anything from Montreal? Is Loki really dead?"

"We don't know for sure," he admitted. "By the end it was hard to tell him apart from the others. I do know the city is in ruins and the giants are still flooding through there, so I fear it may be true that he was killed in the fight."

"Greta is too young to be going to Muspelheim on her own," Brundi insisted. "She has no idea what kind of realm she's heading to. It will be a disaster."

General Pickers nodded. "Perhaps, but she's our best and only hope against the invaders. The transport dropped them off over Machu Picchu earlier today, and they've entered the tunnel to Muspelheim. There is a team of eight soldiers with them, and others are keeping the area secure. We're just awaiting word."

"We're not going to wait," Maya said. She focused on Kai. "If Greta has gone to Muspelheim to free Skuld, then that's where we're going to help her."

The general nodded. "I'd hoped you'd say that. There's another air transport fueling up right now to take you there. Your team will be ready to leave with you shortly."

"Thank you, General," Maya said formally. She turned to Mims and gently handed over Grul. "Would you take care of him for me and see that he gets lots of special love and care?"

Mims nodded. "I will. I promise."

To her grandmother Maya said, "I've never been to Muspelheim before—what can we expect?"

Brundi was wringing her hands. "You're not just going to another realm. Child, you're going to hell."

19

DEEP IN THE TUNNEL TO MUSPELHEIM, THE SERGEANT'S spirit stood beside Freya, looking curiously down at his body. "Wow, that was intense . . . ," he muttered.

The others around him climbed to their feet. "John!" Tina cried.

Freya turned on the sergeant's ghost. "You foolish man—why did you do that? You knew what would happen if you touched me!"

Sergeant Romin looked around in wonder, and then back to her. "I did it to serve my country and my world. I've been in the military for more than twenty years and I'm an experienced soldier. I have skills you need, but I'm no good to you alive. This way we stand a chance of defending Earth against the giants."

"But it's suicide!" Archie cried. "You just killed yourself."

The sergeant shook his head. "No, not suicide. I just changed my skill set for the benefit of the mission."

"Don't you understand? You're dead!" Freya cried. "There is no going home. If we survive this mission and stop the war, there's no getting your life back. It's over! You will either ascend to heaven or stay in Asgard. But you'll never know the love of your family again."

"It's because I love my family that I did this," he insisted. He turned to the other soldiers. "I won't ask you to do the same. But if any of you want to join us, you must touch this Valkyrie."

"No!" Freya shouted as she jumped back. "No one's going to touch me, do you understand? This isn't a game. It's life and death."

"Yes," another soldier said as he stepped forward. "The life and death of Earth. I don't have any family back home, but I love my world and I'm prepared to die for it. Each of us knows the sacrifice we might be called to make. I am prepared to make it right now for this mission."

Freya was struck silent as two more soldiers approached her. "And me," they each volunteered. "You shouldn't have to face those giants alone. Not when we can help."

"This is insane," Freya cried. "You can't all want to die!"

"None of us *wants* to die," Tina said. "But if that's what it takes to defend Earth, we will."

"Greta, listen to me," the sergeant said. "We're grateful for what you're planning to do. You, Quinn, and Skye have amazing powers. But we have skills too. This is too important a mission to risk on just the three of you."

"Four," Archie added. "Don't forget me."

The sergeant nodded. "All right, four of you. Believe me, you need us—you just can't see it. You think because we're human we're weak. But we're not."

Freya shook her head. "I have never considered humans weak—ever! If you really understood what I am, you'd know that Valkyries bring only the bravest fighters of Earth's battle-fields to Asgard to serve in Odin's army. Right now it's dead human warriors who will be taking on the giants when they invade Asgard. So don't think any of us ever thought of you as weak or undeserving of a place in our realm."

"So what's the problem?" another soldier said. "You know we're brave and strong, and like it or not, we're a team. And to stay a team, you've gotta reap us."

Freya's head was spinning. In all her life she'd never encountered a group of warriors *wanting* to be reaped. It went against everything she believed about humans. She looked up at Orus on her shoulder. "What should I do?"

"What does your heart tell you?"

Freya whispered, "That I should do it. But what if I'm wrong?"

"You're not," Archie offered. "We do need their help."

Quinn and Skye both nodded in agreement. Freya looked back at the soldiers. They were standing before her, looking a little frightened by their decision but determined. If she reaped them, there would be no going back—but they could help their mission. If she didn't, they faced a dark future in a world devastated by giants.

"This goes against all the rules," she started. "But the realms have never faced such danger before. Still, it must be an individual decision. No one must feel pressured into joining us. So be warned, I have senses to read people. If you come to me to be reaped and don't really want to, I'll know and will send you away. So think hard. Those who wish to continue on this mission, step forward and I will reap you. Those who wish to serve their world by returning and report-ing what has happened, stay back."

Of the eight soldiers, five were reaped. Their bodies were neatly lined up, sitting against the wall, looking more asleep than dead. The remaining three soldiers returned to the surface.

Freya, Quinn, and Skye had to carry the new ghosts' equipment until their physical presence formed as they passed from Midgard into Muspelheim.

Soon things returned to a strange kind of normal as the soldiers took back their packs and weapons and moved on as though nothing had happened. The only big change was that Freya told them her true name.

Eventually the stink of sulfur increased and Freya's senses

started to pick up on signs of life. "We're getting close," she warned. "I can sense it just ahead."

Quinn nodded and waved his hand in the air. The tunnel filled with light, and a banquet of food appeared before them. "Our powers are back to full strength too."

Knowing this could be their last meal for some time, they stopped for a break and to make their plans. The reaped soldiers were shocked to discover that they could not only eat, but could actually enjoy all the food of the Vanir.

Quinn pulled out the map Verdandi had given to him. He laid it down on the table. "All right, here is where Verdandi said we would emerge from the tunnel." He traced his finger along the map until it passed over a large desert. "And here is where they're holding Skuld."

"How far is that?" the sergeant asked.

"A good day's flight," Quinn responded.

The sergeant looked at Freya. "Now that we're—you know, dead—can we fly?"

Freya shook her head. "No, not unless you could fly when you were alive. Though when you're in Midgard, with no substance, you can learn to fly."

"I tried it," Archie said to the soldiers. "I managed to float for a couple of seconds, but then fell back down to the ground. I wouldn't recommend it."

"That's because you keep thinking like a living human," Orus cawed. *"You're hopeless at letting go."*

"That's easy for you to say," Archie said. "You've got wings. It's harder for me."

"Flying is hard for everyone until you know how to do it," Freya said. She looked at the map again. "If we stay on the ground, it is a good distance over terrain that may be too hot to walk on. But I should be able to carry at least three of you."

"I can carry two," Quinn offered.

A light blush came to Skye's face. "I'll carry Archie again. I—I mean I don't mind, and he's not too heavy for me."

Freya stole a look at Archie and saw the color rise in his face. He was looking at Skye and smiling. Freya gave him a nudge. "Archie, focus!"

"What?" he protested. "I was."

"Yeah, right, and I'm a golden eagle!" Orus teased.

"I've never been to Muspelheim," Freya said, drawing the conversation back to the matter at hand. She pointed at the mark on the map where Skuld was being held. "I don't know what we'll encounter or where this is. It could be some kind of keep, prison, or even like Valhalla. I just don't know."

Archie nodded. "There's only one way to find out what it's like. Go there."

The soldiers checked their weapons as they prepared for the final leg of the journey. The air became hotter and the wall of the tunnel, the root of Yggdrasil, grew thick bark that would occasionally shed away as it developed newer and thicker armor against the hostile environment.

"Now I know what a Thanksgiving turkey feels like," Archie complained as the tunnel started to climb. "I'm being roasted alive!"

"We all are," Freya agreed. She was keeping her wings open because it was too hot to keep them closed and pressed against her back.

"I didn't think we'd feel the heat," the sergeant said.

Freya stopped. "Maybe I should tell you this now. Yes, you are dead, and on Earth, you'd be nothing more than insubstantial ghosts. But here in this realm, you are very much alive. You have bodies and they will feel everything as before. That means you can be hurt. The only difference is, you will heal much quicker, and if you are killed, you will rise again."

"We're immortal?" Tina asked.

Freya nodded. "You are, unless Skuld has been ordered to end your destiny. Skuld holds the power over each of our futures. Which is why this mission is so important."

"Can she kill us?" the sergeant asked.

"No," Quinn answered. "She can't. But what she can do is cut the thread of your future. So if you're killed on this mission and she's cut your lifeline, you won't rise again. If she hasn't cut the line, you will. But you must be killed for any changes she has made to take effect."

The sergeant shook his head. "I don't think any of us realized just how important this is. Stopping the giants won't mean anything if this girl, Skuld, isn't safe."

"Exactly," Freya agreed.

The heat intensified, but so did the smell of fresher air. Before long they saw light filtering down through a narrow gap in the ceiling. The group stopped beneath the gap and looked up.

"Please don't tell me that's where we've got to go," Archie said.

Freya nodded. "That's the entrance to Muspelheim." She looked up at Orus on her shoulder. "Would you fly up there and tell us what you can see?"

The raven cawed and launched from her shoulder. They followed his progress through the narrow gap at the top. After a few minutes, Orus returned.

"You won't believe it!" he cawed excitedly. *"It's not all fire and dead, burnt things. It's beautiful up there. Hotter than I've ever felt before, but it looks just like Asgard. I couldn't see any giants."*

"If everyone is ready, Skye and I will get us up there." Quinn whispered a few words, and they lifted off the ground and floated toward the tunnel exit. As they got near the top, Quinn spoke again and they moved, single file, through the narrow gap.

They touched down on the ground between blades of

grass that rose higher than their shoulders. It was more like walking between trees than grass.

Archie shook his head. "Orus, you said it looked like Asgard. . . ."

"*It does,*" the raven said. "*Yes, the grass is much taller and everything is giant-sized, but it's very similar.*"

"I don't think so," Archie said as he stood amid blades of grass. "Since when does Asgard have red grass? And look at the trees—the leaves are orange." He looked around. "There's nothing green here at all. It's all shades of red, yellow, and orange."

"*It looks the same to me,*" Orus said.

"Then you're as blind as a bat."

"Orus doesn't see color the way we do," Freya explained. "To him this looks the same. To us it's very different. Lovely, but different."

Skye came forward. "I thought everything would be burning in Muspelheim. But it's normal. Just much bigger than I'm used to."

A scream rose from behind them, and they turned to see one of the soldiers standing beneath a fruit tree, bent over at the waist and clutching his hand. "It burns!" he cried.

Freya ran up to the young soldier. "What is it? What burns?"

He lifted his hand and opened his closed fist. The skin on his palm was red and blistering. "I just picked an apple from one of these low-hanging branches. But it was like touching a burning piece of charcoal!"

"That's not an apple," Freya warned. "This is Muspelheim, a giant realm. That's a small berry bush." She looked up at the tall bush and tentatively touched the skin of a berry with the tip of her finger. "Ouch!"

Her finger was blazing with heat.

The sergeant looked at her. "What in the world possessed you to try that? You saw what it did to Jimmy."

"I needed to see if it only affected humans," Freya said, sucking on the tip of her burnt finger. "Now we know it affects Asgardians, too." She looked at Quinn. "Be careful, but try touching something. We need to know if it hurts the Vanir as well."

Quinn raised his hand toward a piece of hanging fruit, and like the others, he was burned. Then he tried a massive leaf and suffered another burn.

Skye reached down and picked up a rock from the ground. She cried in pain and dropped it. "Even the rocks burn us. Be careful not to touch anything!"

The sergeant looked at the sole of his boot. "Uh-oh."

"What is it?" Freya asked.

"We're not feeling the heat yet, but look. Whatever's in this soil, it's starting to melt my boots."

Skye didn't hesitate. She called out a magic spell and lifted everyone off the ground—careful not to brush against the stalks of grass. "It was hurting my feet," she said. She showed them the light sandals she wore. They had been woven from Vanir plants. In the short time she'd been standing there, the soles of her sandals had burned away.

Freya looked around. "This is so bad. Of all the things I was expecting, this wasn't one of them."

"What do we do?" Archie said.

"We do what we came here for," the sergeant said. He turned to the Vanir. "If you two don't mind keeping us in the air, we can continue with our mission unscathed."

Orus cawed and looked up at the sky. *"Unless it rains on us—look at those dark clouds coming this way."*

The sky above them was filled with fluffy pink clouds. But in the distance, angry red and black clouds were forming. There was no mistaking it; a storm was brewing.

"We could go back in the tunnel, but it might fill with water. I suggest we look for shelter up here," Archie said.

"He's right," Freya agreed. "We need to find a safer shelter." She opened her wings. "Skye, let me go—I'll see what's out there. Everyone, stay here. If the skies open, get down in the tunnel. It's not ideal, but it's better than staying out in the open."

Orus joined her, and within minutes of flying, Freya discovered another problem.

"Orus, do your feathers feel strange?"

"Yes. It feels like they're melting, and the air is burning my eyes."

"Me too."

It wasn't disrupting their flight yet, but at this rate Freya was worried the hostile air would eventually eat away all her feathers—leaving her grounded.

"We need to find shelter as soon as possible," she called to Orus. They searched for a cave in an area covered by giant-sized woodland and shrubs. They saw a large trail worn into the ground by giant feet, but there was nothing to offer any kind of protection.

Freya followed the trail farther until they reached the outskirts of a village. Unlike Utgard, with its mishmash of architecture and buildings built on top of buildings, looking ready to fall down in a strong wind, this village was very organized and symmetrical. Homes were built in a circular design, which gave the giants a full view all around.

Freya was surprised to find that nothing was burning. Despite the fact that the giants were always aflame, it appeared that they didn't set their wooden homes or environment on fire.

Climbing higher in the sky, they looked beyond the village and saw the outskirts of a neighboring town. Beyond it was the Great City of Muspelheim. According to Verdandi's map, Skuld was being kept prisoner well past the Great City and deep in the desert. It would be a long flight in this hostile climate.

"We're going to need Quinn and Skye's magic more than

I thought," she called to Orus. "We'll never make it to Skuld without it. . . ."

As Freya glided in the sky, she became distracted by the feeling of something very strange, yet sickeningly familiar, like a prickling on her skin. She sensed a presence she knew—a presence that terrified her. She was so occupied by the feeling that she didn't notice the fast-moving clouds above her.

"Ouch!" she cried. "Something just stung me!" Freya faltered in the sky as she tried to reach the burning spot in the center of her back, between her wings, but before she could, another burn stung her scalp.

Beside her, Orus cawed in pain.

The sky turned black above them, and Freya realized it was the first drops of rain hitting her.

"Freya!" Orus cawed as he was burned again. *"It's raining acid!"*

Freya swooped over to Orus and scooped him up in her arms. She pulled him close to her breastplate to shelter him from the storm before turning to head back the way they'd come.

The raindrops burned through her clothing as she flew. She had to clench her mouth shut to stop herself from howling and alerting the giants to her presence. But with each drop of rain that touched her, it was harder to keep from screaming.

"Hurry!" Orus cried.

The skies opened and the acidic rain poured down. Freya couldn't contain her screams any longer. Her whole body was on fire as the hostile water soaked through her clothes and reached her skin.

Finally the tunnel entrance appeared—there was no time to think, no time to make a proper landing. Freya tucked in her burning wings and dived through the entrance. She smashed down into the floor below and rolled away from the opening, protecting Orus, still in her arms, from the rain pouring in.

"Gee!" Archie cried. He and Quinn were there to drag her away from the growing puddle of acidic water.

Freya was barely aware of the others wiping her dry. She was in more pain than she'd ever experienced in her life. Dirian's blade couldn't compare to the feeling of her skin blistering and melting. There wasn't a part of her that wasn't on fire.

She started to shake all over and, despite the severe burns, shivered with cold.

"Skye, Tina, help me get her out of those clothes," Sergeant Romin called. "We've gotta dry her off."

As Skye and Tina reached for her breastplate, Freya held up her hand. "No! Stop. Skin damaged . . . It will tear away. . . . Leave me. . . ."

"But you're covered in third-degree burns. You need medical help," the sergeant insisted. "We have first-aid kits."

Freya was in too much pain to speak clearly. It was a fight just to keep from screaming and tearing at her skin. "Hu-human medicine—bad—Valkyrie . . ."

Skye understood. "She's saying human medicine won't help her because she's a Valkyrie. But I have something that will." She magically produced a cup of green liquid. "Here, Freya, drink this. It will take away your pain."

Skye pressed the cup to Freya's blistered lips, and she drank the sweet, green liquid. The effect was immediate as the pain dimmed and she felt the drawing of sleep.

Quinn reached down and lifted Freya gently in his arms and carried her away from the risk of getting wet. "Go to sleep, Freya. We'll keep you safe while you rest."

Freya tried to speak, to tell them what she'd seen and felt, but sleep was pulling at her, offering to take her away from the pain. She closed her eyes and surrendered to its embrace.

20

THE SOUNDS OF HUSHED VOICES DREW FREYA FROM sleep. As she came to the surface of consciousness, pain was the first sensation to greet her. It reminded her that she was still alive, but in Muspelheim. Her face felt hot and swollen, and her eyes were puffy and difficult to open.

"Freya!" Orus cawed. "Archie, everyone—she's awake."

Freya was lying on her side, her burnt wings fanned out behind her. She winced as she tried to move her hand to get up. The skin on the back of her hand was blistered and peeling.

"Take it easy," Quinn said, gently but firmly pushing her back down. "You're covered in burns. Just lie still for a bit longer."

"How long . . . ?" Freya coughed and tried to speak through swollen lips and a scorched throat. "How long asleep?"

"All day," Archie said. "The rain stopped, and now it's dark out."

"Too long," Freya rasped. She pushed past Quinn's hand and climbed unsteadily to her feet. She was dizzy and had to lean against the wall to keep from falling. The pressure of standing was making her skin throb, and the pain was nearly unbearable. She tried to fold in her wings, but it was agony. Not only were her wings badly burned, but her back was as well.

When Skye offered her another cup of green liquid, she shook her head. "Can't. It will make me sleep again. We don't have time. We must go."

Archie shook his head. "You can't go anywhere yet. You should see yourself, Gee. You're a big, walking red blister!"

"Believe me, I feel worse on the inside than I look on the outside," Freya rasped. "But we don't have time to waste."

"You need to heal, Freya," the sergeant insisted. "You're no good to this unit as you are."

"And the war will be lost if we don't get moving while it's still dark out. Orus and I have seen where we need to go, and it's a long way from here. There are giant settlements everywhere. We must leave now if we want to avoid being seen." She looked at Skye. "Is there something you can give me to take away the pain but leave me awake?"

Skye looked at Quinn and he nodded.

"It won't take away all the pain; only sleep can do that.

But it will be diminished," Skye said. "And you will heal faster."

"That's all I need."

After Freya drank the new brew, she watched the others pull on strange-looking shoes. Archie brought a pair to her.

"What are these?"

"Skye and Quinn made them from the discarded bark of the Yggdrasil root. Look, this bark hat has been covered in acid rain, but the water didn't hurt it."

Quinn nodded and held up a strange, wide-brimmed hat. "When the storm was at its worst, I went out and tried it. The water couldn't penetrate it, and these bark shoes will protect our feet in the same way."

Freya looked at the odd shoes and strange wooden hats the others were pulling on. "I wish you'd thought of this before I went flying. It would have helped in the rain."

"And I wish you hadn't gone flying in the first place," Quinn countered. He grinned at her and pushed her lightly. "Next time talk to me first—all right?"

Freya felt his genuine concern. She felt something else, too, but was in too much pain to consider it. She nodded and smiled. It split a blister on her lip, and she winced. "Yes, sir," she said, saluting like the soldiers.

When they were ready, the sergeant came up to her wearing a grim expression. "This isn't the time for heroics, Freya. Can you move? I want a full status report."

"That's funny coming from a soldier who heroically reaped himself for the good of his world," Freya said. "But I'll be fine. I promise. I wouldn't endanger this mission. There's too much at stake for unnecessary risks . . ." Freya stopped midsentence and inhaled sharply. She suddenly remembered what had happened right before the rain started.

"Gee, what is it?" Archie said. "You look like you've just seen a ghost!"

Freya could hardly breathe. "How could I forget?" She looked at Skye. "That drink you gave me, it made me forget. . . . We must get out of here now, before they come for us!"

"Who?" Archie said. "What are you talking about?"

Freya turned on her friend and grabbed him by the shirt. "The Dark Searchers! Archie, Dirian is here! I felt him right before the rain started. I felt him and . . ." Her eyes were wild. "He felt me, too. Dirian knows I'm here!"

21

MAYA AND KAI STOOD AT THE BACK OF THE HEAVY, LOUD airship as it approached the jump point over Machu Picchu. The soldiers traveling with them were doing their final parachute checks as they prepared to deploy.

One of the soldiers turned and smiled at Maya. She nodded, smiled back, and then leaned in to Kai. "This feels really strange. Valkyries usually stay hidden from soldiers. I never imagined I'd be working with them."

"We all have something to lose if we fail," Kai said. "We are stronger if we work together—even if it feels strange."

Maya nodded but remained silent. Her shoulder felt empty without Grul sitting on it, and she couldn't get the sight of his broken body out of her mind.

"We're here," a soldier called, giving Maya and Kai a thumbs-up.

Maya nodded and stepped up to the open ramp. "You ready?" she asked her brother.

Kai nodded and fluttered his white wings in preparation.

Maya and Kai jumped, glided down alongside the soldiers floating with their parachutes, and directed themselves to the landing point. It had been a very long time since Maya had been here, and she was saddened to see how much Machu Picchu had changed.

"This place used to be a bustling city," she called to Kai as they soared down to land. "Now it's just ruins."

Kai took in the strange, mountainous environment. "It looks beautiful to me," he called. "But then again, compared to Utgard, anywhere is beautiful."

Despite the seriousness of their situation, Maya laughed. "Wait till you see more of Asgard!"

They soon touched down in the central square of the abandoned city—though it looked far from abandoned; hundreds of people milled around. When they spotted Maya and Kai in the sky, they waved their hands frantically and called to them.

Soldiers were already on the ground and approached them as they landed.

"Mia? Kai?" a soldier greeted them. "We've been told why you're here. Come, the Temple of the Sun is this way;

it's where Greta and the others uncovered the tunnel to Muspelheim."

They followed the soldiers through the parting crowds. People continued to call and wave at them desperately.

"Is this normal?" Kai asked, wide-eyed and staring at the people as they pressed to get closer to him.

"It is now," Maya said. "They're hoping we'll defeat the giants."

"Then we'd better not disappoint them." An expression of determination appeared on Kai's face, and Maya saw traces of a mature Dark Searcher rising from within him.

When they reached the Temple of the Sun, Maya saw her sister's mark cut into the ancient wall. It confirmed what she already knew: that Freya had actually been here. Maya paused and touched the mark.

"This way," their escort said.

Once inside the temple, they found three soldiers waiting for them. They were sitting against the wall, looking weak.

The most senior of the three struggled to his feet. "Mia, I'm Corporal Hillson. I was with Greta and the others in the tunnel. I have to tell you what happened down there. . . ."

As he explained, Maya looked horrified. "She reaped them?" she shrieked.

"She didn't have much choice," the corporal said. "Sergeant Romin grabbed her hand—he died instantly. The moment he touched her, Greta went ballistic and warned everyone else to stay back. But then the others convinced her it was the only way they could complete their mission." He dropped his head. "She reaped five soldiers, but it was under protest. I'm sorry. I just couldn't do it. I have a young family that needs me. I couldn't die."

"Listen to me," Maya told them as she felt waves of shame and guilt coming from the survivors. "There's no need to apologize or feel guilty for thinking of your families first. What the others did broke our Valkyrie rules. In all likelihood Greta was grateful to you all for not asking her to break her oath further."

The corporal shook his head sadly. "But we left their bodies down there. We were just too weak to bring them back with us."

Their failed journey to Muspelheim had taken a terrible toll on the surviving soldiers. Their eyes were sunken and ringed with dark circles, and their skin was sallow. It would take some time for them to fully recover—if they ever did.

"When this nightmare is over, we will bring back their bodies for their families," Maya promised. "But for now no one is to enter this tunnel. Is that understood? It's too dangerous for you."

"But we have our orders . . . ," one of the soldiers traveling with them began to protest.

"And I am changing those orders right now." Kai seemed to grow in height as he stood over the soldier. "You will all stay here and keep this tunnel secure while Mia and I go down. Your deaths will serve no one but the giants."

As Maya drew her sword and stood next to Kai as backup, she mused that he had never looked or sounded more like a Dark Searcher than at that moment.

"Don't make us fight you over this," Kai said darkly. "Not when we are united against the giants."

The soldiers stood back, accepting their new orders. Kai looked at Maya and took the first step into the tunnel. "Let's go."

22

"WHO IS THIS DIRIAN?" SERGEANT ROMIN ASKED FREYA. "I've heard that name before, but I don't know anything about him."

Freya described the rebel Dark Searcher who had killed most of the brotherhood of Dark Searchers because they wouldn't follow him. "He's insane, and is filled with pure hatred for me. He's the one who orchestrated this war and took Skuld. But I never imagined he'd still be here. I was certain he'd be leading the attack on Asgard."

"Gee, wait. I think this is a trap . . . ," Archie said. "Think about it. Dirian stayed here, waiting for you to come after Skuld. He's using her as bait. We've got to go back to Earth."

"That's crazy," Tina said. "How could he know Freya

would come here? You make it sound as if he started the war just to get back at her."

"Exactly!" Archie cried. "You don't understand how Dark Searchers think. They're like the Terminator. They have one function: to obey Odin. When he commands them to retrieve someone or undertake a mission, the Dark Searchers don't stop until they've completed their assignment. He sent Dirian after Freya when she came to Chicago to help me. But he failed in his mission."

"He's become obsessed with me." Freya sighed. "Because of his hatred for me, he disobeyed a direct order from Odin. As punishment, Odin cut off one of his wings and banished him from Asgard. Now Dirian blames me for everything. He killed me once during a competition between the realms, and then he nearly killed me again when I tried to find my brother—if Thor hadn't intervened, he'd have chopped me to pieces. But now, with Skuld under his power, he can order her to cut my life thread so that if he kills me again, I'll stay dead."

Every part of her hurt as she walked to the tunnel exit and peered up. "He knows I'm here and he'll be coming for me." She looked back at the others. "You can't be near me when he does, or he'll get you, too."

"I have an idea," Quinn said. "Dirian being here could actually be good for us."

"How?" Archie cried. "Did you miss the part where Gee said he wants to kill her for good?"

"I know," Quinn said. "But if he's as obsessed as you say he is, Freya is all he's focusing on—which means if we split into two groups, he'll almost certainly go after Freya. So the group without Freya stands a good chance of freeing Skuld."

"That could work," the sergeant agreed. "This mission is more important than each of us individually. Freya, if you draw him out, we can move on Skuld."

"Wait," Archie said. "Are you saying Gee should sacrifice herself so Skuld can be rescued?"

Quinn nodded. "That's exactly what he's saying. And he's right."

Freya listened to the argument heating up. Archie was defending her, and she knew why. He too had fought Dirian—and lost. Apart from her, Archie and Orus were the only ones who had a clue what they were truly up against. The thought of facing the dreaded Dark Searcher again terrified her. Could she really do it? This war was bigger than her, bigger than all of them. She had to put her emotions aside.

Freya walked over to her best friend. "That's exactly what I'm going to do. Archie, we all know the danger. We're not all going to survive. But if I do this, if I can distract Dirian, maybe you guys can get Skuld away from here. Get her back to Vanaheim to her sisters or to Odin in Asgard. Then maybe you can stop this war."

"No way," Archie argued. "You're talking like you're already dead."

"Look at me," Freya said. "I'm burned everywhere, my feathers are damaged beyond repair, and I can't fly. The only reason I'm still moving is Skye's pain potion. This is the best and only solution."

Orus cawed in misery. *"No, Freya . . ."*

"You know I'm right," she told him. "I'm not giving up. I have my sword, and I will fight with all I have left. And I may get lucky and wound him. But even if I don't, while I distract Dirian, you guys can free Skuld."

"I'm staying with you," Archie insisted. "And don't try to tell me no. Dirian knows we're always together. If I'm not with you, he'll suspect something."

"Me too," Orus cawed.

Freya closed her eyes and dropped her head. "You're right; you should come with me. We've gone this far together— let's finish it together."

"Now that that's agreed," Sergeant Romin said, "let's get out of here and get moving before they come after us."

Skye used magic to lift everyone out of the tunnel. The moment the hot air touched Freya's burnt skin, she clenched her teeth and fought the pain. Her hands started to shake, and she shivered all over.

"Are you all right?" Quinn asked, moving closer.

Freya nodded. "It's just the heat. Give me a moment and I'll be fine."

The sergeant called his soldiers together. "All right, you all know your assignments. Quinn, Archie, and Freya will head out first, going in from the right. We'll follow a bit later, from the left. Everyone keep your weapons at the ready and stay sharp. Remember, this mission is everything. If one of us falls, don't stop. Just keep going. There is no room for sentimentality in war. Whoever frees Skuld, get her out of here and don't look back. Understood?"

When everyone nodded, Freya looked at Quinn. "Let's go."

Skye and the Earth soldiers moved in one direction, while Quinn, Freya, and Archie climbed higher in the sky and started to move in the other direction toward the Great City.

With the cover of night to shield them, they passed silently over the villages. The giants' homes glowed with the light of their flames. Occasionally they would see a giant out on the street, glowing like a beacon in the dark. Freya sensed a strange calmness in the air, as though the giants living below didn't know about the war their leaders were waging on Asgard.

The second town was a similar sight: elderly fire giants going about their normal lives, as though nothing had changed. Were they so confident of winning that they weren't prepared for any attacks on Muspelheim?

The giants didn't appear to sense them high in the sky

above them. Although they were very much like frost giants in size, their senses weren't as acute. This filled Freya with hope. Perhaps their mission stood a slight chance of success.

Late into the long night they flew over small and then larger settlements. Soon they reached the outskirts of the Great City. They circled around it and encountered smaller villages that tapered off into single dwellings. It was almost dawn before they approached the edge of the Muspelheim desert.

"He knows I'm coming," Freya called. She tried to suppress a shiver but couldn't. "I can sense Dirian's excitement. He's waiting for me."

"Good," Quinn said. "Let's hope he stays focused on you while the others get to Skuld."

Archie looked over to her. "I still don't like using you as bait."

"*Me neither,*" Orus agreed. "*There has to be another way.*"

"There isn't," Freya said. "But we're not going in unprepared. I have my sword, and Quinn his magic. Together we can fight him."

"*And what about all the other Dark Searchers or fire giants with him? He won't face you alone, and you know it,*" Orus said.

Freya did know it, but she didn't want to comment. She had a feeling this wasn't going to end well for any of them. She buried that thought and focused on what she had to do—draw Dirian away from Skuld.

They started over the crimson sands of the vast desert. The temperature soared, even in the predawn light, and warned of the heat of the day to come. Saying nothing, Quinn pressed on and carried them deeper into the desert.

Skye had given Freya another dose of the liquid that would dim her pain. But as the heat of the sandy desert rose, her skin seared and burned.

"You okay, Gee?" Archie called. "You're looking really pale."

Freya nodded and gritted her teeth. "It's just getting hot."

"We passed hot long ago," he commented. "This is volcanic!"

As they ventured deeper into the desert and with the sun's glow starting to peer over the horizon, Freya began to regret her decision. She was in far too much pain to fight properly. She could barely focus, let alone wield her sword with any accuracy. But they'd come too far to stop now. The others were counting on them to draw Dirian and the Dark Searchers away.

"There," Quinn called as he pointed into the distance to a large keep sitting alone on the crimson sand.

"It looks just like the Dark Searchers' keep in Utgard!" Orus cawed.

"Maybe it's the same one," Archie called hopefully. "If it is, we know a hidden way in."

As they drew near the tall stone structure, Freya's hopes

sank. The stone used to construct this building was deep red. The Keep of the Dark Searchers in Utgard was solid black.

"It's not the same," Freya said, failing to hide her disappointment. "But if we're lucky, the layout might be similar."

"I hope we can get in there without much trouble," Quinn said. "That sun is no friend of ours. If we're still outside when it climbs higher in the sky, we'll be roasted alive."

Freya nodded. "We'll get in. Dirian won't want me roasted outside the keep. He wants to kill me himself."

"You make it sound like we've already lost," Archie said.

Freya looked at him and smiled sadly, knowing she wasn't up to this. It was taking all her strength just to keep moving. She didn't have the energy to fight Dirian. Her only hope now was for Skye's team to make it in and out safely.

"*Be careful, Freya,*" Orus cawed. "*If you let yourself be captured too easily, it will raise suspicion. We must enter as though we're attacking.*"

"Have you been reading my mind?" she asked.

"*No, but I know you better than you know yourself. You're giving up.*"

"No, I'm not—I just know my limits."

"Hello . . . ," Archie said. "I'm here, remember? I haven't trained all this time at Valhalla just so you can surrender. What about Quinn and his bag of magic tricks? This fight isn't over till it's over. You got that?"

Freya smiled again. "Got it." She looked over at Quinn.

"Take us down to the balustrade. He may know I'm here, but we're not going to make it easy for him to catch us."

Quinn maneuvered in the sky and brought them down to the imposing keep. On closer inspection, it was larger than the one in Utgard, with four large towers at each corner and a wide patrol balustrade running along the top.

"There's no one up here," Archie said.

"And I know why," Quinn answered. "In a short while the sun will be up fully. Anyone still out here doesn't stand a chance."

"Over there." Freya pointed to one of the tall towers. She spied a large door that led to the balustrade. "We'll go in through there."

When they touched down on the roof, Freya drew her sword. "Quinn, can you magic yourself a sword? And perhaps a cape to hide your wings? We don't want you to be recognized as Vanir. I want you to conceal your magic until we really need it."

"And a sword for me, too, please," Archie said. "Crixus trained me well. I'm not too shabby at all."

Quinn cast a spell, and two shining silver swords appeared on the ground at their feet. Quinn picked his up and inspected it. "I've never used a sword before."

"Hopefully, you won't have to. It's just for effect. Let me go in first. Use your magic if you must, but hold back if you can. I'm hoping that with your wings covered, they'll assume you're human like Archie."

"*Be careful,*" Orus cawed.

"You too." Freya pulled the handle on the door. She stole one last look at the rising sun, wondering if she'd ever see it again. Taking a deep breath, she entered Dirian's keep.

23

FREYA SWITCHED HER SENSES TO FULL ALERT. SHE COULD feel Dark Searchers inside, but no fire giants. Scanning further, she felt something else—another presence: a very old and powerful presence.

"I can feel Skuld," Freya said. "She's down in the dungeons. But she's surrounded by Dark Elves, dwarfs, and I think I feel some trolls."

"So where's Dirian?" Archie asked.

Freya frowned. "I'm not sure. I can feel him, but it's like he's all around us. It's really strange."

Quinn nodded. "I feel it too. He's using Dark Elf magic to amplify himself—wait . . ." He inhaled sharply. "No, it can't be!"

"What?"

His intense gray eyes settled on Freya. "Do you feel that? She's here."

"Yes, Skuld is here. We know."

Quinn shook his head. "No, not Skuld. I'm talking about Vanir-Freyja—she's here too!"

"Freya?" Archie asked, sounding confused.

"Not our Freya, the Valkyrie," Quinn corrected. "I mean Vanir-Freyja, twin sister to Vanir-Freyr."

"Wait," Archie said. "Are you saying there are two Freyas?"

Freya nodded. "Okay, quick history lesson. Remember I told you about the ancient war between the Aesir and the Vanir and how hostages were traded? Well, the Vanir sent the brother-and-sister twins, Freyr and Freyja. They've lived in Asgard ever since the war but are never seen. My mother named me after Vanir-Freyja, but changed the spelling." She inhaled. "It makes sense now—probably because I have a twin brother."

"But she didn't name your brother Freyr; she called him Kai," Archie pointed out.

"Yes," Freya agreed. "But she might not have been allowed to call him Freyr because he was to be given to the Dark Searchers." She turned back to Quinn. "Is Vanir-Freyr here too?"

Quinn closed his eyes. After a moment he shook his head. "No, just Vanir-Freyja."

"That's strange," Archie said. "You'd think Dirian would capture both—double the magic."

A rock settled in the pit of Freya's stomach as she recalled the stories about Vanir-Freyja. "He's not using her for magic—he could have taken any Vanir for that. No, his intentions are much worse." She looked back at Quinn. "Do you remember any of the stories about her?"

"Not a lot. Just that she's supposed to be the most enchanting woman in all the realms."

"Exactly," Freya agreed. "It's a part of her magic. Men fall instantly in love with her the moment they see her. Throughout the ages, the giant kings have tried to possess her. Dwarfs have used their magic to create jewelry for her, just to see her smile. That's why she went into hiding. It's even rumored that she was the very first Valkyrie, but I don't know for sure."

"No one could ever be that beautiful," Archie said.

"She is," Freya said. "What if Dirian is offering her as a gift to the giant king who defeats Odin?"

Archie shook his head. "That's crazy! Maybe he took her because he's in love with her himself."

Freya shook her head. "I don't think so. He's too evil to feel anything but rage and hatred."

Quinn caught on to Freya's line of thinking. "You're suggesting Vanir-Freyja is the giants' incentive to go to war?" He paused and rubbed his chin. "I've heard they don't care about power or ruling the other realms. . . ." He snapped his fingers. "Of course, it makes perfect sense! Dirian is clever. He's using Skuld as a weapon and Vanir-Freyja as the reward for the giants."

"That is wrong on so many levels," Archie said. "We've got to save her. We can't let Dirian give her away like some kind of prize in a game. It's evil."

"But we must be sure," Quinn said.

"What other proof do you need?" Freya challenged. "No one, not even Dirian, would have the power to unite the giants unless he could promise them something big in return. Our history is filled with stories of how the giants have tried to get hold of her. They even stole Thor's hammer to exchange for her. Now she's here? That can't be a coincidence. Dirian must be using her as a prize."

Freya looked up at the rising sun. "This changes everything. Quinn, get out of here now, before the sun rises fully. Find Skye and the others and tell them what's happening. Send one of the soldiers back through the tunnel to Midgard. We must get word to Thor and the others. Vanir-Freyja is even more important than Skuld."

Quinn shook his head. "I can't leave you; you're in no condition to fight. You can barely stand!"

Freya shook her head. "Don't you understand? I'm not important. None of us are. Only Vanir-Freyja and Skuld matter. If you're captured with us, the others will never know how Dirian is controlling the giants. Don't you see? You must go!"

"*She's right,*" Orus cawed. "*Go now, before Dirian sends his Dark Searchers up here.*"

"I—I," Quinn started. "I don't want to leave you."

"If you don't go now, you'll be roasted by the sun!" Archie pushed Quinn toward the door. "Just get out of here and warn the others!"

Freya felt Quinn's conflicted emotions and realized she didn't want him to go either. But this was bigger than all of them. "Forget about us and go. Archie and I will do what we can to distract Dirian and the Dark Searchers. You and Skye must work with the soldiers to get Vanir-Freyja out of here. Don't you see? If she's no longer the prize, the giants will stop attacking Asgard. That's how we'll do it! That's how we'll stop Ragnarök!"

24

FREYA WATCHED QUINN DISAPPEARING INTO THE
distance and felt a pang of disappointment.

"Earth to Gee . . . Hello?" Archie's voice shook her back
to the moment. "Wow, you've really got it bad."

"What?" Freya frowned.

"You heard me." Archie smiled and shook his head. "You
and Quinn?"

Freya stole a final look into the sky. Quinn was gone from
sight. "Archie, this isn't the time. We're about to face Dirian
alone. The chances of us surviving this are nil."

"I know that," Archie said. "Which is why you shouldn't
deny your feelings. You like him; there's no crime in that."

"We're at war! I don't have time for these feelings."

"But you do feel them," Orus added. *"I've seen it too, Freya."*

"Not you, too," Freya said to the raven on her shoulder. "Can we please focus? Vanir-Freyja is in here somewhere. Until Dirian catches us, let's see if we can find her."

Freya stormed down the tower steps, which ended any further discussion. Of course they were right. There was something about Quinn that she really liked, and she regretted that he had to leave. . . . But this wasn't the time to let feelings distract her. There was too much at stake.

With her senses on high alert, Freya felt Dark Searchers all over the keep. So far, none were making moves to come after them. The tower stairs wound down through each level. At the ground floor, Freya paused before a tall, dark-red wood door. Dirian. She could feel him close by.

"He's through there. What's he waiting for?"

"He's toying with you," Archie whispered. "He must know you're expecting him to move, so he's teasing you."

"No, he's waiting until we get deeper into the keep, where we stand no chance of escaping," Orus cawed softly.

"There's no escape for us anyway," Freya said. "I can't fly."

"But he doesn't know that," Orus finished.

Freya nodded. "Forget him. We must find Vanir-Freyja and Skuld. I can feel them; they're beneath us in the dungeons."

Freya's senses picked up on at least four Dark Searchers entering the stairwell from above. The sound of thudding feet storming down the stairs confirmed her senses.

"They're coming for us—run!" Archie cried, but in the tight confines of the round tower stairs, they were trapped with nowhere to go but down.

Freya forced her aching body to move. Each step was like a hammer pounding on her tender skin as her damaged wings rubbed against her blistered back.

"Faster, Gee," Archie called. He ran past her and caught her by the hand, dragging her along.

At the bottom of the steps they faced a large, closed door. Archie grasped the handle and cried as the metal burned his palm. He pulled his sleeve down over his other hand and grasped the door handle again. It gave without resistance, and they ran through it into a dark corridor.

With the pursuers close behind them, Freya looked around, working out what to do next. She could feel that Vanir-Freyja wasn't on this level, but she sensed an older presence to her left. "Skuld is here—come on!"

They ran down the dark corridor and straight into two large, imposing Dark Searchers. They turned to run back, but the Dark Searchers from the tower stairs were waiting for them.

They were trapped!

Freya and Archie stood back-to-back, holding their swords high.

"Does the foolish Valkyrie really believe she can fight her way out of this?"

The Dark Searchers from the tower steps parted and a Dark Elf walked between them, wearing a forest-green cape and a mask. As it approached, it removed its mask, revealing a green, pinched elfin face and elliptical black eyes.

"You!" Freya gasped. It was the same female Dark Elf who had exposed them in Utgard. If it hadn't been for her, they would have escaped the city with no one knowing about it.

"Oh, I see the Valkyrie remembers me," the Dark Elf said. Her eyes narrowed and focused on Archie. "At least the dead human has stopped pretending to be an elf."

"So you've joined Dirian," Freya challenged, holding up her golden sword.

The Dark Elf shook her head. "Foolish Valkyrie—I have been with him all along. Dirian is the one true leader of all the realms. He will see us into a new and glorious age—seated on Odin's throne."

"He's starting Ragnarök," Freya challenged. "If you can't see that, you're as demented as he is!"

The Dark Elf screeched and tried to run at her. But the hand of a Dark Searcher shot out and caught her by the shoulder. He shook his head.

The Dark Elf struggled for a moment and then became still. "You're right," she said. "This one belongs to Dirian. It is not my right to seek pleasure in her pain." She focused on Freya again. "When Dirian is through with you, you will wish you'd never been born." She motioned to the other

Searchers. "Take their weapons and put them in the cells."

Freya looked around and assessed the situation. She and Archie were completely surrounded. They could fight, but it wouldn't last long and would end with them hurt or killed. It wouldn't give Quinn or Skye the time they needed to get to Vanir-Freyja.

Freya put down her sword and looked over at Archie. "Drop your sword."

"But we can fight them!" Archie swung his weapon at one of the Searchers.

Freya reached out to grab his arm. "Not now," she insisted, hoping he would understand.

Archie looked at her and held her eyes for several heart-beats. Finally he nodded and surrendered his weapon. She could see the message in his eyes saying he hoped she had a plan.

When the Dark Searchers came forward and seized them roughly by the arms, *she* hoped she had a plan as well.

The first thing the Dark Searchers did was separate them. Orus cawed and bit into the Searcher that tried to take him from Freya. He finally launched into the air, flew down the dungeon corridor, and disappeared around the corner.

"I'll get him," the Dark Elf called. She shot a cruel look at Freya. "I may not be allowed to hurt you or the dead human, but I have no such orders for the bird. I'm feeling particularly hungry for roast raven!" She cackled with laughter and took off in a run after the raven.

"Go, Orus!" Freya shouted. "Get out of here. Don't let her catch you!"

"Fly, Orus!" Archie called. "Keep going!"

The Dark Searcher holding Freya shook her into silence. But Freya looked defiantly up into his visor. "He's fast. She won't get him. You'll see. He'll get away from you!"

Deadly silent, the Dark Searchers dragged Freya in one direction while Archie was taken in the opposite. At the end of the corridor, she was shoved into a dark cell. It was almost identical to the one at the keep in Utgard. There were no windows and nothing to sit on but the red stone floor.

The walls and door were newer, but the feelings of dread they instilled were the same. Freya stood at the door, waiting for Dirian. He would come. She knew he would. And when he did, she would face the end with dignity.

After a time she gave up waiting, walked to the corner of the small cell, and lay down. The drug Skye had given her was wearing off, and the pain from her burns was back. With nothing left to do but wait for the end, she closed her eyes and tried to sleep.

It felt as if she had only just dozed off when she heard a key entering the lock. Freya rose and watched the cell door swing open. Standing at the entrance was a Dark Searcher and a troll.

"Come, come," the troll ordered, wagging a crooked finger at her. He was small, round, and gray. Freya couldn't tell whether this was his natural color, or dirt. More than likely dirt, she decided, when she took in his tattered, smelly rags.

The troll could barely walk, but that didn't mean he wasn't dangerous. Freya felt pure evil emanating from him. He stumbled forward and caught her by the arm. "Don't keep the master waiting." Freya had to muffle her nose with her hand to stifle his vile smell.

She snatched her arm from his grip. "If Dirian wants to see me, he can come down here and get me himself!"

The troll squeaked his displeasure and punched her in the midsection, knocking her back and slamming her against the wall. Freya cried out as her damaged wings pressed against her burnt back.

Trolls may be small, but she quickly discovered they packed a vicious punch. Freya righted herself and kicked the troll across the cell. The foul creature squealed as he hit the opposite wall.

"You touch me again and I'll break your arm!" she warned. Freya turned on the Dark Searcher. "Well, what about you?"

He stood staring at the troll. Eventually he drew one of his black swords. "Move . . . ," he rasped with his broken voice. "I cannot kill you, but I have no orders not to harm you. I will if you don't come."

Freya stood defiantly before the Dark Searcher. The troll

had climbed to his feet and took this opportunity to charge at her again. But Freya was too quick for him. She turned her back and struck out with her right wing, smacking him hard in the face. The troll smashed against the wall a second time and fell to the ground, unconscious. Freya sneered at him. "I've never liked trolls!"

"Valkyrie!" the Dark Searcher commanded. He loomed above her with his imposing height. "I am no troll," he said. "You would be wise not to try that with me."

"No, you're a Dark Searcher—and I don't care for them either!" Freya was baiting him. It was dangerous, but at this point she had little to lose.

The Dark Searcher balled his hand into a fist but held it back. "Do not try my patience. I *will* hurt you."

As Freya stood before him, weaponless and wounded, there was no way she could hope to fight and win. She walked toward the door.

Two Dark Searchers, a dwarf, and a male Dark Elf stood waiting for her in the corridor, ready to escort her further. She sensed they'd been testing her, to see how much she would resist. She looked at the Dark Elf. "Sorry to disappoint you. Looks as if you won't be the one to kill me today."

"The day is yet young," the masked elf said lightly, "and I remain hopeful."

As they walked toward the tower steps, Freya stole a look back to see if Archie was being brought with them. He wasn't.

Making it up to the ground floor, Freya looked around. Again, it looked similar to the old keep in Utgard, but somehow it was even darker, as though the evil from the occupants was driving away any light. Their steps echoed as they walked through the wide, empty corridors. They entered a chamber where the ceiling high above their heads gave the large, desolate room a lonely, cavernous feeling.

In the center of the chamber was a long rectangular table with scrolls sprawled across it. Around the table were a few stools. As they walked past the table, Freya saw the papers were maps of the realms and diagrams showing the giants' military movements.

Freya immediately recognized this as a war room. It was here that Dirian was conducting his fight against Odin. There had been no attempt to hide anything from her eyes.

As she tried to get a closer look at the maps, a sound of rattling broke her concentration. She turned as another Dark Elf and a troll came toward her, holding a metal collar and a chain lead.

"If you think you're putting that on me, you'd better think again," she warned the elf. Freya instinctively took a step back, but the Dark Searcher standing behind her blocked her retreat.

The Dark Elf laughed, exposing his tiny, pointed teeth. "Oh, please do try to stop me. I would love to take on a

Valkyrie. I've heard of your fighting skills, Freya, but never witnessed them personally."

"Come closer and I'll show you."

That comment only made the elf laugh harder.

"Enough!"

Freya's heart sank. She knew that broken voice all too well. It was the voice that haunted her nightmares and made her wake in the night covered in a film of sweat. Every nerve in her body told her not to move—to simply close her eyes and await the end. But she couldn't obey. She turned and saw Dirian striding into the chamber.

The Dark Searcher was as terrifying as always. He was wearing his helmet and full armor, with his two black swords strapped to his sides. She couldn't see his face, but she could feel him, could feel his hatred mixed with joy at having her as his prisoner . . . but worst of all was his anticipation. It was all there, offered for her to feel. He held nothing back.

Dirian stood before her—unmoving and silent. Only the slight change in the pitch of his breathing revealed he wasn't a statue.

"Well?" Freya managed. "Come on, get it over with. . . ."

Freya expected many things, but she never imagined she'd hear him laugh. His deep, fractured voice choked on his mirthless laughter as he stepped closer to her. His visor stopped mere inches away from her face.

"I am sorry to disappoint you, *Freya*, but you will not

die this day or any day in the near future. You are to be my special guest for a very, very long time. You alone will bear witness to the defeat of Odin. You will watch Asgard fall to my giants and see all the realms bow to me. You will be there as your Valkyrie sisters are enslaved and traded like coins. I promise you will see it all and will be helpless to stop any of it."

"You're insane!" Freya cried.

"I am only what *you* made me," he replied. "Actually, I should thank you. Were it not for you, I would still be a slave to Odin—blindly serving his every whim. Now I know what it is to be truly free." The large, imposing Dark Searcher slowly turned his back to her. "See how I have freed myself? Odin removed one of my wings. I chose to remove the other."

Freya was horrified by the sight of his smooth, wingless, armored back. "Why would you do that?"

"It was what I chose!" he spat. "Now, to show my gratitude to you, I will share with you that same exhilarating freedom."

Those words chilled Freya to the bone. She tried to deny their implication, but when Dirian ordered his men to grab her and pry open her wings, Freya realized the meaning was clear.

The tall Dark Searcher slowly drew one of his black blades. "Now, you can make this easy on yourself, or you can make it hard. The choice is yours—but have no illusion, I will take your wings."

"No!" Freya cried, struggling in the Dark Searchers' grip. "You can't do this!"

Dirian took a step closer and rasped, "Good. You're going to fight."

He stepped back and pulled his second sword from its sheath. Dirian threw it onto the ground at her feet. "Release her. Let's see if this Valkyrie has learned anything new."

When the two Dark Searchers let her go, Freya snatched up the black sword and faced Dirian. Her eyes scanned the room wildly. Other Dark Searchers, elves, and dwarfs were filing in, blocking her only exit.

The choice was simple. Surrender to Dirian and let him cut off her wings. Or fight, knowing she stood no chance against him. But every moment she delayed, every second she had his full attention, gave the others time to get to Vanir-Freyja.

"Come on, then, Dirian," she challenged bravely. "You want my wings? You're going to have to take them!"

Freya moved first and lunged toward the demented Dark Searcher. But her burns slowed her movement. Dirian easily deflected her sword thrust.

"You can do better than that," he teased.

She sensed his pleasure. He was toying with her, and they both knew it. But each moment bought more precious time for the others to arrive. She would give him the fight he wanted.

Dirian made two halfhearted swipes that Freya easily defended. She could sense he was holding back, not wanting to end the fight too soon. In anger, she launched her own attack, a fraction of a second faster than him. Her blade cut across his breastplate, slicing into his leather armor. It didn't touch his skin, but it was enough to surprise him and make him jump back.

Immediately Dirian's mood changed and the game ended. His swipes became more aggressive. While his blade moved in one direction, his free hand moved in the opposite and struck Freya across her burnt and blistered face with a blow that knocked her off her feet.

Freya opened her wings to slow the fall. The next thing she knew, Dirian's blade flashed faster than she imagined possible. So fast that Freya didn't feel the actual cuts—what she did feel was both her wings coming away from her body and falling to the floor beside her.

Moments later, pain arrived. Sharper than anything she'd felt before. So intense, it sucked the wind from her lungs, leaving her unable to breathe, let alone scream.

Freya was in too much pain to think. She tried to climb to her feet, but Dirian was there, pushing her back. When she hit the ground, he moved in for a final, bone-breaking kick that sent her flying across the room. She hit the wall, her senses overwhelmed. She welcomed the coming darkness and surrendered gladly to oblivion.

25

MAYA AND KAI RAN THROUGH THE TUNNEL TOWARD
Muspelheim as fast as their legs would carry them. They had
to catch up with Freya.

Soon they felt the realm slip from Midgard into
Muspelheim and saw something ahead in the tunnel. As
they moved closer, they made out the bodies of the five soldiers who had been reaped, slumped against the wall. They
looked as if they were napping peacefully.

"What kind of person would ask to be reaped?" Kai said,
studying the soldiers.

"The kind who are devoted to the service of their realm,"
Maya answered. "They knew they couldn't go on any farther,
but they didn't want to give up. It was an extreme but honorable decision."

"Would you have reaped them?"

Maya considered for a moment and then nodded. "Considering what's at stake, I would. I'm sure no one will condemn Freya or the soldiers for what they did."

As they prepared to get moving again, they heard footsteps running toward them. A young soldier emerged from the darkness ahead.

"Can you see me?" he gasped, bending over to catch his breath.

"Yes," Maya said. She immediately recognized him as one of the dead soldiers.

The young man stole a quick look at his body against the wall and then turned away. "I—I'm Private Cornish. I have an urgent message from Freya."

"I'm her sister, and this is Kai, her twin brother," Maya said. "What's the message?"

Taking a couple more breaths, the young private started to speak. He passed on the message he'd been given from Quinn. He went on to explain Freya's plan.

"Freya is handing herself over to Dirian!" Kai cried. "Is she crazy?"

The private shook his head. "She's trying to keep him distracted long enough for the others to free Vanir-Freyja and Skuld."

Kai's eyes were wide and wild. "But he'll kill her!"

"She knows that, but she went in there anyway. In the

short time I've known your sister, I've discovered that she's one selfless but very stubborn Valkyrie."

"She's an idiot if she thinks handing herself over to Dirian can help," Kai said.

The soldier continued. "Quinn ordered me to get back to Earth to try to find your people to ask them to help us. If we can free Vanir-Freyja and Skuld, it will end the war and save Earth."

"We're on our way to Muspelheim now," Maya finally said. "I won't let Freya sacrifice herself. Not to him. But Quinn is right. Thor must be told." She looked back down the tunnel to Earth. "Private, I need you to keep going. Get to Earth and, even though you will be a spirit, do what you can to find Thor and the others. Tell them what you just told us."

The private nodded. "I should warn you, Muspelheim is hot and very dangerous. It's essential that you don't touch anything." He held up his burnt palm. "Everything there burns at the touch. I picked a berry and this is what happened. Freya was caught in the rain and has burns all over her body. Quinn has made extra protective shoes out of the root of Yggdrasil. He has left them farther down the tunnel for you—put them on or your feet will burn to a crisp. And one other thing: The air is corrosive and will eventually destroy your feathers. So be as quick as you can."

Maya looked at Kai. "No wonder Brundi called it hell." She finally turned to the young soldier and took his hand.

"Thank you, Private Cornish, for the message and for your sacrifice in this. With your help, we can move this war away from Earth and take it to where it belongs—the very heart of Muspelheim!"

With each pounding footstep, Maya's head was filled with visions of what could be happening to Freya at the hands of Dirian.

"Faster!" Kai called, as he put on more speed.

Maya's heart felt as if it were about to burst as she kept up with her brother. The air in the tunnel was heating up and burning her lungs, but the urgency to reach Freya was driving them both on.

Soon the tunnel began to tilt up and they slowed to a jog. Up ahead they saw the pile of shoes that Private Cornish had told them about.

They were too tired to speak as they pulled on the shoes. Kai also found a stash of weapons and copies of a map leading to the keep.

"I must meet this Quinn," he said as he strapped several swords to his waist. "He thinks like a Dark Searcher."

Maya scanned their dimly lit surroundings, searching for a way out. She felt a soft, hot breeze on her face and looked up. Her eyes settled on a hole in the ceiling above them. "That's our way out. I can feel fire giants, but they aren't close. Now's the time to move."

They flew through the hole and emerged into darkness. Stars twinkled brightly overhead. Maya looked around to get her bearings and then pointed toward the Great City. "It's this way. . . ."

Kai's sudden screams shattered the stillness around them. He arched his back and then fell to the ground between tall blades of grass.

Maya landed beside him. "Kai, what's wrong? What is it?"

Kai writhed in agony. "I feel Freya," he gasped, barely able to speak. "She's hurt. It's her back. . . ." He struggled to reach the center of his back where his wings joined his body. "Something's wrong with her back."

Maya reached out to her brother. "Listen to me—suppress your connection to Freya before it cripples you. Do you hear me? Break the connection! Do it, Kai. Do it now."

Kai lay on his side, moaning and panting. After a moment he spoke softly. "I—I'm all right now." Maya helped him climb shakily to his feet. "Can you tell me what's happened? What has Dirian done to Freya?"

When he looked at Maya, all she could see was rage. "I'm going to kill him—do you hear me? I swear, nothing is going to stop me from destroying him!"

"Just tell me what he's done."

Kai turned away from her. "That soldier was right—her body's burned and it's agony for her. But what that monster has done is worse."

"Enough!" Maya caught him by the arm and spun him around to face her. "Tell me what's happened!"

Kai balled his hands into fists and then drew his sword. "Dirian has cut off Freya's wings!"

26

FREYA LAY IN A BALL ON HER SIDE. SHE'D NEVER KNOWN such pain. Her burning skin was nothing compared to the searing agony of the stumps on her back where her wings had been severed. She was unsure how long she'd been lying on the stone floor, or even how long she'd been conscious after she'd blacked out. All she knew was pain.

Freya could barely remember the fight with Dirian. Though, she knew she'd never forget the sound of his coarse laughter right after he'd sliced off her wings and kicked her in the side. . . . That memory she would keep for the rest of her life, however short that might be.

Lifting her head, Freya tried to look around, but moving made the pain worse. She could just about make out that she was chained to the floor of the War Room. The heavy metal collar she'd seen the elf holding was now secured around her neck, and the thick chain attached to it was locked to a large metal clamp buried deep into the thick stone floor. Above her, mounted to the wall like a prized trophy, were her severed wings.

Freya retched at the sight of them.

She put her head back down, and silent tears trickled down her cheeks.

"Don't let him see you cry, Freya," a soft, light voice called. "It will only give him pleasure. Just stay still and heal."

Freya's eyes followed the sound and peered across the vast, dark chamber. A young girl was chained to the opposite wall. From what she could make out, the girl was no more than eight or nine.

"Who . . . ? Who are you . . . ?"

"I am Skuld."

"Skuld . . ." Freya tried to sit up, but she was overwhelmed with dizziness and fell back down again.

"You must lie still and heal," Skuld called. "I'm counting on you—we all are."

Freya's head was spinning, and she had to shut her eyes to keep from throwing up again. Her broken ribs hurt almost as much as her wing stumps. She became aware of the tight, thick bandage around her midsection. Her breastplate had been removed and her wounds treated, but they had given her no pain relief. Dirian wanted her kept alive, but suffering.

Each breath she took threatened to bring back the blackness of unconsciousness. But knowing it was Skuld chained to the opposite wall, Freya forced herself to stay awake.

"Where is he . . . ?"

"Resting," Skuld said. "It's night."

Night? Freya tried to focus. Nothing seemed to make sense anymore. How could she have lost so much time?

"Do—do you know why I'm here?"

"Yes," Skuld said. "Please say no more. Evil ears are listening."

"Let them," Freya muttered softly. She lifted her head again. "Whoever's listening, know this—I am going to get away from here, and when I do, I swear you'll pay for what you've done. Do you hear me?"

"Strong words from a broken, wingless Valkyrie." The female Dark Elf appeared from the shadows and crept closer to her.

Pain had blocked Freya's senses, leaving her unable to feel the others around her. But it didn't keep her temper in check. She pushed herself up into a sitting position. "Come closer, Elf. I'll show you how wings don't define a Valkyrie— our strength does."

The Dark Elf snorted with a high-pitched laugh that hurt Freya's ears. "I must say, I do like your new look. Have you thanked Dirian yet? Now you can sleep on your back and wear clothing better suited to you. With a bit of soap and water and a proper dress, you'll be a pretty little addition to his trophy collection."

"I'm no trophy," Freya spat.

"Oh no? Why else are you alive, but to please the master? Have you seen your wings lately? They're his most prized possession!" More laughter followed. "It's too bad the rain damaged the feathers before Dirian cut them off. They would have looked so much nicer on the wall if they were intact."

Freya knew the elf was baiting her to look up at her wings again. But Freya refused. She'd seen them once—that was more than enough.

"This isn't over, Elf. Soon I will be free, and you and the others will be punished for your crimes."

The elf moved closer, but stayed out of Freya's reach. "That's what I like about you, Valkyrie. Even in complete defeat you are too stupid to realize that Dirian has won. Soon all the realms will kneel before him."

"I don't understand," Freya said softly. "Why did the Dark Elves join him? What's in this for you?"

"Nothing much. Just a sweet little realm we've had our eyes on for some time. I'm sure you know it. It's called Midgard."

"You want Earth?"

"Yes, and Dirian has promised it to us. Soon humanity will be our slaves. There will be no more warriors for Valhalla. And you, Valkyrie, will be there to see it all!" Her cackling laughter filled the chamber.

Freya was about to respond when her sense caught hold of her brother. It was only a brief flash before he suppressed their connection. But it was enough. Kai was in Muspelheim, and he was coming for her.

"Oh, Elf," Freya said as she lay back down. "I will see things, that's true. But what I'll see is something that will give you nightmares for the short piece of life you have left."

"Pain has made you delusional." The elf snorted as she returned to her guard post.

"We'll see," Freya muttered as she settled down again.

Kai's arrival did more for Freya than all the healing potions in all the realms. If Kai was here, the others were too. All she had to do was keep Dirian distracted long enough for them to reach the keep and free Vanir-Freyja and Skuld.

She closed her eyes and blocked out the ranting Dark Elf. Freya needed to rest, to heal as much as she could before she faced down Dirian in their final battle.

The sound of voices roused Freya from her troubled sleep. The moment she woke, the pain swooped down on her as a constant reminder of what Dirian had done.

"Do it," the Dark Searcher's broken voice commanded. "Do it or I will make you suffer again."

Skuld was whimpering softly. "Please, no more . . ."

"Do it now!" Dirian commanded.

Freya lay still but opened her eyes. Dirian was standing

with his back to her, leaning over Skuld. The youngest Norn was curled against the opposite wall and weeping as a parchment and quill were thrust into her hands.

"Cross them all out . . . ," Dirian commanded. "Or must I once again prove my absolute power over you!"

Freya was unable to see what Skuld was doing, but by listening to the exchange, she had a pretty good idea. This was how Dirian was ending his enemies. He was having Skuld cross out the futures of those whose names were written down.

After a moment she heard Dirian inhale deeply. "Very good. Now you may eat."

He turned and faced Freya. "I know you are awake," he rasped malevolently. "I can feel you."

Despite the protests from her broken ribs and the screaming from her wing stumps, Freya pushed herself up into a sitting position. She considered trying to stand but knew she didn't have the strength. The last thing she wanted was for him to see her fall.

"Is that how you amuse yourself," Freya said to him. "Tormenting children and cutting wings off Valkyries?"

"I did enjoy taking your wings," the Dark Searcher said as he strode casually toward her. "And there is yet more pleasure to be had in your pain. Let's start with a bit of early-morning reading. . . ."

"You can't read," Freya spat, determined to keep him occupied. "You're too stupid. You can barely even speak."

The only reaction her comment caused was Dirian turning the parchment around and lowering it enough for her to see. "I can read and write well enough to draw up a very special list of names. I'm sure you'll recognize them. These are the names of those who have no future. The moment my giants kill them, they will stay dead."

Dirian bent down closer. "I did this especially for you. It took me a great deal of time and effort to discover all these names. Tell me, have I missed anyone?"

Freya didn't want to see, but she couldn't keep from looking.

Brünnhilde of Skiir—Valkyrie

Eir of Brünnhilde—Valkyrie

Gwyn of Eir—Valkyrie

Skaga of Eir—Valkyrie

Kara of Eir—Valkyrie

Maya of Eir—Valkyrie

Kai of Eir—Dark Searcher

Giovanni Angelo of Brünnhilde—Dark Searcher

Kris of Brünnhilde—Dark Searcher

Myriam-Elizabet of Giovanni Angelo—Valkyrie

Freya's hand flew up to her mouth as she read the names of her family. A bright red line crossed through each of their names. Her senses told her that the red line wasn't ink. It was Skuld's blood. That was how the Norn would destroy the future of everyone Freya loved.

"Of course, your raven and dead human aren't on the list—yet. But there will be plenty of time to add them later, after I take the throne. As for you, Freya, you don't need to worry about appearing on any list. No, you and I will have a very, very long life together."

Freya tried to snatch the parchment away to destroy it, but Dirian was faster and pulled it from her reach. "Temper, temper," he teased.

The Dark Searcher rose and walked toward the chamber door. He reached into his cloak and pulled out Freya's flaming sword. Pinning the list on the end of the blade, he stabbed the sword tip into the wood of the doorframe—posting the list for her to see.

"You're a monster," Freya uttered.

Dirian's broken laughter echoed behind him as he stormed out of the War Room.

"I am sorry." Skuld wept miserably. "He made me do it."

Freya heard the pain in the Norn's voice but couldn't look at her. Her eyes were locked on the list. Dirian had condemned her entire family.

There was only one thing left for her to do, and Freya hated herself for having to do it. "Azrael," she softly called. "Please, come to me. I need your help."

Freya waited for the arrival of the Angel of Death. Last

time she'd called his name, he'd appeared immediately. This time there was nothing. "Azrael, please, I need you."

More time passed and still the angel did not appear. Horrible thoughts went through her head. Had he fallen in battle? Could he not hear her on Muspelheim?

Freya lay down again—crushed by despair. In all her life, she'd never felt so alone.

27

MAYA AND KAI FOLLOWED THE MAP TOWARD THE KEEP, flying high, above the prying eyes of the fire giants. The small villages they flew over grew into towns and then into the massive Great City. Past the city, the terrain gave way to villages and small settlements again. They soared lower in the sky as they approached the vast red desert rolling out before them.

As they flew near the desert edge, the heat rising from the sand hit Maya like a protective wall, designed to keep them out. Grazing against it was like sticking her wing into a blazing fire. It burned her skin and seared her feathers. Just as she was about to warn her brother, her senses picked up on dead humans and the Vanir.

"Kai, wait—I feel something." Maya started to descend.

"Yes, it's the heat from the sand. It's reflecting and magnifying the sun's rays. I've heard about this desert. It's deadly. We have to find another way in."

She shook her head. "I'm not talking about the desert; it's something else. Follow me." Tilting her wings, Maya continued down through the sky. She followed her senses to a single dwelling on the very edge of the red sands. "There," she called to her brother. "The two Vanir are in there. Human soldiers are with them."

They touched down lightly at the back of the dwelling. Maya pulled in her wings. Flying all night and into the day had taken a heavy toll on her feathers—especially her left wing, which had grazed over the edge of the desert sand. The feathers were frayed and tinder dry. If she touched them, they actually snapped.

Feathers weren't the only problem. The intense rays of the sun had burned her arms and hands and any exposed skin. Muspelheim was everything she'd been warned about, and worse.

"I'm not sure how much farther we can go," Kai said, making his own inspection of his wings. "My feathers are ruined."

"Mine too," Maya agreed. "I've heard the Vanir are very powerful. Maybe they can restore them."

Raised voices came from inside the single-story hovel. It was too small to be a giant's home. Low and squat, it looked as if it had been built for a dwarf or a troll. Maya approached the back door and forced it open.

"Help me," cried a troll when he saw Maya and Kia enter the single room.

Maya welcomed the cooler air in the shady hovel as she and her brother entered. A troll was tied to a chair, while two figures stood before him. Maya could make out their beautiful wings. One of them turned around—a boy about Freya's age, with a broad build and finely sculpted features.

"Valkyrie . . . ?" the Vanir boy asked, staring at her. He finally drew his eyes away, and they landed on Kai. "I don't know what you are."

Kai stood to his full height. "I am Kai, a Dark Searcher."

The boy inhaled. "You're Freya's twin brother!"

Kai nodded. "And this is our sister Maya. Are you Quinn?"

The boy nodded, smiling at Maya. "This is Skye." He presented the Vanir girl. She was about the same age but with raven hair and bright, worried eyes. "And these soldiers are from Midgard."

"What are you all doing here?" Maya asked. "Private Cornish found us in the tunnel and told us you were moving in on the keep. Why have you stopped?"

Quinn shook his head. "The desert. I was nearly roasted alive when I flew from the keep. It was still early morning, but the flight nearly killed me. It took all of my magic just to make it out of there alive."

"Same with us," the sergeant said. "When we tried to reach the keep, the sun came up and drove us back. Look how it damaged Skye's wings."

Skye showed them the burnt edges of her delicate butterfly wings. They were tattered and scorched. The skin on her arms and legs was peeling from intense sunburn. "Dirian positioned his keep well. No one can survive that desert during the day. We have to wait until the dark before we can risk going in again."

Maya frowned. "But you're Vanir. Surely your magic is strong enough to combat the sun?"

"Sadly not," Quinn admitted. "I've never known such intense heat. Vanaheim can get warm, but not like this. It's too much for us."

Kai exploded. "This isn't good enough! We must get to the keep *now*. Dirian has hurt Freya. He's cut off her wings and broken her bones. . . ."

"What?" Quinn cried. "Is she alive?"

Maya nodded. "But she's in so much pain, Kai had to break the connection to her just to be able to move."

Quinn's face contorted with rage. "I'm going to kill him!"

"Get in line," Kai said darkly. "I grew up at the keep in Utgard and I've hated Dirian all my life. But now he's gone too far. He will feel the cut of my blade!"

Maya took a moment to smile as she felt their deep feelings for her little sister. "You can both kill him—but first we have to get there."

"She's right," Sergeant Romin said. "You can do whatever you like to him *after* we free Vanir-Freyja and Skuld." He turned his steely eyes toward the troll tied to the chair. "And this guy here knows exactly where they're holding them."

He stepped up to the whining troll. "Listen, little buddy, these people mean business. They won't stop until you tell us where they're holding the others. If you value your skin, you'd better start talking."

The troll shook his head. "I know nothing of what you speak. I am a humble troll."

"Humble?" the sergeant said. "I don't think so."

"I am, dead human, I am. . . . I know nothing of the war."

"Really? And I'm sure you have no idea what we're talking about."

The troll nodded. "It's true. I am innocent. I don't know Dirian or anyone at the keep. I've never even been there."

"Oh no?" the sergeant said. He reached inside the tattered, ragged shirt of the filthy troll. Hanging on a long, leather cord was a single black feather. The edges were singed and fragile. "And I suppose this isn't one of Freya's feathers. . . ."

"Feather?" Kai stormed forward and yanked the cord from around the troll's neck.

The troll squealed and snatched at the feather. "That's mine. Give it back!"

"This is Freya's!" Furious, Kai turned on the troll. "How

did you get it?" When the troll said nothing, Kai slapped him across the face with the back of his gloved hand. "Answer me!"

"Kai, stop," Maya called. She caught hold of his hand before he could strike the troll again. "Torture doesn't work on trolls. You know that."

Kai was panting heavily, fighting to contain his rage. "I must try. He's going to tell us about Freya."

Maya nodded. "He will—"

"No, I won't!" the troll squealed. He spat at Kai. "You can kill me and I still won't speak. The master knows I am loyal."

"Oh, yes, you will, little troll," Maya said darkly. "You'll tell us everything we need to know and more."

"How?" Quinn said. "Nothing we've tried has worked. He doesn't care if we hurt him or not."

"Fear of pain isn't an incentive for them, but I do know a way," Maya said softly.

"If you do, I'd sure like to know about it," the sergeant said.

"There is a dangerous weapon here that you didn't have before. And that will make all the difference."

"Really?" the soldier said. "Would you care to enlighten us and tell us what it is?"

Maya sighed unhappily. "It's me. . . ."

* * *

Maya shooed everyone out of the hovel and asked to be left alone with the troll. When they were outside, she walked back to the smelly little creature.

"What will you do to me?" the troll asked fearfully.

"What I must." Maya retrieved a second chair and placed it before the troll. Turning it front to back, she straddled the chair and sat. She recoiled as the smell of the filthy troll hit her. But she had to focus. She had to do this to get to Freya. "I hate you for making me do this. . . ."

"Do what?"

Maya started to sing.

All Valkyries have the power to charm with their songs. But Maya's family was unique among the Valkyries and possessed even greater powers than this. No one knew why, and throughout their lives, the family had tried to hide their extra abilities.

Freya had been born with unique black feathers and was the fastest flyer in all of Asgard. Her older sisters were the strongest, most powerful fighters among all the Valkyries.

But Maya had an even more extraordinary power—though it was something she had fought against and tried to suppress all her life. She had been born with striking beauty and great power to enchant. No one could resist her when she turned it on. Until now, she had never used it fully—to her, it was a curse, not a blessing. But to save her sister, she would do anything.

Maya poured all that power into the song to cast a spell over the troll. The troll's eyes began to glaze over until he couldn't stop staring at her with complete adoration.

Maya shook her head and rose. She went to the door and called the others in.

"Thank heavens," Tina said. "I thought I was going to melt out there. Being dead isn't much fun when you can still sweat!"

"Well?" Skye said. "We heard you singing—what happened?"

Maya was disgusted with herself. "The troll will answer our questions now."

Kai stepped up to the chair holding the troll. "So, now, troll, you'll give us some answers."

The troll looked at Maya and smiled. "Will I?"

Maya nodded. "Yes, you will. You will answer truthfully, or I will be very displeased."

"No, no, please don't be angry at me," the troll whined. "Ask me anything. I swear I will tell all. . . ."

28

AS THE SUN PASSED DIRECTLY OVERHEAD, THE TEMPERA-
ture in the hovel became almost unbearable. Maya stood at
the small window, watching the waves of heat rolling over the
sand like malevolent living things searching for something to
devour. Nothing could survive in that lifeless, cruel desert.

They spent all morning interrogating the troll. He didn't
hesitate to tell them everything he knew. They untied him
from the chair, and Skye magically produced a quill and
paper, and the troll was instructed to draw up plans of the
interior of the keep.

Nothing was omitted. By the time the troll had finished,
they had the full layout of the keep, including the location
of Vanir-Freyja's cell in the lower dungeon and Archie's cell
on the next level.

The troll went on to tell them that he had seen Freya face Dirian and had personally witnessed him cut off Freya's wings. She was now Dirian's prized possession and was chained in the War Room across from Skuld.

At this point, Kai slammed his fist down on the only table in the room and shattered it to pieces. "I swear he's going to suffer for that."

Quinn nodded. "I will be there with you when he pays."

Maya faced the troll. "If Freya is his prized possession, what are the orders regarding her?"

The troll stared at her adoringly. His voice became dreamy. "No one is to touch or harm her. It is death to anyone who does."

"Good," Maya said.

"Good?" Kai cried. "Didn't you hear what Dirian did to her?"

"Of course I heard," she snapped. Her sister was hurt, the war was raging, and the heat in the small hovel was unbearable—seeing the loving expression on the troll's face only exacerbated her already foul mood. "But didn't you hear what he said? No one is to touch her. That means if we free her, no one can go against her. Freya is safe. Yes, she's suffering. Yes, she's broken—but she's safe!"

Kai and Maya glared at each other for a moment. Finally Kai nodded. "You're right. As much as I hate what he's done to her, Dirian's hatred of Freya will protect her from the others." He turned back to the troll. "You, tell us about all the entrances into the keep—those known and used and those that are hidden."

"Why would they need hidden entrances when they have a large desert out there to protect them?" Quinn asked.

"Because fire giants are immune to the heat of the desert," Kai explained. "And like the frost giants, they can be unpredictable and dangerous. In fact, the keep in Utgard had many secret ways in. They were used as emergency escapes in case the frost giants ever attacked. Dirian may be many things, but he's not stupid. This is the fire giants' realm. He wouldn't have built the keep without a hidden way out—especially now that he's wingless."

"So," Kai barked at the troll. "Tell us how to get in."

Within moments they were staring at the map the troll had drawn. Indeed, there were two hidden tunnels that had been built. One entrance sprang from the lowest level in the keep, crossed the desert deep beneath the deadly burning sands, and exited in the Great City. The other was on the dungeon level and also ran under the desert. It exited through a hidden door in the floor of the hovel—directly beneath their feet.

"Of course," the sergeant said, slapping his forehead. "Why didn't I think of that? This stinky little critter couldn't have walked through that desert on those stubby legs. It would have killed him before he made it three steps from the keep!"

"We all should have thought about that," Quinn said.

"It doesn't matter now," Skye said. "We know about the tunnels. So let's get ready to go before this war destroys all our realms!"

After the troll revealed the entrance to the tunnel, they drew up a plan. Again, they would split into two groups. Maya, Skye, and Tina would access the dungeon to free Vanir-Freyja while the troll would lead Kai, Quinn, and the remaining soldiers to Archie's cell and then make their way up into the War Room to free Freya and Skuld.

Though their weapons were checked and rechecked, Quinn also issued daggers to the soldiers in case their weapons failed in the harsh Muspelheim climate. Once those were secured, they started down the stone steps into the tunnel. The air became much cooler, and everyone breathed a great sigh of relief.

The tunnel was wider than Yggdrasil's roots. Kai stepped forward and opened his blazing white wings. "It's wide enough for the Dark Searchers to fly through. We must be on our guard. They might try to engage us down here."

"And we'll be ready," Skye said.

Quinn and Skye cast a spell to lift them off the ground and carry them swiftly through the long, torch-lit tunnel. Eventually the tunnel slanted up and Maya began to feel a dark presence. "Be careful, everyone," she whispered softly.

"There are Dark Searchers in there. I didn't realize just how many followed Dirian, but it's got to be at least forty."

"Forty?" one of the soldiers cried. "I saw the Dark Searchers on Earth—they're unstoppable!"

"Quiet!" Sergeant Romin ordered. "What did you expect? That we'd just stroll in and take the keep without opposition? We're in for the fight of our lives. And each of us must realize that there's a strong possibility we won't be coming out again."

"But we're already dead," Tina said.

"True," Maya hushed. "But your body can be killed again. So we must all be on our guard."

"This is what we signed up for," the sergeant reminded them, "so let's get moving."

Before they separated, Maya gave the troll his final orders. "Remember, you will do everything Kai and Quinn tell you to. Then, when you find Freya, *you* will keep her safe. Do you understand?"

The troll nodded. "As you command."

Maya said to her brother, "I emptied his mind and altered his loyalties. He is to serve our side now. But be careful in there."

"You too," Kai said.

They approached the hidden entrance to the keep. It was a thick stone arch, supporting the weight of the keep far above. Built into the arch were two tall doors, cut of the same stone.

As Quinn used his magic to open the doors, Kai turned back to Maya and whispered, "Remember, the moment you free Vanir-Freyja, get her out of here and go back to Midgard. Don't wait for us." His eyes settled on Skye. "I want you to use your strongest magic to seal these doors after you leave here."

"But you'll be trapped."

"Yes," Kai acknowledged. "And so will the Dark Searchers. They won't be able to follow you through this tunnel, and the other one will take them only to the Great City. It's too hot for them to fly after you when the sun's out. It will give you time to escape."

"What about you?" Maya said.

"We'll free Freya, Skuld, and Archie, and then Quinn will open the doors again. But even if we don't make it out, Vanir-Freyja is the most significant hostage."

Reluctantly, Maya nodded her head. Vanir-Freyja was the most important part of their mission. She would have to trust Kai and Quinn to save her younger sister.

The moment Quinn raised his hands and cast his spell, the two heavy stone doors swung open and a blast of hot, dry air blew into their faces. Powerful evil emanated from deep inside the red stone keep, causing Maya to shiver despite the heat. Freya was trapped in there with it. Maya also sensed a presence older than she'd ever felt before: Vanir-Freyja.

They entered the secret passage and followed the low

tunnel to a crossroads. "That way goes to the tunnel beneath the dungeon." The troll pointed and then turned his filthy finger in the opposite direction. "The stairs going up into the keep are that way."

Maya nodded to her brother a final time as he and his team drew their weapons and disappeared down a dark, arched corridor. She motioned for Skye and Tina to keep low and follow her as they walked in the opposite direction.

Senses on full alert, Maya freed her sword and padded softly down the dimly lit corridor. She held up her hand as she neared the first bend. "There are two Dark Elves and a dwarf just ahead," she whispered.

They paused and listened to the slurred voices of the Dark Elves mumbling before one called out loudly, "Where have you been? We've been waiting ages. . . ."

A dwarf's voice responded, "This barrel is heavy. If you two had stopped drinking long enough, you could have helped me carry it down here. . . ."

The drunken argument continued as Maya looked back at her team. "Tina, don't use your gun just yet—we don't want to alarm the keep. Let's keep it quiet. Skye, you use magic, and I'll use my sword."

Skye nodded. The wide-eyed, butterfly-winged Vanir reminded Maya of Freya. She was young, determined, and ready to surrender her life for the protection of others.

With a final nod, the three crept around the corner.

Maya pulled in her senses and tried to suppress her powers to mask her presence from the two drunken Dark Elves, but it didn't work.

The Dark Elves felt her and turned. Maya and Skye had no choice but to charge at them. There was no time for the elves to give alarm or even draw their weapons before Maya cut one down with her blade and Skye obliterated the other with magic.

The dwarf squealed in rage and ran at Maya. Even before he could raise his sword, Tina stopped him with the dagger Quinn had given her.

Maya nodded to the human soldier—acknowledging her ability with the blade.

"This way." She motioned as she led her team deeper into the keep. Maya followed her senses, taking the sandy trail toward the keep's most important prisoner. After turning down another, narrower corridor, she stopped and looked up at the ceiling. "Vanir-Freyja is directly above us. Skye, any chance you can cut through the ceiling to get into her cell?"

When Skye nodded, Maya looked at Tina. "Vanir-Freyja is surrounded by female Dark Elves and trolls. More than I can fight with my sword alone. I hate the noise it's going to make, but you must use your weapon. We're going to need all your skills as a fighter. After we get Vanir-Freyja, we'll bring her back down through here and out of the keep the way we came in. Understood?"

"I'm ready," Tina said.

"Me too," agreed Skye. "I'll open a hole above us and lift us up through it. Be prepared—it's going to happen quickly."

Skye closed her eyes and started to whisper. Moments later, a large hole appeared in the ceiling and two trolls fell through it. Maya silenced them with her sword before the three of them shot up through the hole.

They arrived in a heavily secured cell. Within a fraction of a second, Maya took in the entire scene. She saw a still, shrouded figure lying on the bed against the far wall. At the head of the bed perched a Dark Elf, whispering a spell. Maya's senses told her the figure on the bed was Vanir-Freyja. The actions of the Dark Elf suggested that she was being kept in a deep sleep by some sort of magical charm.

The rest of the cell was filled with more female Dark Elves, trolls, and dwarfs serving as guards for their ancient, powerful prisoner.

With no time to think, Maya flashed her blade and cut down the Dark Elves charging at her. A loud explosion of gunfire burst to life behind her and echoed through the dungeon level. Tina was taking on the guards outside the cell who were working to get in through the door.

"There are too many!" Tina cried. "Skye, seal the cell door!"

After the final Dark Elf fell to Maya's blade, Maya ran forward and killed the elf keeping their prisoner asleep. Maya scooped up the ancient Vanir in her arms and was shocked to discover that the wings on Vanir-Freyja's back were feathered like the Valkyries' and not insectoid, like most other Vanir.

Maya turned and watched Tina shooting through the bars and taking down guards while Skye used magic to secure the cell doors. Moments later three large Dark Searchers appeared outside the cell and roared at the sight of the intruders.

"Come on!" Maya clutched Vanir-Freyja close and jumped through the hole.

A second later, Skye landed on the sandy ground beside her. She looked up and immediately closed the hole in the ceiling.

"Where's Tina?"

"The Searcher threw one of his swords at her through the bars," Skye cried. "She's dead. They're sounding the alarm—we have to go!"

For an instant Maya felt conflicted. Freya was still trapped in the keep, but Vanir-Freyja was safe in her arms.

"Please forgive me, Freya," Maya whispered up to the ceiling.

With Skye by her side, they headed toward the exit.

29

THE ONLY WAY FREYA COULD TELL THE DIFFERENCE between night and day was through the temperature of the War Room. It was hot at night but stifling during the day.

She passed in and out of sleep as her body slowly healed, with the pain from her back and ribs a constant reminder of her loss.

Lying on her side, she tried her best not to reveal the emotions raging through her. Dirian's latest torment had been the most effective yet. His words cut more than anything he could have done with a sword.

The rebel Dark Searcher had taken great pleasure in informing her that his giants had broken through Asgard's outer wall and were now marching on Valhalla. He was preparing to leave the keep and join his generals there to capture the throne.

"This won't take long." Dirian leaned in close to her and rasped, "When I return, I will bring a special gift, just for you. . . ." He rose and headed for the door but paused before passing through to look back at her. "I will bring you Odin's head."

When he was gone, Freya lay her head down. Part of her wished Dirian had killed her, so she wouldn't have to witness Odin's defeat and the destruction of her home.

"Do not cry, Freya." From across the War Room, Skuld's voice was like a soothing lullaby in the long, terrifying night. "Things seem their darkest now, but the future is in flux. Nothing is set. Many things can happen, and fortunes can still change."

Freya raised her head and sniffed. "How? Dirian will march on Asgard with the giants. He'll kill Odin. How can the future be anything but awful?"

Skuld leaned back against the wall. "Because nothing is ever as it appears. Just as you are not as you appear—"

The arrival of a Dark Elf guard interrupted her midflow, and the change in the Norn was instant.

"Release me, you wretched creature!" Skuld screeched. "Never in my life have I been treated so disrespectfully. If you do not free me this instant, I swear I will erase you from existence!"

Freya watched in stunned silence. This was the first time she had heard Skuld raise her voice, and the Norn sounded a lot older than she looked. Every word dripped with threat. Freya's senses told her that the young Norn meant everything she said.

"Erase me from existence?" the elf repeated. "Those are powerful words from a child, especially one chained to a wall. Tell me, Skuld, how do you hope to achieve my demise?"

"I have my ways. Do not doubt . . ."

As they argued, Orus flew silently into the War Room. He landed unseen behind Freya and was hidden from view by her body. "Orus!" Freya was so relieved to see her friend. "What's happening—do you know what they did to Archie?"

"Don't worry—Archie has not been harmed. He remains here in the keep, but Dirian and his generals are on the move—they're heading to Asgard!"

Freya nodded. "It's awful," she whispered. "The giants have breached the boundaries of Asgard and are pouring in. Soon Odin will fall. . . ."

"Don't give up yet," Orus cawed softly. *"He won't be easy to beat."*

Freya was about to speak when her wounded senses picked up on something she'd never thought she'd feel again. She inhaled sharply. Maya and Kai! They were in the keep—deep down somewhere below her. And then she felt the presence of Quinn and Skye.

"You!" the Dark Elf called, hearing Freya's gasp. She

stepped away from Skuld and walked closer to Freya. "What are you up to over there?"

"*Careful,*" Orus whispered. *"Don't let her know I'm here."*

"If you must know," Freya shouted, wincing at the pain it caused her, "I'm in agony. What do you expect—me to sing with joy? Every time I breathe, it is like Dirian's blade cutting through me again." She knew that would please the evil elf, and her senses told her it had. "I need something for the pain."

"The Valkyrie is in pain? Good!" the Dark Elf cried with glee. "You deserve it, and much more. Why the master spares your life is a mystery to me. But I am sure he has more plans to make you suffer."

Freya's lips went tight. "You're the one that's going to suffer. . . ."

The Dark Elf laughed as she made her way to her seat—a posting where she could keep an eye on both Freya and Skuld.

Freya became silent and unmoving as the Dark Elf's beady eyes kept their watch on her. She kept her emotions well hidden while she inwardly celebrated. Across the room, Skuld gasped and started to smile. She too must have seen the arrival of the rescue team.

"What is it, Norn?" the Dark Elf demanded suspiciously. "What have you seen?"

"Leave her alone!" Freya shouted, forcing herself up

into a sitting position. She was still weak and dizzy from her wounds, but feeling her family close was giving her strength to keep fighting.

"What is this?" the Dark Elf shrieked. "Is the Valkyrie giving *me* orders?" She ran across the room and tried to kick Freya, but despite her wounds, Freya's reactions were faster. She caught hold of the Dark Elf's foot and twisted it back so quickly, she felt the delicate bones snap.

The elf cried out in pain and fell to the floor. Freya kept hold of her foot and pulled her close, quickly finishing her off.

"That's for threatening to eat Orus!" Freya spat. "I hope your head really hurts when you rise again."

"She won't rise again," Skuld said darkly.

Across from her, the Norn bit the end of her finger and was writing the Dark Elf's name on the stone floor in her blood. She swept her finger through the name, as though to wipe it out. "There, you horrible creature. You deserved that!"

Freya stared in stunned silence at the small Norn. The youthful expression had vanished from her face to reveal a powerful, ancient being with more than a trace of malice. Just as quickly, this disappeared and Skuld sat back, looking as innocent as ever.

Moments later an alarm bell started to chime from far above. Shouts filled the corridors of the keep. Stomping feet could be heard just outside the War Room.

Freya felt her sister somewhere beneath them; she was with Vanir-Freyja. She could feel Maya's excitement—this was a good sign. Suddenly there was hope that not all was lost.

"*Freya,*" Orus cawed, drawing her attention back. "*Check the elf's pockets. Does she have the keys to your collar?*"

"Don't," Skuld called quickly. "We only have a moment before the others discover what's happened in here. When I told you the future was in flux, I meant it. I have just seen something and must share it with you. You are no ordinary Valkyrie. You have power way beyond your knowledge, but you don't know how to use it. You must learn as quickly as possible—the future depends on you."

"I don't understand. What power?" Freya cried. "What are you talking about?"

"The power of the Vanir."

30

MAYA AND SKYE CHARGED THROUGH THE NARROW corridor deep in the bowels of the keep. Clutching Vanir-Freyja protectively, Maya navigated her way back to the tunnel entrance.

Just as they passed through the doors, Maya felt an unwelcome presence. "Searchers are coming," she cried. "Skye, seal the doors!"

Skye nodded and waved her hand. The thick stone doors started to swing shut just as the Dark Searchers arrived and began to pound and push against them.

"Seal them!"

"I'm trying!" Skye cried as her hands moved quickly through the air to cast the locking spell. "But the Dark Elves are using their own magic to force them open. They're too strong for me—the doors won't hold!"

Maya shifted Vanir-Freyja to one arm and pulled out her sword. Just as the heavy stone doors started to give, a hand shot out from under the shroud and grasped Skye's arm.

"Calm yourself, child. Focus your powers and let me help you . . . ," a soft voice said.

Skye inhaled sharply and recast her spell on the door. The heavy stone doors slammed shut.

As Maya started to put Vanir-Freyja down, the ancient Vanir's soft voice spoke again from beneath the shroud. "No, Maya, take me away from here, please. . . ."

How did Vanir-Freyja know her name? "Of course," Maya said respectfully. "Anything you say." She settled Vanir-Freyja in her arms again and spread her wings wide. She looked back at Skye. "I hope you can keep up with me."

"I'm right behind you," Skye said, casting her magic to lift off the ground.

Maya flapped her large white wings and took off through the deep tunnel running beneath the burning sands of the desert. She flew harder and faster than she'd ever flown in her life. Before long the tunnel ascended, and Skye lifted them through the hidden entrance in the hovel. When they were safe, Maya kicked the trapdoor shut. She looked around the small room for somewhere to lay her charge.

As if in answer to her thoughts, Skye waved her hand, and a narrow, soft bed appeared.

Maya lay Vanir-Freyja down gently. She reached for the shroud and pulled it away. Maya gazed down into the face that had the power to start wars. She was too stunned to speak.

Beside her, Skye was doing the same. Her mouth was hanging open as her eyes passed from Vanir-Freyja to Maya and then back to Vanir-Freyja again.

"Maya, she looks just like you!"

Vanir-Freyja's ice-blue eyes fluttered open. When she saw Maya, she smiled gently. "No, Skye. My great-great-granddaughter looks just like me. . . ."

Maya fell backward and landed awkwardly on her wings as Vanir-Freyja sat up. Maya's mirror image fluttered open her white wings and reached out to Maya. "Come, my child. Take my hand."

Struck silent by the sight, Maya climbed to her knees and crawled forward. She took Vanir-Freyja's hand.

"I'm so sorry that you've borne the curse of my image," she said softly. "But you are my blood, my direct descendant, and it was too great a power to lay dormant for very long."

"I—I don't understand," Maya mumbled. "How is this possible?"

"In Asgard, anything is possible," Vanir-Freyja said. "When my brother, Freyr, and I were traded as hostages in war, we settled in Asgard. It became our home and we flourished there. But when I arrived, I was already with child. I had one daughter, the first Valkyrie—a full-blooded Vanir, but born in Asgard. And then she had a daughter, and so on.

"As each new generation came, my brother and I cast a spell that would stop most of our powers from being inherited. But recently we've felt the tension in the realms growing, and we realized that Asgard needed special defenders. When you and your sisters were born, we did not cast the suppression spell. You all have our powers, and you, my dear heart, are the closest to me in looks. But your beauty has been a curse, hasn't it?"

Maya lowered her head.

"Of course it has, especially in Valhalla with all those warriors. I have seen how they've all fallen in love with you."

"You have?" Maya whispered.

Vanir-Freyja smiled, and it lit her whole face with a beauty that Maya had seen reflected in her dressing mirror many times before.

"Oh, my sweet child, I never left Asgard. I live there still and have watched over you and your family—my family—closely. I have seen my namesake, Freya, and her restless, unstoppable spirit. I've watched Gwyn's, Skaga's, and Kara's fighting skills develop, and I've seen you grow into the powerful beauty that you are."

"How can this be?" Maya asked. "Surely we would have seen you?"

Vanir-Freyja waved her hand over her face. Suddenly her beauty vanished and an old crone in a thick, tattered cloak was sitting before her. The cloak hid her wings and gave the appearance of a painful hump. Her voice cracked with age. "This is the only way I could ever find freedom from my curse."

Maya instantly recognized the sweet-seller from the market her family regularly attended. For as long as she could remember, the old woman had given her and her sisters treats whenever they visited. "You're Old Maave?"

The old crone nodded. "It was the only way I could see my family without causing mayhem. How I have longed to hold you all and tell you who I am. Your uncle Freyr has felt the same. You know him as Rathgar."

Maya didn't think anything could be more shocking—but finding out that her great-great-grandmother was Vanir-Freyja and that her great-great-uncle was actually the old blacksmith working at the stables of the Reaping Mares was almost too much to take in.

"Rathgar," she repeated softly. "He's always been so nice to me and takes extra-special care with my Reaping Mare when he makes her shoes."

"Of course. He loves you. He loves all of you as much as I do, which is why we stay close and do what we can to protect you."

"You know everything about us?"

Vanir-Freyja nodded. "Everything and everyone. Including the birth of Vonni's baby."

Skye was sitting beside Maya, listening in silence, but finally reached out. "I am sorry to break this up—but the war. We must stop the war."

"What war?" Vanir-Freyja said.

Maya shook her head and focused on the immediate. "Of course." She turned back to her ancestor. "Don't you know about the war? What Dirian has done?"

Vanir-Freyja shook her head. "I know nothing. From the moment the Dark Elves discovered my secret and caught me in Asgard, I have been kept under a sleeping spell." She looked around the hovel. "I can see and feel that we're in Muspelheim, but I don't know why."

Maya told Vanir-Freyja everything she knew, including the giants' arrival on Earth and how Dirian had caused it all. She finished with what he'd done to Freya.

"He cut off my baby's wings!" Vanir-Freyja raged. "I'll crush him!"

"There are many of us waiting to do that," Maya said softly. "But before that, we must stop the war in the realms from turning into—"

"Ragnarök," Vanir-Freyja finished.

Skye nodded. "We believe Dirian has been offering you as the prize for the giants when they help him defeat Odin. You are to be given to their kings."

As the news sank in, the crone facade slipped away and was replaced by Vanir-Freyja's outstanding beauty—beauty tinged with pain. "It's this cursed face of mine," she said miserably. "Because of it, war in the realms has started."

Tears rimmed her eyes, and seeing her pain was almost too much for Maya to bear. She shook her head. "Listen to me. This isn't your fault, and it's not Freya's either, though she still argues it is. Dirian is doing this, no one else. It's obvious your face hasn't captured his heart. He was going to give you away to those who served him. So it's his crime, not yours. But *you* are the only one who can stop it."

"Me? How?" Vanir-Freyja said miserably.

Maya rose and reached down for her distant grandmother's hands. "By coming with us to Earth and showing the giants that you are free and will never be anyone's prize."

Vanir-Freyja nodded. She stood and wrapped her arms and wings around Maya. "We will do this together. You and I, my great-great-granddaughter and mirror twin. We will use our beauty like weapons and lead the giants away from Midgard and send them back to their realms."

Maya smiled. "For most of my life, I've resented how I look and been envious of my sisters' fighting skill. But that ends today. If beauty started this war, then together we will use our beauty to stop it!"

31

THE KEEP WAS IN UPROAR AS DIRIAN AND HIS GENERALS charged back into the War Room. Freya didn't need to use her senses to know how furious the Dark Searcher was. He stormed over to the table and slammed both his fists down. The enormous table buckled beneath his rage, and the maps went flying and then settled on the floor around the room.

"Find me the map with the tunnels to all the realms!" Dirian shouted to his men. "If Vanir-Freyja thinks she can find sanctuary back home, she's in for a rude surprise. We'll unleash fire giants on Vanaheim—and as their realm burns, they'll plead for mercy and surrender her to me!"

The map was found and Dirian called his generals forward. He stole a glance over his shoulder and caught Freya watching him.

"You!" he raged, taking three long strides to reach her.

The body of the Dark Elf was still beside her. Dirian took one look at it and kicked it aside as though it meant nothing to him. "That sister of yours has stolen my prize! But it won't save her or your realm. I will find Vanir-Freyja, and when I do, Maya will pay for her crimes—and I will make you watch!"

"You've lost, Dirian!" Freya shouted.

"Freya, stop!" Skuld warned frantically. "Say no more!"

Freya knew she should keep her mouth shut, but she couldn't. She was in pain, and hearing that Maya had freed Vanir-Freyja was the best news possible. Even if Dirian killed her now, she could die happy.

"Without Vanir-Freyja, you have nothing to offer the giants. They'll turn on you and squash you like the insignificant bug that you are!"

Dirian's fury soared and washed over her in waves. He drew his black blade and lifted it over his head.

Freya closed her eyes. This was it. She would not live to see the end of the war. Archie, Orus, and her family would be lost to her, and she'd never learn who her father was. It would all end now—and she was ready. . . .

Freya waited one heartbeat, and then two, but nothing happened. She opened her eyes. Dirian had put his weapon away and knelt down close to her.

"Thank you . . . ," he rasped with his fractured voice.

"Thank you, Freya. Once again you have made me see things clearly. Were it not for you, I would have made a terrible mistake and followed Vanir-Freyja. But now I realize I don't need the giants anymore. Asgard has already fallen. Only Odin stands in the way of my ruling all the realms."

He reached out to her, and Freya flinched back. But instead of striking her, Dirian patted her lightly on the head as though she were a young child being praised by a parent. "You will make an excellent part of my war council."

Dirian rose and walked back to his men, his whole demeanor changed. He pointed at one of the generals. "I want you to take a team of Searchers and go after Vanir-Freyja. The giants don't know she's free yet—use that to your advantage. Take a group of fire giants with you to Vanaheim. I want her found and brought back here. Now that Vanir-Freyja has sealed our primary tunnel, it's useless to us. Take the secondary one. It's longer, but you will come out in the Great City. Go from there."

He turned to the others. "You're with me." Glancing back once more at Freya, he said to his men, "While they go after Vanir-Freyja, we will go to Asgard. Before another day has come and gone, Odin will be dead!"

"Freya, what have you done?" Orus emerged from his hiding spot.

Freya was shaking her head, trying to understand what had just happened. "I wanted to make him really angry, to distract him and give Maya time to get Vanir-Freyja away from here. I was ready to let him kill me."

"Dirian is too clever for that," Skuld called. "I tried to warn you."

"I know. I'm sorry," Freya said, bowing her head. She looked miserably at Orus. "Why don't I ever listen?"

"It's not in your nature," the raven said sadly. *"Most of the time your instincts work."*

"Not this time," Freya said. "I've made things worse."

"Then you are going to have to fix it," Skuld called.

"How?"

"By acknowledging your mistake and moving on."

Freya looked at Skuld, chained to the opposite wall. She appeared to be so young, but she sounded older than anyone else Freya had ever met before.

"Freya, hear me," the Norn continued. "You are alive, and while you are, there is hope. I told you, the future is in flux. Many things are happening at once. Nothing is clear, not even to me. Remember what I told you. You must summon a part of you that you've never used before. You have strength, and power. Now is the time to use it before it's too late."

"What power? I just don't understand."

"Yes, you do," Skuld said cryptically.

Freya cast her mind back to the beginning—when they were still in Midgard, preparing to leave for Muspelheim.

What was it Quinn had said after she'd helped them lift the stone altar? Something about her Valkyrie blood having a lot of power in it.

Was that what Skuld meant?

Did she have Vanir powers? There were times in her life when things had happened that she couldn't explain—when she'd achieved things and she couldn't possibly understand how or why, like defeating the much bigger and stronger Dirian at the Ten Realms Challenge. And being the fastest flyer in Asgard. She'd always believed it was her wings carrying her forward, but perhaps there was more to it.

Freya sat very still for some time, considering Skuld's words and all the occasions in her life when strange, unexplained things had happened. She closed her eyes and pushed back the pain from her severed wings and broken ribs. Taking a deep, cleansing breath, she reached out with her senses. She could tell that all the Dark Searchers had now left the keep as they made their final push in the war.

Apart from one. Kai was still alive, somewhere in the keep. She could feel him. As she reached out further, she felt Quinn and the soldiers with him too. There weren't as many as before, but a couple remained. They were with . . . Freya inhaled. She could feel that they were with Archie!

"Calm," Skuld called. "That's it. Remain calm and breathe deeply. Focus on what you want to do."

Freya took another long, deep breath and ignored the

pinching from her ribs. She reached up and grasped the metal collar around her neck.

Orus moved closer and climbed up onto her knee as she sat cross-legged on the stone floor. *"You can do it, Freya,"* he coached. *"You can do anything."*

With Orus and Skuld offering encouragement, Freya started to pull at the lock securing the collar around her neck. The heavy metal seemed to move a fraction, but when she felt it shift, it broke her concentration and everything stopped.

"Try it again," Orus cawed.

"But it's so hard." Freya panted from the strain. "I can't break metal, at least not this kind."

"Then you are already defeated," Skuld said. "If you don't believe in yourself, how can you expect others to have faith in you?"

Those words stung. "Just because I can't break metal doesn't mean I don't believe in myself!"

"Why are you trying to break the lock?" Skuld asked. "Surely you can't. But what you want to do is open it."

"Open it? How?"

"Haven't I told you already?"

"All you've said is that I have the power of the Vanir. But you didn't say how! If you know so much, why don't you tell me?"

"That is up to you to discover," Skuld said.

"You're talking in riddles now?" Freya fumed. "Just as

Dirian is moving in on Asgard? Skuld, if you know something I don't—and you do, because you're the Norn of the future—for Odin's sake, tell me!"

Skuld's expression dropped as if Freya had struck her. "I can't tell you how to do something I don't know how to do myself." It sounded as though she were on the verge of tears. "All I know is I've seen you use the power. But that doesn't mean I know how to teach it to you."

Freya felt as if she'd stolen a treat from a child. "Skuld, I'm sorry. I didn't mean to yell at you. But this is so important, and I just don't know what to do."

Orus pecked Freya in the leg. *"You're overthinking this. You always do your most amazing things when you don't have time to think about it. So stand up, open that collar at your neck, and save Odin!"*

"How?"

"Don't ask how. Just do it!" Orus shouted.

Freya put Orus down and climbed slowly to her feet. This was the first time she'd stood since Dirian's attack. Her balance was way off because she didn't have the weight of her wings on her back. Everything felt strange and wrong. She leaned against the wall for support until she found her balance and stood straight.

"That's it," Orus cawed, flying up to his proper place on her shoulder. *"Now pull the collar's lock to the front and do like Quinn or Skye would do, and open it."*

Freya was filled with doubt. This was insane. But with so much at stake, she had to believe that deep down inside, somehow, she had the power of the Vanir.

Once again Freya clasped both sides of the metal collar. Instead of straining to use her strength to pull it open, she focused all her thoughts on "wanting" it open.

It was impossible to know who in the War Room was the most shocked as a loud *click* echoed through the large empty room.

As the collar fell away, Freya's eyes went wide. "Orus, I did it!"

"*I knew you could all along!*" Orus said as he playfully nipped her ear.

Freya reached up, caught him by the beak, and gave him a big kiss. "Thanks, Orus."

Free of her chains, Freya took two unsteady steps forward. Without the weight of her wings for balance, walking felt strange, and she wondered how long it had taken Brundi or even Dirian to get used to being wingless.

Freya could sense that the corridor directly outside the War Room was empty and that they were alone. The first thing she did was walk over to the door where Dirian had posted the parchment with the list of her family names on it.

Catching hold of her golden flame sword, Freya pulled it out of the wall, freeing the list. She caught the parchment in her hands and shivered as she read the names of her family again.

"Skuld, can you take this back? Can you give my family their futures again?"

The young Norn nodded. "Bring the list to me."

Freya never imagined that walking across a room could be so difficult or awkward. But now that she was upright, the wounds on her back were throbbing and her balance was still way off.

As she drew closer to the Norn, Freya was finally able to see her clearly. Skuld did look like a child. But as Freya came closer to her, she saw that Skuld's eyes were solid white.

"Skuld, are you blind?"

"I am the Norn of the future," Skuld said. "I must be blind to the past and present; otherwise I wouldn't be able to see the future."

Freya's heart immediately went out to her. "I'm so sorry. Why didn't you tell me?"

"What difference would it make? Yes, I'm blind and I can't see you right now, but I am no less the person I was before you knew, and you shouldn't treat me any differently."

"Why would I?"

"Some do," Skuld said. "That I am without present sight makes some believe I am less than they are. But I often ask them, 'Can you see the future?' and that makes them think."

Skuld reached for the parchment. "Freya, before I do this, you must know—I can't help those who have already fallen from this list. They will not rise again."

A dagger of fear cut through Freya's heart. "Do you know who's fallen?"

The Norn said nothing, but nodded.

"Please, you must tell me."

Skuld shook her head. "I can't. To tell you would distract you from the trial you must now face. But I will say there have been only two losses. Everyone else on the list is alive."

Freya's heart raced as she scanned the parchment again. Her mother, grandmother, sisters, brother, cousins, and uncles were there—almost everyone she cared for most in all the realms was on that list. To know that two had fallen was unbearable. "You must tell me!" she cried. "Don't you understand? I can't go on without knowing. Please, who have I lost?"

Tears rimmed the Norn's eyes. "I am so sorry, Freya. Your grandmother, Brünnhilde, and your sister Skaga were killed in separate incidents. Skaga was defeated by a fire giant. I promise you; it was quick and painless. She died bravely, surrendering her life to save humans."

The Norn paused and then inhaled deeply. "Brünnhilde and her raven were killed when two frost giants attacked the mountain she and your cousins were hiding in. Myriam and baby Michael are alive. I do see a future for them, but until this war ends, that future is in flux."

At her shoulder, Orus cawed in grief. But Freya was silent. She felt the air sucked out of her body as her legs gave out and she collapsed to her knees. Her amazing sister Skaga was dead for good. Brundi, who had suffered so much and had risen above it all to do great things, was gone.

"You shouldn't have told her, Skuld." A Dark Searcher entered the War Room. "Knowing never helps anyone . . ."

Freya gasped, fighting to hold back tears. The Dark Searchers would never see her cry. Instead she let rage overwhelm her senses as she reached for her sword. Driven mad by fury, she rose and turned.

Silenced by grief, Freya stalked the Dark Searcher. Clear thinking was gone. She felt no pain from her wing stumps, burns, or broken bones. She felt nothing but an overwhelming desire to share with him the agony she was suffering. She lifted her sword, unwilling to wait for him to defend himself. Skaga and Brundi were dead; soon he would be too.

The Searcher stumbled back and held up his hands. "Freya, stop!" Suddenly the Dark Searcher shimmered and melted into a familiar form, standing before her in green armor holding a Vanir staff in one hand.

"Loki?" Freya staggered and dropped her sword, unable to trust her eyes. But her senses quickly confirmed what she couldn't believe. "Is that really you?"

Loki nodded. "I am sorry for your loss—for our loss. Brundi was a very special woman. She meant everything to me."

Tears that she'd fought so hard to hold back flooded her eyes. "You're alive . . . ?"

Loki nodded and opened his arms to her. Freya ran forward and embraced him as though he were the only real thing left in her life.

"Let it out, Freya," he said softly into her hair. Loki held her tight but was careful not to touch her wing stumps as he rocked her like a father comforting a suffering daughter. "Just let it all out."

32

MAYA WAS FILLED WITH MIXED EMOTIONS AS THEY
entered the Yggdrasil tunnel and left Muspelheim behind.
She had rescued Vanir-Freyja, but leaving her sister, Kai, and
Quinn behind was the hardest thing she'd ever done in her life.

Vanir-Freyja cast a spell to carry them through the roots
of Yggdrasil to Midgard.

Traveling at speed, Maya was barely aware of passing
from one realm to the next. It was only when they rounded
the corner and saw a cluster of soldiers before them that she
realized they were entering the domain of Midgard.

"Maya! I'm so glad to see you! We didn't know what to
do, so we've been waiting here for you."

"Tina?" Maya called. Three other soldiers from their
journey to Muspelheim were there as well—including the

one whose ghost she'd sent back to Earth to warn Thor about Vanir-Freyja. But as she reached out with her senses, she realized that none of them were ghosts anymore. They were very much alive and healthy.

Not much farther down the tunnel, the body of Sergeant Romin sat against the wall—looking unchanged and alone. Private Cornish scratched his head. "I don't know what happened. One moment I was talking to Thor, passing on your message about Vanir-Freyja, and the next, I was back here."

Another private said, "I was at the keep with Kai and Quinn, and some Dark Searchers came. Then I woke up here."

Tina nodded. "All I remember is entering the cell with you. . . ." She frowned. "But then everything went blank and, just like the others, I woke up here."

Maya remembered perfectly well what had happened to Tina. "You don't remember being killed by the Dark Searchers as they tried to enter the cell to stop us?"

Tina frowned and shook her head.

"Maya," Private Cornish said, "these are our bodies, right? I mean, I know that Freya reaped us, but we're alive again, aren't we? How is this possible?"

"I really don't know," Maya admitted. "You were dead. I know you were. But now you're alive, and I don't understand how."

Vanir-Freyja nodded. "I believe I do. Tell me, when Freya reaped you, were you here in this tunnel?"

"Yes," Tina said. "And our bodies were left right there, just like John's is now. Our ghosts went to Muspelheim with Freya and Skye to try to free you."

Vanir-Freyja nodded. "Your bodies were held in the embrace of Yggdrasil. The World Tree kept them safe for when you needed them again. When each of you completed your task, Yggdrasil returned your spirits to your bodies and restored you to life."

The ancient Vanir came forward and touched Tina's face. "But you have changed. You are no longer a human of Midgard. Nor are you Aesir, or Vanir, or of any one realm. You are part of all realms—you are the children of Yggdrasil. It is a great honor she has bestowed upon you. You must use this gift wisely."

Behind them came the sound of a deep inhalation and a cough. Everyone looked back and saw the body of the sergeant stir. His eyes opened as he took another deep breath. Confusion rose on his face.

"John!" Tina cried. She ran over to him and helped him climb to his feet. "Nice and slow. It takes a moment to adjust."

Sergeant Romin shook his head, and then his eyes flashed open. He ran over to Maya. "I don't know what just happened or how I got here, but we have to go back."

"Calm down," Maya said. "If you are here, it means you must have been killed at the keep. Yggdrasil has restored your spirit to your body."

"I—I'm alive?"

When Maya nodded, the sergeant shook his head. "No, no, I can't be. They need me!" He reached out and took Maya's hand. Nothing happened.

"Maya, reap me!" he cried.

Maya looked down at where they were touching and back up to the sergeant, baffled to see that he was still alive.

"She can't," Vanir-Freyja said. "Yggdrasil has changed you. You aren't human anymore and are immune to a Valkyrie's touch."

Tina approached him. "John, she says we can move through all the realms."

"Is this true?" he demanded of Vanir-Freyja.

"I believe so."

The sergeant nodded. "Good." He looked back at his men. "Just like before, this is a volunteer mission. Those of you who want to come with me, do. Those who want to return to Earth, you can go with no charges or blame against you."

"Come where?" Tina asked.

"Back to the keep. Just before I passed out, Kai, Quinn, Archie, and I were on our way up into the War Room to get Freya and Skuld. Outside the door, we heard Dirian and his men making plans."

"Did you see Freya?" Maya demanded. "Is she all right?"

"I couldn't see her, but I could hear her. Dirian was furious that the exit tunnel was sealed after you left. Freya started baiting him, making him even angrier. It sounded like he was going to kill her—"

Maya inhaled. "No . . ."

"It's all right," the sergeant said quickly. "He didn't. From what I could hear, he actually thanked her for making him think clearly. He sent some of his men to take the other tunnel out of the keep and gather a group of fire giants together. They're going to Vanaheim to burn it down and force you to hand Vanir-Freyja back over to him."

"But we're not going to Vanaheim," Skye said.

"He doesn't know that. They're on their way there now."

"What of Dirian?" Vanir-Freyja asked.

The sergeant's eyes landed on Maya. "That's why I wanted you to reap me. I've gotta get back there. Dirian is on his way to Asgard right now. He told Freya it's fallen and he's going to kill Odin." The sergeant paused and started to frown. He rubbed his neck. "I—I can't remember what happened after that. We—we heard them coming out of the War Room and hid in the tower stairs. I think other Searchers found us. . . ." He continued to rub his neck as though it hurt.

From this Maya was sure he had been killed in the tower by a sword strike to the neck. "Can you remember if Kai was hurt?"

Sergeant Romin's brows furrowed deeper as he tried to recall his final moment. He shook his head. "I just don't know. I can't remember anything after that."

"Just as well," Vanir-Freyja said. "Remembering how you died will not serve you going forward."

"We must go back," Maya said. "Dirian must be stopped."

Vanir-Freyja shook her head. "No, child. Our first priority is stopping the giants from destroying Midgard, Vanaheim, and all the realms in between. When they are on our side, we'll move on Asgard and go after Dirian."

"But he could kill Odin!" Maya insisted.

"It is a risk," Vanir-Freyja said. "But Odin is powerful and resourceful. I doubt many alive today will remember what a fierce fighter he can be. It won't be easy for Dirian to kill him."

The sergeant stepped closer to the ancient Vanir. His eyes were filled with passion. "There is nothing I would love to do more than follow you wherever you go. . . ."

Maya felt the sergeant and all the soldiers in the tunnel reacting to Vanir-Freyja's beauty. They were all under her spell and would do anything she said. Or so Maya thought. She was stunned when the soldier continued. "But with all due respect, Odin must be protected. I've seen what that monster Dirian can do. We have to stop him from claiming the throne."

"Of course." Vanir-Freyja smiled at him, and her smile commanded all the soldiers' attention. "Our paths lie in different directions." She turned to Skye. "The choice is yours, my young, brave friend. You may stay with Maya and me as we go after the giants, or lead these Guardians of Yggdrasil to Asgard to protect Odin."

"We won't make it there without you," Sergeant Romin said. "Skye, only you can help us."

Skye's eyes moved from Maya to Vanir-Freyja and then to the sergeant. Finally, determination rose on her young face and she nodded. "What Vanir-Freyja says is true. Our paths do lie in different directions. I will go with the soldiers and use my magic to help defend Odin."

Maya walked up to the young Vanir girl with the badly tattered butterfly wings. "You remind me so much of Freya. Please, take special care of yourself." She gave her a powerful hug. "When this is over, if we are all still standing, there will be great celebrations in Asgard and we will all know such joy."

Skye nodded. "And all the Vanir will be there."

Maya stood with Vanir-Freyja and watched the brave soldiers departing down the tunnel with Skye. She could sense that the change in realms was not affecting the soldiers. It was true, Yggdrasil had altered them and made them all part of the Great Cosmic Tree.

"Do you think they'll be all right?"

"I hope so," Vanir-Freyja said. "Yggdrasil is counting on them."

"We all are," Maya agreed.

Once again the Vanir used her magic to move them swiftly through the tunnel. Finally, their long journey came to an end when the ground beneath them started to tilt up toward the entrance in the Temple of the Sun in Peru.

"Now, before we start, we must be set on our course." The ancient Vanir took Maya's hands. "This will not be as easy as you might think, my child. We are going to cast a spell that will never be broken. In doing this, we will unleash your greatest power—power that has lain dormant within you until now.

"After this, anyone who hears you—be they giant, human, elf, or Asgardian—will become as obsessed with you as they are with me. The life you knew will end. You will know no peace, freedom, or respite from their pursuit. Not in Asgard, Midgard, or any realm. They will always be looking for you—not to do harm, but to love and possess you. Trust me. This is a great burden to carry, much greater than you have known. To find peace, you will have to do as I have done and live the rest of your life in hiding."

Maya considered her words carefully. "If we do this, will it end the war?"

Vanir-Freyja nodded. "I believe so. When the giants are

enchanted, they will do our bidding and return home. All that will remain will be to stop Dirian and his men from taking the throne. Even if they succeed in killing Odin, they must never rule. If needs be, we will command the giants to stop them for us."

"I understand," Maya said somberly. She took her great-great-grandmother's hand and nodded. "Let's do this."

33

KAI, QUINN, AND ARCHIE RAN INTO THE WAR ROOM BUT stopped short when they saw Loki holding Freya.

"Loki?" Archie cried. "What are you doing here? We saw you die in Montreal."

"Get away from my sister!" Kai demanded, charging over.

Loki gave Freya a final squeeze and whispered gently, "Dry your tears and don't tell them about Brundi or Skaga. It can't help them to know just yet."

He turned on Archie. "You might wish I had died, ghost, but it will take more than a few giants to end me. So what took you so long to get here? Or were you hoping Freya and I would take Dirian down by ourselves?"

That set Kai off, and he furiously explained what they'd been through.

While Kai talked, Archie approached Freya. "Gee, are you all right?"

Freya nodded, still unable to speak without breaking down and telling him what had happened to her family. Instead she stumbled into his arms, grateful that he was unharmed.

"It's gonna be all right. I promise," he reassured her. "I know what Dirian did to you. But you're alive—that's all that matters."

Freya nodded and pointed to the place where she'd been chained. Posted on the wall were her black wings.

"That monster! He's mounted them like a trophy!" Archie left Freya and ran over to the wall. Jumping up, he caught hold of her severed wings and wrenched them down. "I'd rather see them burned than left up there for him."

"I'm so sorry." Quinn approached her cautiously. "Do you want me to get rid of them so Dirian can't have them?"

When Freya nodded, Quinn put his hand on her shoulder and gave it a squeeze. "You're sure?" he asked gently.

Was she sure? Her wings . . . They were so much a part of her life. How was she going to live without them? "They're not really mine anymore. They're just useless wings that will never fly again. Yes, please, destroy them."

"*Your beautiful wings . . . ,*" Orus moaned.

"They're gone," Freya whispered to him.

Quinn took the wings from Archie and frowned.

"They're much heavier than I expected," he said. "No wonder you could fly so fast—you had an unfair advantage when we raced. No one could beat these!"

Archie shook his head. "Not now, Quinn . . ."

"Archie, it's all right," Freya said, knowing Quinn was trying to make her feel better. As she watched Quinn put her wings down on the floor, Freya realized that was another thing she would grieve over for the rest of her life. She wondered how long it would take to get used to being grounded.

"You might want to look away," Kai warned.

"C'mon, Gee," Archie said, taking her by the hand. "Let's check on Skuld."

When they walked over to the Norn, Kai looked back to where Quinn was casting the spell that would destroy Freya's wings. "I swear I am going to kill Dirian for doing that to you."

"We all are," Archie agreed.

Freya wiped away the last of her tears and swallowed down her pain. There would be time enough to mourn later. She took a deep breath. "If we're going to find Dirian, we'd better get moving. He and his men have gone to Asgard to kill Odin."

"We heard," Archie said, still holding her hand tightly. "And we will . . ."

"Just as soon as we get you and Skuld to Vanaheim," Quinn added as he rejoined them.

Freya stole a quick look back, but there was no longer any evidence of her wings. They were gone. Just like Skaga and Brundi. "I don't want to go back to Vanaheim. . . ."

"You must," Quinn insisted. "They'll take care of you and help you heal. And Skuld must be returned to her sisters."

"I'm afraid there's no time for that," Loki said. "Dirian and his men already have a good head start. If we have any hope of getting to Asgard before he does his worst, we must all go now."

"No. You're wrong," Quinn said. "Freya and Skuld must be taken to safety first."

Freya could feel that Quinn cared for her, and it warmed her heart. In this—the worst moment of her life—she realized she felt the same for him. But this wasn't the time for emotions. Freya shook her head. "After *everything* Dirian has taken from me, I want to be there when we stop him. I *have* to be there. All I need is a bit of that potion of yours—the one that takes away pain. Then we can go."

"But it's too dangerous," Quinn insisted.

"*She has to do this,*" Orus cawed. "*And for once I agree with her. Freya must face Dirian one last time if she's ever to get past this.*"

"It'll be all right, Quinn," Archie said. "Nothing's ever too dangerous for our Gee. Just give her the potion. We don't have time to argue."

"Finally the ghost has something intelligent to say!"

called Loki as he knelt beside Skuld. "And when you're finished making the potion for Freya, get over here and open Skuld's lock."

Once Skuld was free, she looked even younger and more vulnerable—standing no higher than Freya's shoulder and staring forward blankly. Despite her seeming youth, she was the oldest among them, and the expression on her face made it clear that no one was going to tell her no, or risk angering the tempestuous Norn. "I will go with you to Asgard," she said firmly. "There will be no arguing with me."

"Of course," Loki said. His expression made it clear he was cautious around the ancient Norn.

They headed out of the War Room and entered the corridor.

"Freya, look out. It's the troll that attacked you!" Orus cawed in warning.

Freya simultaneously realized two things. One, she wasn't in pain anymore and could move quickly again. Two—and perhaps most important—although Quinn's potion did relieve her pain, it dulled her senses. She hadn't felt the troll lingering in the corridor.

Freya raised her sword to dispatch him.

"Gee, no!" Archie cried, grabbing her arm. "Don't. He's with us."

"With you?" Freya frowned and looked from the troll to

Archie. "He attacked me when I was in the dungeon. He's no friend of mine!" She pulled her arm away. "Let me do this!"

"Freya, stop!" Skuld commanded. "He has a purpose to fulfill in the future. You must not harm him."

"But—"

"I swear he's with us now," Archie said. "Maya reprogrammed him. He's here to protect you and will show us the way out."

The troll nodded. "Maya told me I had to protect you. I am your slave. . . ."

Freya felt pity mixed with disgust as she watched the sniveling, round troll appear to be happy to be her slave. She took a step back. "All right. All right. You can protect me— but you're not my slave, and you're never to call yourself that again! Do you understand?"

The troll nodded. "I do. I do understand. I will be a good slave."

Freya sighed and shook her head. "How did Dirian get out of here?"

"I will show you!" the troll squealed, jumping gleefully to his stubby feet. He caught Freya by the hand. "Come, come, this way. It will be faster, and I can keep you safe!"

Freya was repulsed by the touch of the troll, but she let him lead her forward. The silence was disturbing as they walked through the long corridor. Where was everyone? Surely their escape couldn't be this easy. Not too long ago, the keep was teeming with Dark Searchers and Dark Elves. When she asked the troll, he shrugged. "They're with Dirian on his mission to kill Odin. Only a few were left, but we've killed them to protect you."

Freya looked back at her brother.

Kai nodded. "We encountered a couple of Dark Searchers and a few Dark Elves and dwarfs. They killed Sergeant Romin before we could stop them. But it seems the keep is now empty."

Freya wasn't sure if this was a relief or a worry. Just how bad was it in Asgard?

"This way," the troll cried, leading them to the tower stairs. "We all go down."

Everything about the keep was eerily quiet. Only the sounds of their footfalls on the thick stone steps disturbed the overwhelming silence.

When they reached the next level, Freya saw the remains of the Dark Searchers and elves Kai was talking about. By the looks of things, the fight had been quick but deadly. As she studied the bodies, she couldn't see the sergeant. She also noted that some of them had no obvious wounds and wondered if Quinn had used magic to dispatch them. She looked back at the Vanir. Quinn simply nodded, confirming it was true.

At the bottom of the stairs, the troll led them forward into another dark, low-ceilinged tunnel. They walked single file, Quinn keeping close to Skuld and acting as her eyes as they reached a narrow archway, with an even narrower corridor beyond it. At the end of that corridor, they faced another set of steps going down. The air around them felt stale and the temperature seemed to be rising, despite their being underground.

"This was only to be used in emergencies . . . ," the troll said. "But now that the other tunnel is blocked, it is the only way out during the hot day."

The potion kept most of her pain under control. But the heat of the still air around them made Freya's burnt skin prickle. She didn't like this one bit. As the troll started to descend, she had no choice but to follow.

At the bottom, they stood before two wide double doors.

Kai tried to push them open but failed. "There's magic keeping them sealed." He looked back at Quinn. "Can you open them?"

Quinn left Skuld in Loki's care and came forward. He brushed past Freya, smiled, and reached for her hand. "With a bit of help, I can."

Freya blushed under the intensity of his stare and took his hand.

"Oh, please," Loki cried. "I think I'm going to be sick. Just open the doors already."

"You ready?" Quinn asked.

Freya nodded, recalling how she had unlocked the chain

around her neck. She took a deep breath, forcing down all her grief, pain, and rage, and focused only on finding calm. She closed her eyes, breathed softly, and thought of nothing but opening the doors.

Holding tightly to Quinn's hand, she felt his presence so close, it was almost as though they were one person. His powers flowed into her, and her own power entered him and then came back into her again. Merged together, their combined powers were directed toward the doors.

The doors didn't just open; they exploded into tiny bits that rained down into the exit tunnel.

"Wow," Archie cried. "That was awesome!"

Orus cawed and flapped his wings. *"You did it!"*

Quinn kept hold of Freya's hand. "Someone's been practicing."

"Freya, is there something you should tell us?" Loki asked with a raised eyebrow.

"It's nothing," Freya said quickly. She released Quinn's hand, suddenly feeling awkward, and stormed into the tunnel.

"Freya, calm down," Orus said. *"You should celebrate what you can do."*

What could she do? That was the question. Until now she'd been just a plain Valkyrie. Yet there was no denying that she possessed the power of the Vanir. Nothing in her life made any sense anymore.

She looked up at the raven on her shoulder. "Orus, stop. I don't want to think about this or anything else!"

Archie ran to catch up with her. "Gee, what is it? Something's wrong—and don't tell me it's just your wings. I know you too well. It's more than that."

Freya refused to look at him and kept moving. Archie was her best friend and knew her better than anyone else. She wanted nothing more than to share with him her grief over the loss of her sister and Brundi, and her confusion over her Vanir powers. Instead she said, "Please don't ask me now. I can't tell you; it hurts too much. Ask when this is over."

"Okay," he agreed reluctantly. "But you know, don't you, when you're ready to talk, I'm right here."

Freya stopped and gave him a sad smile. She nodded. "I know."

"Enough chatter," the troll called. "Come, come, we must move. It is a long walk to the Great City."

"We're not going to walk," Quinn said. He cast a spell that lifted them up and carried them swiftly through the tunnel. They were moving so fast, the torches posted on the wall flashed by them like twinkling candles.

They stopped when they reached the entrance to the Great City. "We're going to need a disguise, and I know just the thing." Quinn magicked clothes for them out of thin air.

"Dark Elves again?" Archie moaned as he held up a mask and cloak. "We're going to cook in all this clothing."

"It's better than being roasted alive by the fire giants," Quinn said. "Just imagine what that would be like."

His words stabbed through Freya's heart like a dagger as she thought of Skaga being killed by a fire giant. It took all her strength to fight back the tears that lingered painfully close to the surface.

"He couldn't have known about Skaga and didn't say that to hurt you," Loki whispered to her as the others were busy changing into their disguises. "You'll get through this, Freya. I know you will, and you'll be stronger for it."

Freya looked up into his dark eyes and for a moment saw beyond the troublemaker she had known her whole life. So this was the man Brundi had cared for and called family. As he winked at her and walked away, she wondered if this was the real Loki, and whether the mischief-maker of Asgard was just the mask he wore.

Kai pulled the Dark Elves' cloak over his white wings and took the lead going up the steps. He reached a closed trapdoor and drew his sword. "I can feel others are up there. Wait here. I'll call when it's clear."

Kai shoved open the trapdoor and disappeared through it. They heard the sound of a scuffle and then two loud grunts.

Kai appeared at the trapdoor again. "All clear—you can come up now."

Two Dark Elves lay in a heap. Kai reached for one elf

and called to Archie, "Grab the other one. We'll hide them behind this barrel."

Freya looked up at the high ceiling and enormous doors around them and realized that they were in the cellar of a fire giant pub. Just across from them was a stack of enormous kegs of mead. The stench of the strong drink in the intense heat was almost overwhelming and threatened to make Freya sick. From above came the loud sounds of drunken laughter and heavy dancing.

"What is it with secret tunnels and pubs?" Archie demanded, brushing off elf blood. "This is just like the one in Utgard."

"Pubs and inns are the best places to hide tunnels," Kai said. "Most of the patrons are too drunk to realize the tunnels are here."

Quinn looked up at the noise from the merrymaking. "It sounds like they're celebrating."

Freya nodded. "Yes, the fall of Asgard," she said darkly. "Dirian told me they'd broken through the defenses."

"Then we'd better hurry." Loki walked over to the giant-sized stairs leading up to the main floor of the pub. The first step rose high above his head. "It's going to take a giant to get you out of here safely without alerting the others to our presence."

"Why?" Archie asked. "We're dressed like Dark Elves. We can just walk out of here."

"You may look like an elf, but you stink like a dead human," Loki said sarcastically. "Don't you ever wash?"

Archie took a step closer. "I've had it with you, Loki. We didn't ask for your help and we don't need it. We were doing just fine without you!"

"Yes, I can see. You were doing so fine, Dirian cut off Freya's wings!"

"Loki, Archie, stop it," Kai said. "We're facing enough danger already. We don't need to hear you two bickering as well."

"Then tell the ghost to keep his mouth shut," Loki spat.

Archie opened his mouth to reply, but Freya stopped him. "Let it go, Archie. We don't have time for this."

"Exactly," Loki said. He turned to Quinn. "Can you work some of your magic to protect everyone from the heat and flame of a fire giant?"

Quinn nodded. "I could, why?"

"Because you're all going to need it if you're going to travel in my pocket." Loki stepped away from the group and started to shimmer. "You'd better start casting that spell now. It's about to get very hot in here. . . ."

Freya took Skuld's hand and escorted the blind Norn back a safe distance from Loki as he started to grow in size. His color changed to bright orange as his clothes started to burn.

"Quinn, hurry with that spell!" Orus cawed. *"My feathers are roasting!"*

"Everyone, grasp hands," Quinn cried.

While Loki turned into a full, flaming fire giant, a bubble of protection formed around the others, very similar to the one they had traveled in under the frozen sea. Inside the bubble, the air was refreshingly cool, even though just outside it was scorching.

Loki now stood high above them, looking very much like a fire giant version of Loki, with a bulbous nose and exaggerated features. His long dark hair was ablaze and his clothes were a raging inferno. His hands were huge, and each finger was on fire.

"I really hope he's on our side," Archie said.

Freya looked up at Loki. "He is. He just doesn't always know how to show it. But Loki isn't the one I'm worried about." Her eyes settled on the troll who was holding Kai's and Archie's hands. "You, I still don't trust. If you let go and break the spell, the moment we feel the first bit of heat, I swear I'll use my sword on you!"

"No—no—no, I am your guardian," the troll whined. "Maya told me to protect you and I am."

"Maya isn't here," Freya said.

"But I promised. And I always keep my promises."

Loki bent down and put his hand on the floor, inviting them into his palm.

"Remember," Quinn said. "No matter what happens, we must keep hold of each other to keep out the heat. Does everyone understand?"

They all agreed and walked as one onto Loki's hand. As he lifted them up to his enormous giant's face, his now golden eyes indicated his pocket.

Freya nodded and called, "Go ahead."

Being surprisingly gentle, Loki pulled open the breast pocket on his tunic and placed them inside. Before they disappeared into the burning depths, he brought a massive finger to his lips and hushed them.

"Say nothing, but hold tight to each other," Quinn whispered. "The spell will hold, but being this close to his burning clothes means it will get hot in here."

It was already getting hot and very uncomfortable for Freya as her burnt skin protested and wing stumps throbbed under the heat and tight confinement. Every nerve in her body screamed to be freed from the confines of the pocket. Freya closed her eyes and leaned her head back, forcing herself to remain calm. At her shoulder, Orus pressed in tight and lightly closed his beak on her earlobe, to let her know he was with her and understood better than anyone else what she was suffering. Beside her, Quinn squeezed her hand reassuringly.

They felt each step Loki made as he climbed the cellar steps and made it to the main floor of the pub. Loud music played, and people sang and danced.

As Fire Giant Loki moved through the crowds, he was being bumped and shoved by the other giants around him. The mood was boisterous as the fire giants celebrated the fall of Asgard. A large hand slapped Loki on the back, and they all jolted inside Loki's pocket.

"Everyone keep still," Freya hushed, and they each held their breath as the fire giant embraced Loki.

"Have you heard, my friend?" a voice boomed. "Asgard has fallen—soon it will be ours!"

"I have, friend," Loki's giant voice replied. "Odin will die and we will know a new and prosperous age!"

The fire giant laughed, and they could hear his breathing getting louder as he leaned in close to Loki's ear. "After Odin, we will conquer Utgard and the frost giants, once and for all. Fire giants will rule all the realms!"

Freya inhaled and looked at Kai and Archie. She had never imagined that the fire giants had such ambitious plans.

"We've gotta stop them," Archie whispered.

Giant Loki started to cough and pounded his chest, nearly crushing his pocket. His message to them was understood. *Keep quiet.*

Soon the music faded and they heard sales traders calling out offers of goods at reasonable prices—so they knew that Loki had stepped safely out of the pub and was now walking the crowded streets of the Great City.

Time stood still in Loki's pocket as he moved through the city streets and eventually out of town. When all they could hear was the crackling of burning clothes and Loki's heavy breathing, they knew they had made it.

Loki stopped. Light poured in from above as he opened his pocket. "Quinn, lift everyone out of there." His voice boomed like thunder.

The bubble of protection floated out of the pocket and drifted toward the ground. By the time they touched down, Loki had changed back to his normal form.

"I'm sure you heard," Loki said. "They're already celebrating Asgard's defeat."

"And they're planning to attack the frost giants next. If we don't stop this now, it really will be Ragnarök," Kai said.

"We have got to get moving before it's too late." Loki stepped up to the troll. "You, tell us, where's the tunnel Dirian is using to get to Asgard?"

The troll looked back to Freya.

"Speak," she ordered.

Within minutes Quinn had them in the sky and on their way to the tunnel. The sun was high overhead and mercilessly hot in the clear, cloudless sky. Freya's skin seared under its scorching intensity. If they somehow managed to survive this, she swore she would never return to this wretched realm again.

As day turned into early evening, there was only a slight respite from the heat. They passed over the flatlands and a large, steaming lake. In the distance rose a series of mountain ranges covered in red- and orange-leaved trees—their destination.

The troll directed them to touch down by a hidden cave. The entrance was almost completely obscured by giant leaves that grew on the thick vines draping down before it.

"Look," Quinn said as he walked to a small area of cleared vines. "They've been here. This vine has been recently cut. . . ."

Kai stepped forward. "With a hole just large enough for Dark Searchers to fit through. This is the right place."

"Then what are we waiting for?" Freya asked as she held Skuld's hand and led the blind Norn forward. Just before she passed under the cut leaves, Freya warned Skuld to keep her hands and head down. "Don't touch anything," she warned. "The leaves here will burn you worse than fire."

"I understand," Skuld said as she pressed closer to Freya. "You lead and I will follow."

Freya raised her sword and passed through the opening into the dark cave. Immediately the temperature dropped and she breathed a great sigh of relief.

"Ah," Archie sighed when he entered. "That's much better. Gee, remind me never to come back here."

"I will," Freya promised. She looked up at Orus. "And I want you to bite me if I ever suggest we do."

"Don't worry, I will."

"You never will come back here," Skuld said cryptically.

Freya looked down at Skuld and wondered what the Norn of the future meant. Was it that Freya would never return? Or was it that she had no future left in which to do it? They were about to head into a war zone. Would that spell the end for her?

"What have you seen?" she finally asked.

Skuld smiled, and there was a sense of mischief about her. "That's for me to know and you to find out."

"Freya, do you and Skuld want to stay here and talk and maybe have a picnic, or are you coming with us to Asgard to save Odin?" Loki challenged.

Freya smiled, grateful for his sarcasm. It gave her the first trace of normalcy she'd known in a long time. She held on to Skuld with one hand and raised her sword with the other. "Oh, don't you worry about me not coming. I've got a very special date with Dirian!"

34

"REMEMBER," VANIR-FREYJA WARNED MAYA AS THEY rose through the opening at the Temple of the Sun in Peru, "sing as loud and as strong as you can." Vanir-Freyja had taught Maya the song that would unleash her powers fully. They were now back in Midgard and ready to cast their spell over the giants.

The moment they emerged from the temple, Maya felt her new powers affecting the people who greeted them. Vanir-Freyja had had to lift them high up into the sky to keep the crowding soldiers from touching Maya and being reaped.

"When you finish the song, start over again. Just sing and fly—that's all you need to do. Your powers will do the rest. And when you reach the tunnel entrances that the giants are using to enter Midgard, sing even more. And when they are yours, command them to return to their realms. Make them love you, child, and they will do anything you say.

"If we fly at our top speed and circle the globe, we should finish quickly. Then I will meet you at the tunnel entrance to Asgard—the one in northern Canada. If I am not there, wait for me. Together we will return to Asgard and stop the giants."

Maya felt the weight of responsibility pressing down heavily on her. "I understand."

Vanir-Freyja hugged her tightly. "I am so proud of you. Asgard will sing of your bravery and Odin will bow to your beauty."

Maya shook her head. "I don't care about that. I just want this war over."

"Indeed," Vanir-Freyja said. "Go now, my mirror twin. Go and do as you were born to do."

Maya opened her wings and lifted off. She looked back and watched Vanir-Freyja fly in the opposite direction. They had been together only a short time, but already Maya felt the anxiety of separation from her powerful ancestor.

Rising high above Machu Picchu, Maya started across the Andes, keeping alert for any giants. It wasn't until she headed farther north that she felt a familiar prickling on her skin. Giants. Taking a deep breath, Maya started to sing. At first the words of the song were unfamiliar and awkward, as they were from an ancient language unknown to her. But then a strange wave of heat and a kind of calmness washed over her, and everything changed.

Like a dam bursting, powers that Maya had been unaware of were released. She understood the ancient words she was singing and felt the full power of the Vanir coursing through her veins.

This power fed her voice, and the song that sprang from her became louder and reached farther. She was calling to others, enchanting them—commanding them to love her and do as she bade.

By the time she reached the tunnel entrance from Utgard in the Florida Everglades, Maya was heartbroken. The area had been reduced to ruins. The main cities of Florida were gone, trampled under giants' feet and revealing a steady path of destruction leading north.

Circling over the tunnel entrance, Maya sang her heart out.

"Come to me. . . ." Her haunting notes were filled with yearning. The frost and fire giants halted their northern march. They turned and looked back at her longingly.

It was working! The giants were drawn toward her and were calling her.

Maya put even more of herself into the song. "Come to me . . . ," she sang. "Love me. Serve me. . . ." They reached up, trying to catch hold of her from the ground.

Drawing them back toward the tunnel, Maya changed

the song. As Vanir-Freyja had taught her, she kept up the melody but changed the lyrics.

"You have been used as weapons of war!" she sang to them. "But that is over now. Go home. Return to your families and tell the others in the tunnel that they will please me by leaving this realm forever. . . ." She sang of Vanir-Freyja's freedom, and how she had never been a prize for the kings.

One by one, as though in a trance, the giants started to descend into the tunnel.

Heartened by success, Maya kept singing. Following the path of devastation, she flew farther up the coast and called the giants home. She soon learned that she didn't have to escort them back to the tunnel. At her command, they went on their own.

Along the route, Maya saw signs of fighting. Defeated frost and fire giants lay on the ground, waiting to rise—but her heart sank when she saw the number of military vehicles and soldiers who lay among them. The humans had fought hard to defend their realm, but had failed. There would be no rising again for them, as they had been taken by the Angels of Death.

Farther up the coast, where human soldiers were still fighting the marching giants, Maya's song halted everyone. Giants and humans alike paused to listen. As she passed overhead, the humans called to her, while the giants turned around and followed her commands to go home.

After Maya reached as far north as she needed, she

changed direction and headed back toward California and the tunnel entrance out in the Pacific Ocean.

"Follow my words," she kept singing. "Return to your realms and make war no more. . . ."

Day turned into night, but still Maya kept singing. She crisscrossed the United States and ordered the giants home.

By dawn, Maya's voice was breaking and she was exhausted from the exertion, but she was overjoyed. A simple song was the most powerful weapon they had against the giants. She had to keep going. As she made her way north, Maya kept singing and watched the steady stream of creatures heading south. Male or female, frost or fire giant, dwarf, elf, or troll, it didn't matter. They all moved as though in a dream—reaching up to her, calling out to her, but always obeying her command to go back home.

As Maya crossed into Canada, her voice was weakening and she needed to rest. She glided down into the ruins of a small northern town. Touching down in the center of the street, she spied an abandoned diner that had somehow survived the giants.

Once her senses assured her that she was alone, Maya entered the diner. The place was eerily silent. Food and drinks lay abandoned on tables. Some meals were partially consumed while some lay untouched by those who had ordered them. Maya took a seat on one of the counter stools and reached for the abandoned food.

In all her life, she had never felt so exhausted. Her body was shaking, her wing muscles were sore, and her throat felt raw. But it was worth it. The giants were leaving Midgard.

Maya lay her head down for just a moment. Before long, she drifted into a deep, much-needed sleep.

"Maya . . ." Someone was shaking her arm. Groggily opening her eyes, she saw the face of her mother hovering above.

"Mother?"

Tears filled Eir's eyes as she pulled Maya into a tight embrace. "My beautiful girl, you've come back to us. We feared the worst!"

It had been a long time since she'd seen her mother cry. "I'm all right," she soothed.

"Maya, I don't understand," Eir said. "I heard you singing, and then felt compelled to find you. What's happened?"

As Maya looked at her mother, she sensed a deep grief coming from her. Her mother had been through a lot; she could feel it.

But before she could find out more, the door of the diner opened. For the first time in a long while, Maya smiled as the familiar faces of her sisters Gwyn and Kara appeared, followed by her uncle Vonni, who was being supported by Kris. Vonni's left leg was wrapped in a thick bandage and his arm and face were cut. It felt as if she hadn't seen them in a thousand years.

Behind them were Dark Searchers. When their eyes landed on Maya, they rushed toward her, trying to get as close as possible.

"Please, stop!" Maya cried, pushing the Dark Searchers away. They were pressing in so close, she couldn't breathe. "What you're feeling isn't real. It's a spell, that's all. Please, stand back."

The Dark Searchers immediately obeyed her command and took a step back. But their emotions didn't change. They loved her.

"How did you find me?" Maya asked, reaching back for her mother.

Vonni's eyes were glazed, staring at her. "You called to us and we had to obey."

"It's just a spell," Maya explained. "You must get past it. Asgard needs you."

Vonni shook his head. "What kind of spell? Why do I feel this way?"

Maya took her mother's hand and started to explain. "Our family are the direct descendants of Vanir-Freyja and Freyr. For generations they've used a spell to suppress the power in our family line. But for our generation, they didn't. We possess the powers of the Vanir. I inherited Vanir-Freyja's beauty and power to enchant. That's what you're all feeling. I cast a spell to send the giants home, but it's affecting you, too. Vanir-Freyja is here in Midgard and is doing the same thing in Europe and the rest of the world. It's working. The giants are leaving."

Vonni shook his head to clear it. "You're defeating the giants with magic?"

Maya nodded. "Vanir-Freyja warned me that using magic would have a price. I've enchanted everyone." She looked at all the Dark Searchers beginning to get close to her again. "That's what's happening to you. It's not real. You must fight past it."

"What of Freya? Have you seen her?" Her mother's voice shook.

Maya dropped her head. "Mother, Dirian has Freya. He's cut off her wings and is holding her in his keep in Muspelheim."

Her mother gasped, and the shock of hearing what had happened to Freya broke part of the spell over everyone.

"I—I swear I didn't want to leave her there," Maya implored, "but freeing Vanir-Freyja was the only way to end the war."

"You did right, my daughter. Freya knows that too. This war has cost us all dearly. . . ."

Once again, Maya was struck by her mother's suppressed grief. As she pressed further with her senses, she felt something terrible. Maya's eyes shot up to her sisters. "Gwyn, Kara, where's Skaga?"

Tears rimmed her sisters' eyes. "A fire giant killed her and—and . . . she didn't rise again," Gwyn struggled to say.

Maya inhaled sharply and shook her head. "No . . ."

"Your grandmother is gone too," Vonni added with a pain that ran deep. "The frost giants attacked the mountain in Colorado. I've been told Mims and the baby are safe, but the military has moved them. . . ." His voice broke. "I know what happened to my Sarah. Eir says because you and Mims reaped her, she is still with Mims, but I don't know where they've been taken."

"We'll find them," Kris rasped with his broken voice. "It will be a grave mistake if the humans try to keep them from us."

Maya couldn't breathe. So much pain and loss, all because of Dirian. She rose from her stool and staggered, finally over-whelmed. Two Dark Searchers darted forward to support her. But their touch only added to Maya's distress.

"No, I'm all right." She pulled away and looked at the large gathering of Dark Searchers and her family. "This isn't the time for our tears. Come, we must go."

"Where?" her mother asked.

"Vanir-Freyja told me to meet her at the tunnel the giants are using. We're going home to declare war on the giants in Asgard!"

35

QUINN'S HEALING POTION WORE OFF SOMEWHERE IN the tunnel between Muspelheim and Asgard. But Freya found the pain wasn't as bad as it had been. Her burns were healing, and her bones felt stronger. It was her wing stumps that still throbbed and stung. She wondered if that pain would ever end.

But with the clearing of her head, her senses returned. She could feel Yggdrasil all around them as they moved within its root. But something was wrong—the vibrations from the tree had changed and were becoming sporadic. The green lichen that grew on it was turning pale and its glow was fading. The Cosmic World Tree was in distress.

"How much farther?" she asked the troll.

"Not far now. We will be there soon."

"I miss Bifröst," Archie grumbled from beside her. "I don't ever want to travel through a tunnel or root again!"

"Me too," Freya agreed.

"I've heard Bifröst is beautiful and filled with the colors of the rainbow," Quinn said.

"It is," Freya agreed. "That's why they call it the Rainbow Bridge. If we manage to survive this, I'll take you there."

"Well, aren't you just a little ray of sunshine," Loki teased. "What do you mean, 'If we survive this'? Of course we will. Soon everything will get back to normal."

When Freya looked at him, he winked at her. They both knew things could never return to normal. But she appreciated him saying it. Freya hated to admit it, but she liked this new version of Loki.

"We are here," the troll called excitedly.

As Quinn slowed them down, Freya felt the presence of other Valkyries, citizens of Asgard, and Light Elves, and was filled with hope. But her heart sank when she also picked up on a large number of frost and fire giants.

"It's true," she said. "The giants have broken through the defenses. I can feel them here. I also feel Dark Elves and more dwarfs and . . ."

"And Dirian," Kai finished. "I feel him too. He and all his Dark Searchers are here."

"Then what are we waiting for, a written invitation?" Archie said. "C'mon, let's go kick some Dark Searcher butt!"

"Hear, hear!" Loki cheered as he led them forward.

They climbed up the incline that led into Asgard and exited through the base of a large, fallen ash tree. Freya stood in stunned silence as her eyes took in the sight of her home realm. They were in the Asgard forest, just outside the city. Before them, the wall that surrounded the city had been partially knocked down. In places it was gone completely.

Beyond the wall, plumes of smoke rose in the air above the many buildings. In the distance, she spied the damaged spires of Valhalla. The flags were down and smoke billowed from its windows. She was sickened to realize that the Great Heavenly Hall was burning.

"They breached the walls," Orus cawed, as stunned as she was. *"The walls have stood for thousands of years and now they've fallen. Asgard is burning!"*

"Look at it," Archie said in shock. "How long have the giants been here?"

"Too long," Freya cried. "C'mon, let's get them!"

Forgetting herself, Freya took three long strides and leaped into the air.

"Freya, stop!" Orus cried. *"You can't fly!"*

Just before she hit the ground, Freya stopped and floated in midair for a moment, before being lowered to the ground by Quinn. "You must remember your wings are gone."

Freya's spirit crashed to the ground, even if her body didn't. The horror of her new life cut as badly as Dirian's blade. She was grounded and felt helpless. "I can't believe I just did that," she muttered softly.

Skuld reached for Freya. "It is understandable considering the circumstances. It will take time for you to adjust."

"Time we just don't have," Kai said. He opened his wings and drew his black swords. "Quinn, can you bring the others with you? I'm going ahead to find Dirian."

"No, Kai. Wait for us!" Freya called. But he was already in the air, winging his way toward Valhalla.

"Kai's not going to be the only hero here." Loki started to shimmer and grow. "I'm going to fight fire with fire." Soon his staff and clothing started to burn as he turned back into a fire giant. Loki bent down and he smiled at Freya. "See you on the other side!"

As Loki started to run toward the destroyed wall around Asgard, Quinn lifted them in the air and carried them toward what was left of the walled city.

"Freya, where's Dirian?" Quinn called.

Freya cast out her senses until she started to shake. She felt Dirian's evil presence like a foul touch on her burnt skin. "He's that way." She pointed. "Moving toward Valhalla from the opposite side."

When they passed over the damaged outer wall and reached the outskirts of the city, they encountered the worst of the fighting. The reaped human warriors from Valhalla were fighting side by side with Light Elves and faeries as they took on renegade dwarfs and Dark Elves.

"We trained for this at Valhalla"—Archie gazed around himself in awe—"but I never imagined it could happen. I hope Crixus is okay. He's the toughest warrior in Valhalla—and crucial to our fight."

Freya tried to take it all in but couldn't. Her home realm, everything she'd known, was being destroyed.

The sounds of battle were coming from every direction. Everywhere they looked, they saw Asgardians and friends from other realms fighting to defend Odin.

"Gee, look up there," Archie cried.

Freya followed his gaze and saw a cluster of Valkyries taking on a frost giant. Their swords flashed as they went after the giant's head. Despite the enormous size difference, working together, the Valkyries quickly defeated the giant and he fell to the ground with an impact that rattled buildings. Not stopping to rest or celebrate, they flew like a squadron toward the next giant.

The sounds of thunder and lightning rose in the air. For a moment Freya hoped it was Thor, back from Earth, but as she listened, she could tell the sounds were different. "That's Odin!" she shouted. "He's still alive!"

Freya strained her senses to feel Odin. "Quinn, forget Dirian. Head in that direction as fast as you can. Odin's in trouble—we must protect him!"

While they flew over the battleground that had once

been Asgard, Freya caught hold of Skuld's hand and placed it in Archie's. "Stay close to Archie," she said. "This is going to get very dangerous. and I don't want you hurt."

"It is you I worry about," Skuld said. "You have so much rage in you; it might make you reckless."

"I'll be careful." Freya looked at Archie. "You have your sword. Be ready to use it. Skuld must be protected until we can get her back to her sisters."

Archie nodded. "Don't worry about me—Crixus trained me well. You just focus on protecting Odin."

"And I will protect you," the troll added.

Freya had almost forgotten about the troll. She fought to hide her revulsion of him as they approached the partially destroyed Valhalla. She gazed down to the large training field surrounding it. Not too long ago, that field had hosted the Ten Realms Challenge, where members of the realms competed against each other in friendly contests. Now some of those same participants were back, fighting against each other for real.

"It's a nightmare," Orus cawed mournfully. *"How can we hope to beat them?"*

"We don't have any choice," Freya said grimly.

Thousands of human warriors were gathered on the field, battling against the invaders. As they moved closer, Freya was overwhelmed by the number of fighters on Dirian's side. Apart from the giants, Dark Elves, dwarfs, and trolls, there were also faeries, Dark Demons, and creatures she'd never seen before that must have been dredged up from the deepest depths of the darkest realms.

Large spiders, snakes, and serpents fought alongside the giants. Freya's eyes landed on Sif among the throng. Thor's wife held two swords and fought with bravery and expertise as she stood back-to-back with another Asgard fighter. Freya also spotted Heimdall, the bulky Guardian of Bifröst, fighting against a frost giant. Though the giant was bigger, he was felled by Heimdall's might.

Freya took it all in, realizing that this fight was bigger than just Dirian's bid to dethrone Odin. They had to stop it from becoming Ragnarök—or none of the realms would survive.

As they scanned the immense battlefield and listened to the sounds of roaring voices and clashing swords, Freya's eyes landed on a group of Dark Demons, Dark Elves, and Searchers moving in on a Valkyrie and one other fighter she couldn't quite make out. Despite her fighting skills, the Valkyrie was taken down swiftly by demon magic. When she hit the ground, the dwarfs pounced on her, tearing out her feathers and breaking her bones.

The other figure tried his best to defend himself against the attackers. His back was to her, and Freya saw him for only a flash before he was swamped by the invaders. But she'd seen enough. The flash of a gold eye patch, blazing red hair, and familiar armor, now dented and covered in the many shades of elf, dwarf, troll, and giants' blood, made it clear who it was.

"Odin!" Freya cried.

"Where?" Archie asked. "I don't see him."

"Down there!" Freya pointed. "Near that fallen Valkyrie. They've overwhelmed him and somehow captured his staff. Without Gungnir, he doesn't stand a chance!"

"Freya, give me your hand!" Quinn cried as he reached for her.

Using their combined powers they blasted away Odin's attackers and lifted the leader of Asgard off the ground. A large serpent launched itself into the air after him—as it went for Odin's foot, Freya reached down and cut off its head with her sword.

"Freya!" Odin roared when he saw his rescuers. "What are you doing here?" His shock grew more intense when he saw Skuld. "What's happening?"

"Great Odin," Freya cried. "We're here to protect you. Dirian is behind all of this. He's back in Asgard and coming for you. He plans to kill you and take your throne."

"He'll never take the throne!" Odin boomed. "Take me into Valhalla. I will face him there!"

"No, sir, you can't," Archie cried. "It's too dangerous. The giants will capture you in there. We must take you away from the danger."

"Abandon the battle?" Odin cried furiously. "Never! I am more than the leader of Asgard—I am its protector! If it falls, I fall with it. Do as I command and get me inside Valhalla—now!"

Freya looked at Quinn. "We'll take him into the banquet hall. It's in the very center of Valhalla and looks like it hasn't been damaged."

Quinn carried them over the raging battle secured in the magical bubble. Swords, spears, and weapons flew at them from below but were deflected away. When the group approached a large, gaping hole in the side of Valhalla, they had a close-up view of what the giants had done to the Heavenly Hall. The entire front had been torn open by giant hands. Towers lay in rubble on the ground, and many of the doors had been ripped off.

Most of the roof had been burned away, as well as all the warriors' sleeping quarters. Acrid smoke billowed out of the windows and holes from the parts of Valhalla still on fire.

As they drifted down to the ground, Freya was left speechless.

"In here," Odin commanded. His one blue eye focused on Freya. "If you really want to redeem yourself, Valkyrie, follow me." Just as he was about to move, Odin frowned. He caught Freya by the shoulder and roughly turned her around.

"Who took your wings?"

"Dirian," Freya said. "I was a prisoner at his keep."

"He held me and Vanir-Freyja there as well," Skuld added.

Odin was stunned by the news. "Where is this new keep?"

"In Muspelheim," Orus cawed.

Freya continued. "He's been forcing Skuld to end the futures of fallen warriors and using Vanir-Freyja as a prize for the giant kings who served him."

Skuld nodded. "He had me cross out your name, Odin, but I restore you now. He cannot keep you dead."

For the first time in her life, Freya watched Odin bow deeply. "Thank you, Skuld."

"It is not me you must thank. Freya, Archie, Quinn, and many others have served and sacrificed for you without you knowing it. They are the ones deserving of your thanks."

Odin was looking at Freya as if seeing her for the first time. His one remaining eye lost its hardness. "Where is Vanir-Freyja now?"

"In Midgard," Freya answered. "Maya and a Vanir called Skye rescued her from the keep. They took her to Midgard for safety."

Odin took in the information but gave nothing away. He turned and started to climb over the rubble outside Valhalla.

"Come," he commanded. "It's time we faced Dirian!"

36

THEY FOLLOWED ODIN THROUGH THE RUBBLE.

"*Valhalla is gone,*" Orus moaned.

"It can be restored," Odin said.

They wound their way deeper inside and reached the banquet hall. Tables were overturned and chairs toppled, but the walls and high ceiling were intact. On the dais, Odin's throne remained standing.

"Up there," Odin said. "If Dirian wants my throne, he's going to have to take it from me!"

They followed Odin up onto the dais and took protective positions on either side of his throne. The sounds of the battle raging outside echoed through the ruins of Valhalla.

No one spoke. They all knew there was nothing left to say. This was it, the final confrontation. Soon they would have to fight Dirian and his Dark Searchers for ultimate control of the realms.

"My sons, Thor and Balder, are dead . . . ," Odin said softly, breaking the silence.

"Dead? When? How?" Freya cried.

"They went to Utgard to learn of the giants' plans. They were killed at the keep just before the war started."

"Wait," Freya said, shaking her head. "They weren't at the keep at the start of the war. They were with us in Midgard."

Odin's head turned sharply to her. "What are you telling me? Speak!"

"Thor and Balder weren't killed at the keep. They and a few loyal Dark Searchers followed us to Brundi's farm."

"My sons are alive?"

Freya nodded. "The last time I saw them, they were planning to fight the giants in Midgard. I promise you, they were very much alive."

"And they still are," Skuld added.

Odin roared in joy and jumped to his feet. He scooped up Freya in his massive arms and nearly squeezed the life out of her. Freya was too stunned to cry out that he was crushing her wing stumps and fragile ribs.

"I was told they were no more," Odin said in disbelief, and put Freya down.

"I assure you, they are unharmed," Skuld said. "They still have a future. I can see them in it."

"I don't understand. What were they doing in Midgard?"

Freya dropped her head. "They were coming after me and my twin brother, Kai. We were . . ." She stopped as she felt as if her stomach had been punched. It was Kai. Her brother was in pain and struggling. Then Freya felt something else pull at her. She forced herself to block Kai's pain for the moment and focus. She stepped down from the dais and raised her sword. "Dirian and his Dark Searchers are approaching."

Among everything she felt, Freya also sensed Odin's renewed energy. Hearing that his sons were alive put the fight back in him. "Let him come. I'm ready for him," he roared.

Then Odin held his hand out to Quinn. "Vanir, give me a sword, a large one."

Quinn nodded and cast a spell to create a large broadsword that looked almost too heavy to lift. Odin picked it up as though it weighed nothing and nodded his head. "Very good, thank you."

Kai staggered into the banquet hall, his white wings covered in blood. He had a deep wound on his side, and he was limping from another gash to his upper thigh.

In moments Freya was by his side. "He's hurt," she called to Quinn. "Please! We need more of your pain potion!"

"I'm all right," Kai said. He lifted his head to see Odin standing before his throne. He pulled himself up with Freya and Archie's help.

"Odin." Kai struggled to bow before him. "I am at your service. My swords are yours."

Odin's one eye moved from Freya to Kai and back again. "The twins are united."

Freya nodded. "And we'll never be parted again."

"Agreed," Odin said.

Quinn helped Kai drink the potion, but there was little time to pause.

"ODIN!" a broken voice rasped.

Freya turned and watched Dirian enter the hall with a troop of at least ten Dark Searchers. They were followed by a stream of Dark Elves, dwarfs, and demons. She felt a large number of giants encircling Valhalla on the outside, poised to strike at anyone who tried to flee.

They were trapped.

Dirian came closer and focused on Freya. "You? How? I left you chained and broken in my keep."

"You can't stop me from protecting my realm or my leader!" Freya spat.

Dirian's visored head nodded. "It seems I made a mistake in letting you live. I should have taken your head, not your wings. I won't make that mistake again."

The troll squealed and ran at Dirian. "You won't hurt Freya!"

The Dark Searcher cut him down with a single blow. "You have trolls fighting your battles now?"

Freya looked at the troll that had sacrificed himself for her. His death fed her anger. She handed Kai over to Archie and raised her golden sword. "It's over, Dirian."

Dirian slowly drew his two swords. "Over? Not quite— Odin is still alive. You know, Freya, I may actually miss your sense of humor. But not enough to let you live!" He ran at her with murder in his heart.

Freya tossed Orus into the air and released her own rage to meet him halfway across the floor. Unlike their last fight, she felt stronger, and this time, there was more at stake. Odin had to be protected at all costs.

Freya charged into his attack, her sword flashing. Her Vanir power coursed through her veins as she defended against Dirian's every blow.

As she fought, Freya became aware of the others fighting around her in the banquet hall. Odin was taking on all the Dark Searchers at once, while Quinn and Kai fought against demons and elves. Archie remained with Skuld, fighting two Dark Elves who were trying to reach the ancient Norn.

"*Freya, be careful!*" Orus cawed as he flew at Dirian to block his vision.

This move had worked at the Ten Realms Challenge, but now the Dark Searcher was ready for him. As Orus dived a second time, Dirian's blade flashed, cutting Orus out of the air.

The raven fell to the floor.

"Orus, no!" Freya howled.

"Your raven is dead," Dirian rasped. "Soon you will follow him!" His swords flashed against her even faster. One cut sliced across her abdomen, but Freya kept fighting through her mounting pain.

With grief and fury driving her on, Freya matched Dirian move for move as they fought all through the banquet hall. Seizing an opening, she thrust forward. Her sword hit its mark and cut into his chest. She immediately followed with another slice across one of his arms.

As Freya went for a third, lethal strike, Dirian lunged forward and caught her in his arms. They encircled her and started to squeeze. "This ends now," he rasped.

Freya felt as if she were caught in a dragon's mouth as Dirian's arms gripped her, tighter and tighter. She couldn't move, couldn't breathe, and bones snapped as he slowly crushed her. Freya's head felt as if it were going to explode under the pressure, but still Dirian squeezed tighter.

Just as she felt herself slipping away, Dirian whispered into her ear, "No—not yet, little Valkyrie. I won't free you until you've witnessed my victory! Watch, Freya. Watch your beloved Odin die!"

He released her, and Freya collapsed to the floor. Gasping for air, her ribs broken again, it took all of Freya's strength to lift her head and see the deadly Dark Searcher advancing on Odin.

The leader of Asgard was displaying every fighting skill

he possessed against the Dark Searchers. He was able to duck and dive against the blades that cut at him, while simultaneously cutting down Searchers one by one. When most of the Searchers were defeated, the Dark Elves and demons moved in, casting their magic. The sword was ripped from Odin's grasp, and a blow from one of the remaining Dark Searchers knocked him to the floor. Freya focused on Odin until she felt her brother fall in battle at the blades of two Dark Searchers. She couldn't imagine a pain worse than losing Skaga—until now. Kai was more than her brother. He was her twin, a living extension of her. As Kai died, a big part of Freya died with him.

Across the hall, Dirian stood triumphantly over the restrained Odin, his two swords hovering above him and poised to strike. "You have lost, Odin of Asgard," Dirian rasped. "I, Dirian of Utgard, claim the throne and all the realms, in the name of the Dark Searchers!"

Freya raised her head as a blind rage overwhelmed her. She climbed to her feet and charged at Dirian with every ounce of energy she had left.

Cutting her way through the Dark Elves and demons, Freya dashed under Dirian's blades as they started to move. She pushed Odin behind her and turned to face the Dark Searcher. As her golden sword thrust up and into Dirian's heart, his blades cut down into her.

"Gee!" Archie howled.

Freya felt no pain. There was nothing.

With their swords interlocked, Freya and Dirian fell as one. They hit the floor together and lay sprawled beside each other.

As the world around her started to fade, Freya felt Dirian go first. The enemy she had made so long ago and had fought so hard, was finally dead.

Freya was barely aware of the fighting going on around her. First she heard gunfire, which made no sense to her fading mind, as there were no human weapons in Asgard. After that, she was sure she heard the boom of Thor's hammer.

Just as her mother reached her side and called her name, she was swallowed into oblivion.

37

FREYA WAS DRAWN SLOWLY BACK TO CONSCIOUSNESS, only to taste a bitter liquid at her lips that drove her back into sleep. This happened many times before she was allowed to rise to the surface for a moment.

There was pressure on her chest. Opening her eyes, she saw Orus lying on her. Her raven was covered in bandages and unconscious—but his faint breaths told her that he was alive.

She looked up to see that she was lying in a tent. Loki was standing beside her bed. With his arms crossed casually over his chest, he was grinning at her. "Welcome back."

Freya's lips were dry and her throat too parched to speak.

"Don't try to talk." Loki knelt beside her and brought a cup of cool water to her lips. "What a journey we've been on, you and me."

"Wha—what happened?"

"We won," he said, gently brushing hair back from her face. "If you tell anyone I said this, I'll deny it. But I want you to know, I'm proud of you."

He rose. "Now, get back to sleep and heal—it's no fun picking on you when you're down." Loki grinned, shimmered into a bumblebee, and buzzed his way out of the tent.

Freya tried to follow him with her eyes, but they were too heavy to keep open. She surrendered to the draw of sleep.

It was two more days before Freya woke and stayed awake. This time Archie and Quinn were at her side.

"Orus, you're alive . . ." Her feathered friend was perched on Archie's shoulder, looking a little rough, but very much alive.

The raven cawed and flew to sit on Freya's stomach. *"We both are!"*

"Freya, it's time to get up. You mustn't put pressure on your wings any longer; they need to be exercised."

Freya followed the voice and saw Maya on the other side of her bed. There was a man beside her who looked like an older version of Kai or even Vonni—with dark, neatly styled hair and eyes of blazing sapphire blue. His features were finely sculptured, and he had a dimple in his chin. If it were possible, he was even more handsome than her uncles.

"Maya, my wings are gone. Dirian cut them off."

"Gee, that's not Maya." Archie started to grin. "It's Vanir-Freyja and her twin brother, Freyr. They're your family. They saved your wings and were able to reattach them."

Freya heard the words, but they made no sense. Vanir-Freyja? But she looked exactly like Maya! And what had Archie said about her wings?

Now that she thought about it, she became aware of the discomfort she always felt when she slept on her wings too long. "Wings?" she cried.

"Freya, get off your wings," Orus cawed as he limped up to her shoulder. *"You don't want to break them when you've only just gotten them back."*

Freya was helped to her feet by Archie and Quinn. She felt weak and dizzy as she stood for the first time in days. She smiled as she felt the familiar weight of the wings on her back. She opened them and fluttered them lightly. "H-how?"

Vanir-Freyja smiled and walked around the bed to embrace her. "Quinnarious didn't destroy them in Muspelheim. He hid them and brought them back to us. Our Vanir magic restored them to you."

Freya could hardly believe what she was hearing, but the black wings on her back proved it true. She looked at Quinn. "You did?"

Quinn grinned. "Course I did. I wasn't about to destroy a perfectly good set of wings. Yes, the feathers were a bit burnt, but otherwise they were beautiful—just like you."

Lost for words, Freya threw her arms around Quinn and held him tightly. "Thank you!" she wept into his long brown hair.

"Come, my little Freya." Her uncle Freyr gestured to her. "There are a lot of people outside waiting for you."

It was only then that Freya looked around and saw she was the only patient in the private healing tent. "The war?" she quickly asked.

"It's over," Archie said. "Maya and Vanir-Freyja enchanted the giants and sent them home. You killed Dirian." He paused and frowned at her. "But you and I are going to talk about that stunt you pulled with him. I've never been so scared in all my life!"

"In all your death, you mean," Quinn teased.

Archie punched Quinn and chuckled. "All my death . . ."

"What happened to Dirian?"

"You mean after you killed him?" Archie asked. "Skuld wrote down his name and crossed a big line through it. She really enjoyed doing that."

Freya was almost too frightened to ask. "And Kai? Is he all right? Why isn't he here?"

Vanir-Freyja nodded. "Like you, he rose again. He's been with Odin and Thor, giving his full report. He'll be here shortly."

Freya felt as if she were asleep, in the most wonderful dream. Her brother was alive, her wings were back, and Dirian was dead. If it was a dream, she didn't want to wake up.

Her great-uncle Freyr smiled. "No, little Freya, it's no dream," he said, reading her thoughts. "You're very much awake."

"C'mon, Gee," Archie said, taking his rightful place at her side. "Let's not keep everyone waiting."

With Archie supporting her on one side, and holding tightly to Quinn's hand on the other, Freya walked toward the entrance of the tent. Once she was outside, her eyes flew open and she couldn't take it all in. Everyone was there, including Vonni and Sarah—bearing the mark of Mims on her hand. Then there was Mims with Skaga's raven nestled on her shoulder. She was grinning and holding her baby brother. Beside them stood Skye and her team of human soldiers from the tunnel. . . . Her senses told her they were alive, but not human anymore.

Archie started to laugh. "You should see your face! Breathe, Gee," he teased. "Keep breathing."

Her mother was standing with Freya's surviving sisters. When Freya's eyes landed on Maya, she welled up and ran to her.

"I felt you in the keep," Freya said, holding her tightly. "Thank you for saving Vanir-Freyja!"

Maya's eyes misted. "I didn't want to leave you. . . . It was the hardest thing I've ever done."

"I know," Freya said, as they laughed and cried together. "You did right."

As the two sisters embraced, their ravens, Orus and Grul, started to argue about who had the worst wounds and who had suffered the greatest.

"*Yes, well, a frost giant broke my back,*" Grul said. "*I was completely paralyzed! I nearly died!*"

"*You call that suffering?*" Orus cried. "*I did die. Dirian cut me in two! The healer almost failed putting me together again!*"

"*Too bad she didn't keep your beak shut. . . .*"

Freya looked around at the gathering of those she cared for most and was completely overwhelmed. She didn't know who to hold or talk to next.

Suddenly a hush fell over the gathering and everyone parted. Kai, looking pale but very much alive, was walking toward them with Odin and his wife, Frigg, and Thor and Balder. Odin was out of his armor and displaying his new battle scars proudly.

"Freya," Odin said informally. "We have much to discuss, but for today I want only to say thank you—thank you for saving Asgard."

"I—I," Freya stuttered. "I didn't save Asgard. It was you."

Odin's eye darkened. "Even now you wish to argue with me?"

"No! I'm sorry, Great Odin," Freya rushed to say.

Odin held the stern look for a moment longer but then burst into laughter. "You will never change," he said, shaking his head.

"And I hope she never does." Frigg smiled. "We have a gift for you. It is our way of thanking you for everything you've done." She stood back and motioned for someone to come forward.

Freya recognized the dark hair, blazing eyes, and muscular build of the strongest warrior in Valhalla. It was Archie's gladiator trainer, Crixus. He walked forward and nodded to her.

Frigg said formally, "Normally, this is forbidden, but today we will make an exception. Freya, daughter of Eir, twin sister to Kai, I would like you to meet your father, Crixus of Midgard."

Freya inhaled sharply. Her eyes flashed over to her mother, who was smiling and nodded her head. Kai was also nodding.

"Gee," Archie breathed. "Crixus is your dad? That's awesome. . . ."

For so long Freya had yearned to know who her father was. Now that he was standing before her, she didn't know what to say or do.

Crixus opened his arms. "Daughter . . ."

Freya ran into his arms.

"How I have longed to tell you it was me," he whispered into her ear. "All these years, watching you grow into a powerful, accomplished Valkyrie and I was forbidden to say anything or claim you as mine. All I could do was train your best friend and hope that he would help you when I couldn't. I am so proud of you. . . ."

"Father . . . ?" Freya whispered.

Crixus nodded and held her tighter.

With her arms around her father, and all her family about her, Freya finally felt whole.

EPILOGUE

THE FIELDS OUTSIDE OF VALHALLA WERE ONCE AGAIN decorated with colorful banners, as all Asgard welcomed the end of the war. Though the Great Heavenly Hall lay in ruins, plans were already under way for its restoration.

Invitations were sent to Vanaheim, and many of the Vanir traveled to Asgard via the newly opened Bifröst to join in the celebrations and renewed union of the two realms.

Urd and Verdandi arrived, and for the first time in recorded history, the normally somber Norns laughed and danced as they were reunited with Skuld.

Over the following days, Freya and Orus stayed close to their family. Vonni, Sarah, Mims, and the baby moved into their large home in Asgard, while Vanir-Freyja and Freyr also took their place among the family. Plans were being set for

Maya to spend time away with her great-great-grandmother, to learn to use and control her newly released powers.

"Gee," Archie called to her. Skye and Quinn were with him with big grins on their faces. "We need you to come with us for a minute. Someone needs to speak with you urgently."

"Who?"

"You'll see," Skye said as she put her arm around Archie and lifted him lightly into the air. Her butterfly wings had recovered from their burns and fluttered lightly in the blazing blue sky.

"This way," Quinn said.

Freya looked at Orus on her shoulder and shrugged before launching into the air behind them to fly to Valhalla. When they landed, they crossed over the rubble and into the Great Heavenly Hall.

They led her to the banquet hall. Just outside it, Archie nodded. "In there."

"What's in there?" Freya asked.

"You'll see."

"Why don't you guys come in with me?"

Quinn grinned but shook his head. "Because it's for you."

"*That's right,*" Orus said as he flew off her shoulder and landed on Archie's. "*We'll be right here.*"

Freya frowned suspiciously at the raven. "What are you up to?"

"*Me?*" Orus cawed. "*Why do you always blame me?*"

"Because it's usually you." She laughed and stroked his smooth black feathers.

Then Freya turned and entered the banquet hall alone, curious as to what awaited her.

"Azrael!" she cried.

The Angel of Death threw his arms around her and wrapped her in his stunning white wings. "I'm so sorry I couldn't help you in Muspelheim. I heard you calling for me, but I couldn't come. It tore at me to know what Dirian did to you."

Freya held him tightly. "It's all right."

"No, it's not. I promised I would always help. But Muspelheim is the only realm we angels can't survive in. To know that you were there and suffering . . ."

"Azrael, I understand. I really do," Freya said. "I'm just so glad you're alive. When I didn't see you again, I feared the worst."

"Never fear for me. I will always come for you. . . ." He grinned and playfully tweaked her nose. "Unless it's in Muspelheim again."

Freya shook her head. "I have no plans to go back there."

"Good." Azrael's face became somber. "Freya, with all you've endured and lost, I can't bear to see you grieving." The Angel of Death waved his arm in the air and a beam of light appeared. Freya squinted until she could make out two figures emerging from the center of the beam. Dressed in the same brilliant white as Azrael, Skaga and Brundi appeared.

"Skaga!" Freya cried.

The two sisters greeted each other noisily. When Skaga released Freya, Brundi bundled her into her arms.

"I don't understand. How is this possible?"

Azrael started to chuckle. "Skuld isn't the only one with powers over people's destiny. When Skaga and Brundi were killed, there was no returning them to their lives as Valkyries. But there was nothing to say that I couldn't claim them for my angels."

Skaga started to laugh and opened her angel's robes. "Can you believe it? Look, they let me keep my Valkyrie armor!"

Freya laughed with her sister. "A Valkyrie Angel of Death . . . only you, Skaga, only you."

Skaga held on to Freya's hands. "Heofon is so beautiful. I hope you can come and see it."

"I hope so too," Brundi said. She smiled and opened her new white wings. "Look at this. I can finally fly again." She looked up at her raven. "And did you see who came with me?"

"Pym!" Freya cried, reaching to stroke her grandmother's raven. "I'm so glad to see you again."

"*And I you, child,*" Pym said.

Freya looked at Azrael. "Can I tell everyone? Mother and Vonni are really suffering."

He nodded. "Of course. I'm sorry we can't stay for the

celebrations. Earth still needs us. It took quite a pounding in the war, and people are suffering. But when our work is finished, we'll have a proper reunion."

Azrael gave Freya a final smile and then disappeared with her sister and grandmother.

Freya stood watching the empty place where her sister and grandmother had been standing. She was overwhelmed. So much had changed in her life. Loved ones lost and new friends found. Would anything be the same again? Did she want it to be the same?

Probably not. After a few minutes, Quinn and Orus entered the banquet hall. Quinn used his dragonfly wings to fly to her. "Are you all right?"

Freya nodded. "I am now." She looked past him. "Where are Archie and Skye?"

Quinn grinned. "Archie is giving Skye a personal tour of Asgard. Those two really like each other."

Freya nodded. "Archie and I went shopping earlier. He bought a necklace to give to her."

"*Archie has got it bad for her,*" Orus said.

Quinn tilted his head to the side. "What do you think about that? I mean, Archie bears your mark. He should be with you, shouldn't he?"

"No, it's not like that. Archie is my best friend, and nothing can ever change that. But he's free to be with whomever he wants."

"Just like you?" Quinn asked.

"Exactly."

Quinn stood beside her and smiled. It lit up his whole face and started Freya's heart racing. With so much happening, she hadn't allowed herself to feel anything. But now that the war was over and they were here alone, she realized how much she cared for him.

"Want to go back to the party?" Quinn asked.

"In a minute," Freya said. She lifted herself up on tiptoes and gave Quinn a tender kiss. She smiled shyly and knew that this was just the beginning.

"*Freya,*" Orus cawed. "*What is your mother going to say about that?*"

As Quinn took her hand, Freya looked up at the raven on her shoulder and stroked his smooth feathers. "Orus, I think she'll be fine." Her eyes trailed over to Quinn. "We'll all be fine now."

A GUIDE TO THIS WORLD

Norse mythology is old. It's not just old; it's really, really old! It's also known as Scandinavian mythology and was created, retold, and loved by the Vikings. The Vikings, or Norsemen, settled most of Northern Europe and came mainly from Denmark, Norway, Sweden, Iceland, the Faroe Islands, and Greenland.

As you get to know the Norse myths, you might notice there are some similarities to the ancient Greek myths (including flying horses—but not my sweet Pegasus). Here's a simple comparison.

In Greek mythology, you have the Olympians and the Titans. The "younger" Olympians, in fact, came from the "older" Titans, and yet, there was a war between them and the Olympians won.

In Norse mythology, you have the Aesir and the Vanir. The "younger" Aesir came from the "older" Vanir, and yes, there was a war! But the difference is, in Norse mythology, neither side won—they called a truce.

Here's a big difference. In Greek myths, you have the place called Olympus. But in Norse myths, there are in fact nine worlds, or "realms" as they are sometimes called. In each of these realms, you have some really weird and wonderful creatures. And you know what? *We* are part of those nine realms. We're in the middle bit. And instead of Earth, our world is called Midgard.

Now, some of you may think you don't know Norse mythology at all. You do, but what you have learned may not be correct.

What's the biggest mistake I hear all the time? Okay, here is a really big one. I mean *big*. He's huge. He's green and has a bad temper. Yes, I'm talking about the Hulk. He is *not* part of Norse mythology. Neither are Iron Man, Hawkeye, Black Widow, nor many of the other characters from the Avengers movies. But no matter how many schools I visit, the moment I mention Thor or Loki, the students immediately think that the Hulk and the other characters are part of Norse mythology.

Trust me, they're not.

Don't get me wrong: I love the Avengers and Thor movies as much as anyone. But they are the creation of Marvel, Paramount, and Disney. The real Norse myths are much older and have a much richer history.

So, as you enter the world of Valkyrie and Norse mythology, I would like to introduce you to some of the characters you may meet along the way.

Some will appear in this book; others will appear in the

later books in this series. But I also encourage you to go to your local library or bookstore and check out more books on Norse myths. Believe me, with all the heroes and monsters you'll meet, you will soon love them as much as I do!

—Kate

NAMES AND PLACES IN NORSE MYTHOLOGY

YGGDRASIL—Also known as the Cosmic World Tree, Yggdrasil sits in the very heart of the universe. It is within the branches of this tree that the nine realms exist. Yggdrasil is supported by three massive roots that pass through the realms. It is said that the fierce dragon Nidhogg regularly gnaws on one of the roots (when he's not eating corpses— don't ask). The Well of Urd, where Odin traded his eye for wisdom, sits on another root. Water from that well is taken by the Norns, mixed with earth, and put on the tree as a means of preventing Yggdrasil's bark from rotting. They also water the tree. It is said that a great eagle sits perched atop the tree and is harassed by a squirrel, Ratatosk, who delivers insults and unpleasant comments from the dragon Nidhogg, who resides at the base. Yggdrasil gives the nine realms life. Without it, they and we would cease to exist.

AESIR—This is the name of the group of younger gods, like Odin, Thor, Loki, Frigg, and the Valkyries. These are warrior gods who use weapons more than magic.

VANIR—This is the name of the older gods. Not much is known about them, but there are some familiar names. Vanir-Freyja and her twin brother, Freyr, are two well-known Vanir who were traded to Asgard in a peace exchange after the war. The Vanir are more earthen/forest-type gods who deal with land fertility and use a lot of magic.

ODIN—He is the leader of Asgard, the realm of the Aesir. A brave, strong, and imposing warrior, he presided over the war with the Vanir. He has many sons, most notably Thor and Balder. Odin carries a powerful spear, Gungnir, and wears an eye patch. It is said that Odin journeyed to the Well of Urd, where he exchanged his eye for wisdom. Each night Odin can be found in Valhalla, where he celebrates with the fallen heroes of Earth's battlefields. His two wolves sit loyally at his side.

FRIGG—The devoted and very beautiful wife of Odin, she is the mother of Balder and is known for her wisdom. Sadly, not a lot more is known about her, other than that she knows everyone's destiny. In later mythology, she is often confused with Vanir-Freyja and their deeds are mixed.

THOR—The son of Odin, he is known as the thunder god and is often compared with Zeus from the Greek myths. Thor is impossibly strong, with flaming red hair and a raging temper. He is known for being a fierce but honorable warrior. Thor is a sworn enemy to the frost giants, but calls Loki (who is part frost giant) a friend. They had many adventures together. Thor is also known for his mighty hammer, Mjölnir, which was created by the dwarf brothers Sindri and Brokkr on a mischievous bet with Loki. After its creation, they gave it to Thor, as he was one of the few strong enough to wield it. (By the way, Loki lost the bet and the two dwarfs sewed his mouth shut.) Thor is actually a married man—his wife is Sif, and they have three children. Note: We use the name Thor every week, as Thursday was named after him. Just think: Thor's day.

BALDER—Son of Odin and Frigg, he is known as the kindest of Odin's sons. Balder is a devoted brother to Thor and can calm his brother's fearsome temper. Sadly, within the mythology, Balder died, and it is widely believed that Loki caused his death and was responsible for keeping him dead.

LOKI—He is the trickster of Asgard. His origins are a little unclear, but it's said that both of his parents were frost giants. He is by turns playful, malicious, and helpful, but he's always irreverent and self-involved. Loki likes to have fun! He enjoys getting Thor into trouble, but then he helps Thor out of the same trouble. Loki is a shape-changer and appears in many disguises. For all his troublemaking ways, it is written that Loki is tolerated in Asgard because he is blood brother to Odin.

HEIMDALL—Ever vigilant watchman of Bifröst, Heimdall has nine mothers but no father. He is a giant of a man and amazingly strong. Heimdall requires less sleep than a bird, and his vision is so powerful, he can see for hundreds of miles, day or night. His hearing is so acute that he can hear grass or wool grow. It is written that he carries a special horn, Gjallarhorn, that he will sound at the start of Ragnarök when the giants storm Bifröst.

VALKYRIES—Choosers of the slain, the winged Valkyries are an elite group of Battle-Maidens who serve Odin by bringing only the most valiant of fallen warriors from Earth's battlefields to Valhalla. There, the warriors fight all day and feast all night, being served food and mead by the Valkyries. In early mythology, the Valkyries could decide who would live or die on the battlefield, but later this was changed to only collecting them for Odin. The Valkyries arrived on the battle-fields riding blazing, winged horses, and their howls could be heard long before their arrival. It is written that the Vanir goddess Freyja, who was traded after the war, was in fact the very first Valkyrie. Again, within the mythology, she gets to keep half the warriors she reaps—but it's not written what she does with them. The other half go to Odin.

FROST & FIRE GIANTS—Throughout the mythology, the frost and fire giants often appear, and there are many stories about Thor's encounters with them. Fearsome, immense, and violent, they each live in their own realms. Frost giants are from Utgard in Jotunheim, and the fire giants come from Muspelheim. Though there are some peaceful giants, most seek to conquer Asgard. To offer an idea of size, there is one story in which Loki, Thor, and two humans venture to Utgard to meet the frost giant king, but get lost in a maze of tunnels. It is later discovered that these tunnels were, in fact, the fingers of a frost giant's glove.

DWARFS—Both good and bad, dwarfs play a large part and fill an important role in Norse mythology. They are the master craftsmen and architects of the building of Asgard. It was dwarfs who created Thor's mighty hammer, Mjölnir, and Odin's spear, Gungnir. There are many stories of the dwarfs and their amazing creations.

LIGHT & DARK ELVES—These are the two contrasting types of elves. Dark Elves use dark magic, cause a lot of trouble, and can be very dangerous; they are hard to look upon and seek to do harm. Whereas the Light Elves are fairer to look at than the sun, use their magic for good, and help many people.

MIDGARD SERPENT—Also known as Jormungand, the Midgard Serpent is the son of Loki and his giantess wife, Angrboda. The Midgard Serpent is brother to the giant wolf Fenrir and Hel, Loki's daughter and ruler of the underworld. It is written that Odin had Jormungand cast into the ocean, where he grew so large, he could encircle the Earth. There is an ongoing feud between Thor and the Midgard Serpent. It is written that Jormungand is big and powerful enough to eat worlds.

RAVENS—Ravens play a large part in Norse mythology, and Odin himself has two very special ravens, Huginn and Muninn, who travel through all the realms and return to Odin at night. They sit on his shoulder and tell him everything that is happening in the other realms. They are known for their wisdom and guidance.

VALHALLA—Odin's Great Heavenly Hall for the heroic dead has a curious problem. In the mythology, there is a question of where Valhalla actually is. Most say it was part of Asgard, but others suggest it is in Helheim, the land of the dead. One thing is clear: Valhalla is a wondrous building where the valiant dead from Earth's battlefields are taken. Here they are served and entertained by the Valkyries who delivered them there. They drink and feast with Odin and continue their training until the day comes when they are called back into service to fight for Asgard during Ragnarök.

BIFRÖST—Also known as the Rainbow Bridge, this is a magnificent, multicolored bridge that links Asgard to Midgard and some of the other realms. It is said to have been created by the gods using the red of fire, the green of water, and the blue of air. Bifröst is guarded by Heimdall the Watchman.

THE NORNS—There are three Norn sisters who dwell at the Well of Urd at the base of Yggdrasil. The oldest is Urd, the middle sister is Verdandi, and the youngest is Skuld. These are the goddesses of destiny, similar to the Greek Fates. Urd is able to see the past, while Verdandi deals with current events. Skuld is able to see everyone's future. It is said that they are weavers, weaving people's destiny. If a thread is broken, the life ends.

RAGNARÖK—Also known as the apocalypse of the Norse gods and the end of everything, Ragnarök (in the mythology) is said to have been started by a very insane Loki and his wolf son, Fenrir, along with the frost and fire giants. They took on Asgard, and during the war all the gods were killed. Odin was killed by Fenrir, who was then killed by another of Odin's sons. Thor and the Midgard Serpent fought a battle to the death in which they managed to kill each other. Heimdall was the last to fall at the hand of Loki. It is during Ragnarök that Odin called on the warriors of Valhalla to fight for Asgard—but there were no winners. And it was from the ashes of Ragnarök that a new world was formed from the survivors—the world that we inhabit today.

DARK SEARCHERS—The Dark Searchers did not actually exist in Norse mythology. They are my creation because, in all my research, I couldn't find a mention of Odin's police force. So I created them for that purpose.

AZRAEL & THE ANGELS OF DEATH—Now, some of you may already know that Azrael and the Angels of Death don't come directly from Norse mythology. That's very true. But as they are known all over the world in almost every culture, and since they do similar jobs to the Valkyries and have wings just like the Valkyries, I thought it would be fun to mix things up a bit. To avoid confusion, I set it up so that the Valkyries only deal with the most valiant warriors reaped from Earth's battlefields, who are then taken to Valhalla—thus staying true to Norse mythology. Azrael and his Angels of Death deal with everyone else—thus staying true to many other cultures.

ACKNOWLEDGMENTS

Life is filled with many challenges.

This was never more evident to me than when I was writing this book. I had only just started it when two of my brothers (one here in the UK, the other in New York) became unexpectedly but gravely ill. One came out of it—scarred but alive. The other didn't. I lost my oldest brother, Pat, before Christmas 2014. And for the first time in my life, I found I couldn't write. The words were gone.

This is why I want to thank my editor, Naomi Greenwood, and everyone at Hodder Children's Books for their patience and for letting me take the time I needed to heal—so the words would return. They did. This book was so late being delivered, but not once did I hear a word of complaint from my publisher.

My wonderful agents, Veronique Baxter and Laura West, were equally supportive during this dreadful time, and continue to be just as supportive as the rough waters finally start to calm.

This just goes to show the resilience of our hearts and spirits. Terrible things do sometimes happen, but somehow we get through them—even when we think we can't.

ACKNOWLEDGMENTS

Should you, my sweet readers, ever face these terrible times—and a lot of you will—just know the days do get better. I promise. You are not alone.

Normally about now, I would start talking about protecting horses, dogs, marine animals, all endangered species, and doing all you can to protect our Mother Earth. But for now, instead, I will leave you with a few words to my brother. I have never claimed to be a poet, but for you, JP, I will try.

Seek Me Not

Seek me not, where the seabirds fly,
Or tempest ocean crashes to lonely shore
Do not look for me on a windswept cliff
Or where caverns sing, or rain will pour.
I am there with you, no further than a whisper
Not lost, or hiding behind eternity's door
So search no further than your own wounded heart
For there I reside, forever more.